The Wrack

John Bierce

"Bierce's knack for worldbuilding and realism crafts a remarkable, fascinating story with a terrifying illness at its core. The Wrack is heartwarming, clever, and horrific in equal measure, and it's like nothing I've read before."
- Travis Riddle, author of Balam, Spring

"The Wrack is brutal, fascinating, relentless. The realities of plague have often been shunted to the boundaries of fantasy, but here they're unveiled in all their awful glory."
- Sarah Lin, author of The Brightest Shadow

"The Wrack is one of those rare fantasy books that remains in your thoughts long after you've finished the last page, that send chills down your spine as you read it and calls to you ever time you set it down. It is a sobering reminder that even in worlds rich in magic, the ordinary can still be terrifying, and that not all problems can be solved by the swing of a sword."
- F James Blair, author of Bulletproof Witch

For all our own missing names.
And for all the amazing epidemiologists, public health workers, and healthcare professionals out there. We owe you all big-time.

Author's Note

Several months into the writing of The Wrack, reports starting coming out of China of some sort of new strain of coronavirus. Four days after I sent the manuscript of The Wrack off to my editor, the WHO declared COVID-19 a pandemic.

To say the writing of The Wrack was a weird experience is seriously understating things.

Fair warning- The Wrack is a weird, depressing little book. If you came looking for something along the lines of my Mage Errant series, this definitely isn't that. But if you're in the mood for a weird, depressing little book, then I hope you enjoy The Wrack!

CHAPTER ONE

The Castle Below the Mist

The first victim of the Wrack was Prince Arnulf of Lothain.

In general, when one's prince collapses at a luncheon and begins convulsing and screaming, one can safely assume the involvement of poison. When said prince is a warrior in his prime, who lived with wild abandon and had never been known to be sick a day in his life, it tends to strongly reinforce the possibility that poison has been involved.

The residents of Castle Morinth, unsurprisingly, assumed exactly that.

Castle Morinth was swiftly locked down, and none were permitted to leave, save for three guards judged to share the twin virtues of being particularly trustworthy and of having lacked the opportunity to have poisoned Arnulf.

The latter virtue was, to be honest, the more important of the two. If you'd asked anyone in the castle an hour before, none would have imagined that *anyone* would poison Arnulf. He was much beloved by his soldiers, the servants, and even the villagers farther down the pass.

Prince Arnulf, the fifth son of King Sigis IV, had been sent to Castle Morinth to take up the mantle of the Mist Warden by his father, and had had done a far better job than any other Warden in generations.

It would seem odd for any other kingdom to maintain a sizable armed force far from its borders, but other kingdoms lacked the Maze of Mist.

Castle Morinth sat at the base of a high pass leading up into the Krannenbergs— the jagged mountain range that marked Lothain's north-eastern frontier. The pass Castle Morinth guarded, however, didn't cross the Krannenbergs. In fact, no one ever entered it if they could possibly help it.

A massive wall of mist hung just a few miles up the pass from Castle Morinth. Even in the heat of a late summer afternoon, the mist never burned away. It just hung between the walls of the pass, always shifting and twisting. If you watched it long enough, you could begin to almost make sense of the twisting patterns of the mist.

Almost.

Those few who had entered and returned spoke of a twisting maze inside the mist, narrow paths where the miasma could be seen through. Those who strayed off these paths into the thicker mist were never heard from again.

As if that weren't bad enough, the paths were always moving, shifting, merging and splitting.

If that were the extent of the Mist Maze's dangers, it would hardly be more than a lethal curiosity. Far from it, however.

Because *things* also came out of it. Beasts of twisted forms, of vile temperament, of uncouth demeanor.

Sometimes it would be weeks or months between incursions, and sometimes the denizens of the maze would flood out like the tide.

The maze beasts varied wildly in form. In the last year alone there had been a snake the size of a tree, a flock of predatory flightless birds, some sort of hideous tentacled boar-horror, and a voracious land-eel with the eyes and legs of a centipede.

Past kings had tried merely ignoring the maze and hoping the beasts would stay near it, but eventually, the threat grew severe enough that the kings of Lothain had constructed the fortress to keep the rest of the kingdom safe. The commanders of the fortress became known as the Mist Wardens.

Though others would deny it, all those who fought the beasts from the mists knew their work had the blessing of the ancestors.

Many past Mist Wardens had stayed safe in the castle while their men defended the pass, but Prince Arnulf had personally led the charge against each and every one of the beasts that emerged under his watch. His men adored him for it. The villages below the castle grew to love him as well, for allowing their children and herds to roam more safely.

His generous nature, handsome face, and booming laugh did their share in making him so beloved, of course. As far as those around him were concerned, Arnulf was a living legend. He could ride twice as hard, fight twice as long, and eat twice as much as a normal man. Given that, and the fact that Castle Morinth was far enough from the capital that it rested almost untouched by court politics, no one should have had any reason to poison Prince Arnulf.

The three desperate guards that left the castle that summer day all rode down the pass towards the villages below in search of the castle healer, in the vain hope of saving their prince.

Captain Oson, the highest ranked of the three soldiers, was the one to find Healer Benen, who was riding his horse back from one of the herder's villages.

"Hail, Oson!" the grizzled, burly healer called, then adjusted his leather eyepatch.

Captain Oson drew his horse alongside Benen's as he caught his breath from the swift ride down.

"Something come out of the Maze?" Benen inquired, offering Oson his waterskin.

Oson drank gratefully from the waterskin. He hadn't thought to bring his own in the rush, and he wasn't as young as he used to be.

"I must admit, to my shame," Benen said, "that I've been looking forward to some action. It will make a welcome change from farmers insisting that their cattle are acting strange."

Captain Oson shook his head. "It's Prince Arnulf. He's been poisoned."

The affable healer had kicked his horse into a gallop before Oson could even offer the waterskin back.

"Tell me everything," Benen demanded, as he stormed through the castle halls.

"The prince was halfway through his luncheon, then he just… fell over," the head maid said, wringing her hands. She looked on the verge of tears. "He started making this awful noise in the back of his throat, and kept shaking like he'd lost control of his body."

"What was he eating?" Benen asked.

"Stew with barley bread and cheese, nothing unusual," the maid said.

Benen frowned. Nothing unusual for Arnulf, perhaps, but the prince was the only noble Benen knew that preferred coarse barley bread over wheat bread.

"I'll need you to fetch the prince's food to his chambers," Benen said.

"My lord?" the maid asked.

Benen, for once, ignored being referred to as a lord. His parents were honest craftsfolk, not nobles, but the servants and village folk up here were convinced that seers were somehow a step above them, and wouldn't dream to treat them any different than they'd treat lords and ladies.

Benen hated it, but he'd been unable to convince them to stop.

"I need to check the food for poison, and I daren't leave the prince's side once I get there," Benen said.

The head maid nodded. As they crossed the great hall, she snagged a guardsman, and the two of them began gathering the remains of Arnulf's luncheon.

The healer ignored them for the moment, going through the door at the back of the great hall.

There was a short hall leading to a spiral staircase through the door. The guards at its base let him through wordlessly, and he quickly ascended to the prince's chambers above the great hall.

He could hear shouting and screaming coming from Arnulf's chamber as he climbed the stairs.

Benen was hardly expecting the sight of Arnulf thrashing about in his bed, a half dozen of his soldiers trying to hold him down. He varied back and forth between incomprehensible muttering and horrid, rasping screams.

"Seer Benen!" a soldier called. "The prince is"

Benen pushed past the woman and marched straight for Arnulf. He slipped in between two of the soldiers holding the prince down, and rested his hand on the prince's forehead.

The prince was feverish, but nowhere near as much as his symptoms would seem to warrant.

"His fever is low," Benen muttered.

"That's good, right?" one of the soldiers asked. "It means he's more likely to survive?"

"Fever is the body's first weapon against contagion," Benen said, quoting the Moonsworn holy book. Many of his fellow healers would frown at him quoting the Moonsworn, but they could all have their names forgotten, for all Benen cared. Whether they were southern spies or not, the Moonsworn could save three patients for every one that his fellows could. If the Moonsworn said humours and vapours were nonsense, they were nonsense, and if they claimed fevers were the body's weapon, Benen believed them.

Frowning, he pried open Arnulf's eyelid. His pupil was constricted almost to nothing. "Any illness bad enough to do this should have triggered a much stronger fever. Some poisons are known to cause low fevers along with their other symptoms, however."

"You can cure him?" another soldier asked, desperately. "You can use your magic on him?"

Benen had opened his mouth to explain for the thousandth time that magic didn't work like that, when Arnulf tore his arm free from the soldier's grasp. The prince convulsed, screaming as he clawed himself across the face hard enough to draw blood.

After Benen had helped the others pin and tie the prince down, the healer carefully cut off Arnulf's tunic, taking care not to cut the thrashing prince as well.

He did his best to ignore the blood dripping down into Arnulf's beard.

Once he had the tunic free, he realized that it wasn't just Arnulf's arms and legs clenching. The muscles across his entire body appeared to be twitching and spasming violently.

This… this wasn't anything Benen had seen before. A thought occurred to him.

"Did the mist-beast the other day bite or sting him?" Benen demanded of the soldiers around him.

"The big armored beetle thing?" one soldier said. "Didn't even come close to touching him before he planted his lance in its eye."

Perhaps some of the beast's ichor had splashed onto Arnulf and poisoned him?

Benen sighed, then reached for his eyepatch. The soldiers around him edged away, as though afraid he'd curse them or some such nonsense. Superstition reigned supreme this far from the capital.

The healer pulled away the eyepatch, revealing the polished, light green peridot sphere in his eye socket. Delicate lines were engraved into its surface in precise patterns, and it seemed to glow slightly from within.

Benen took a deep breath, shut his living eye, and dove into the spirit realm.

Despite what the peasant folktales claimed, Benen had never seen any actual spirits in the spirit world. No ghosts of the dead, no demons, and no horrible creatures that preyed upon the living.

No, the spirit realm was far more peaceful than the real world.

Benen knew that if he opened his good eye, he'd still be able to see Arnulf writhing in his bed and the soldiers clustering worriedly. He knew everyone else in the room would just see him standing there stock-still, his peridot eye faintly aglow.

Benen felt like his hair and beard should be drifting in the gentle currents of the spirit realm, but they had no power over the material world.

Around and above Benen stretched an endless, restful sea of transparent, pale green energy. Gentle streams of spiritstuff drifted past him, like currents passing through a gentle river. It looked serene at first, but his vision quickly adapted, and he began spotting the turbulence where the physical world impinged upon the spirit realm.

As an apprentice, it had been months before he could dive into the spirit realm on command. It had been months more before he could stay there— he kept getting vertigo, feeling as though he were about to plunge into the infinite abyss of the spirit realm.

Now, though, he could dive on command and hold there as long as needed.

As his vision continued to adjust, he carefully measured the distortions against the lines that crossed his vision— the very lines carved into the crystal sphere of his eye. Despite what the peasants and soldiers thought, the markings weren't any sort of magic rune. They were merely reference marks, to help him better get his bearings in the spirit realm.

After about a minute, he started parsing the turbulence in the spirit currents. As spiritstuff flowed, its currents were churned by the material world. A seer could learn to interpret that turbulence, to use it to see within solid matter.

Learning that art was by far the most challenging part of the endeavor. Scrying presented the human mind with far, far more information than it could ever use, so the most important ability of the seer was learning to filter out unnecessary turbulence in the spirit realm.

Having one's eye put out as a youth to gain the ability to see the spirit flows was also rather a challenging aspect of learning magic, of course.

Gradually, slowly, the world came into focus. The stone walls sheared the spirit currents according to their mineral crystals. The wooden bedposts twisted the flows around their own grains. The threads of the blanket fuzzed and disrupted the flows.

And there was Arnulf.

To a seer untrained in healing, the currents flowing through the human body — or that of any animal — appeared to be pure chaos. This was largely because bodies didn't have the simple composition of baser matter, but were instead filled with a hundred different materials. Bone, blood, bile, fat… the list went on and on.

Compared to a human, a block of stone or board of wood was hardly so complex.

The diversity of their constituent parts was far from the only difference, however. The internal movement of the blood, the flow of lightning across the nerves, and the strange chemical processes of the gut all further changed the shape of the body in the spirit realm.

It had taken Benen most of a decade to learn to properly read the spirit flows as they passed through the human body.

He frowned as he passed his gaze over Arnulf. The prince's wild muscle spasms were making this far more difficult than it should have been, distorting and hiding the turbulence from his organs.

Benen contemplated giving Arnulf tincture of the poppy for a moment, but he decided against it. It would settle the prince's muscles so he could see past them, but he had no idea what poison ran through Arnulf's veins. The mixture could hasten Arnulf's death, for all he knew.

He briefly wished for an eye of emerald. Peridot was a poor replacement for true green beryl — an emerald eye could discern the turbulence of poisons with ease.

There were, however, only three emerald eyes on the whole continent, and none had set foot in Lothain for centuries.

Benen reached up and rotated the peridot eye in his socket, adjusting the reference marks.

He relaxed his focus a little. It was counterintuitive, but it made the spirit current ripples from deeper in Arnulf's body stand out more. It was, some seers theorized, to do with the fact that the essential core of scrying wasn't one of trying to see more, but trying to see less. The most useful gems limited a seer's vision to specific types of spirit turbulence. Peridot did much of that work for the human body, but there was so much of it that a seer had to learn to ignore. There were countless little creatures living within the human body to ignore, countless normal functions of the body that looked bizarre and terrifying to a new seer. Training oneself to only see the harmful creatures and the abnormal functions took years.

He frowned, then opened his good eye. He felt briefly nauseous for a moment as he tried to overlap the spirit world and the material world, before his vision stabilized. The angle of the spirit current was off a bit, so he shifted his body to take better advantage of it, then ran his eyes down Arnulf's body again.

There.

The spirit current passing through Arnulf's liver looked wrong. It was a subtle thing— ripples a little shorter and more chaotic than usual, curves a little too sharp— but it was definitely there.

Arnulf popped out his peridot eye, and the vision of the spirit world collapsed into faint flickers visible in his empty socket, like the flashes you might see when you clenched your eyelids too tight.

"What did you find?" one of the guards asked.

Benen ignored him as he wiped down the crystal sphere, then tucked it away in a protected pocket of his satchel. Peridot might be cheaper and more common than emerald, but peridot crystals of sufficient size for artificial eyes were still worth more than most prosperous craftsfolk would make in several years. He withdrew another sphere— also peridot, but with a cunning glass lens fastened to its front. Ironically, though it required a smaller peridot crystal, this eye was far more expensive— it required an exceptionally skilled jeweler and an even more skilled lenscrafter to craft. The lens couldn't be glued to the crystal, for glue would interfere with spirit sight. Rather, it had to be attached with cunning slots and pins.

He carefully wiped down the sphere with a clean cloth, then slipped it into his empty socket. He blinked a few times and dropped back into the spirit world. This eye magnified his view, letting him see much smaller, finer details of the spirit currents, at the expense of the bigger picture.

It was no surprise, given he didn't recognize the poison's symptoms, but the spirit currents gave him no clues as to what poison had been used either. The poison was most densely concentrated in Arnulf's liver, but the healer found traces of it in all of the prince's twitching, convulsing muscles, and, to Benen's distress, the quantities seemed to be actively increasing, as though it were leaking out into the rest of the body from his liver.

To his surprise, however, none of the poison could be seen in Arnulf's stomach.

Scowling, Benen turned to the side-table where Arnulf's food had been set. He was no culinary seer— indeed, he found their entire practice to be ostentatious and wasteful in the extreme— but he was no stranger to examining food for poison via spirit sight.

And there was no poison in Arnulf's food.

"His luncheon wasn't poisoned," Benen said. "It might be a slow-acting poison. There are a few, like starweb leaf, whose symptoms come on all at once. It could also have been a faster poison delivered to the prince by some other means, as well. If we could…"

Arnulf screamed and convulsed. Benen had never heard sound kin to it from a human voice before— it sounded as though it were tearing the prince's very throat apart. Most of the soldiers and servants in the room stepped back in fear, but two brave souls— a soldier and a chambermaid— dove atop the Prince, in an effort to still his thrashing.

To no avail, however. The massive warrior, even tied to his own bed, threw both off like they were mere children. His eyes were open but unseeing, and spittle flecked his beard and mustache. He strained forward, as though trying to escape some terror.

There was a *crack*, and Benen's eyes, both living and crystal, shot to the bedposts, thinking Arnulf had broken one.

It wasn't the wood that had broken.

Arnulf had shattered his own bones in his convulsions. His left forearm seemed to have grown a new elbow— one lumpy and deformed. Even with the wrong eye in his socket, Benen could clearly make out the rapids in the spirit currents where they passed through the break.

"Hold him down!" Benen shouted over the prince's inhuman screams, and dove for his medicines.

By the time the soldiers had pinned Arnulf down, and Benen had retrieved his tincture of the poppy, Arnulf's screams had become awful, rasping whispers, as though the man's throat really had torn apart. Benen roughly splashed a little of the powerful sedative in Arnulf's mouth, hoping it would quiet the screams, so he could get the man to drink more.

It took nearly half an hour to get enough of the concentrated poppy down Arnulf's throat to force him to slumber. It took more of the tincture than he'd ever given to any man or woman before, save for in easing the death of the mortally wounded.

Part of Benen feared that if the poison didn't kill the prince, the sheer amount of poppy might do the job.

The exhausted soldiers and servants were pale and terrified, and Benen feared he didn't look much better. His false eye had rolled a little in his socket somehow, and the reference lines were strangely askew. He took a deep breath and adjusted it, as much to gather his wits as anything.

Even as he slumbered, Arnulf twitched and writhed, like a man tortured with hot coals.

Prince Arnulf's death wasn't a gentle one.

The massive doses of poppy tincture Benen provided barely alleviated the prince's suffering. Twice during the endless night that followed his collapse, he managed to shatter the splint they'd put on his broken arm. Past midnight, Arnulf bit off the tip of his own tongue in his convulsions. The tips of his fingers and toes began to blacken horribly, and every time he awoke, the same dreadful, pained rattling echoed out of his broken vocal cords.

The healer did what he could for the prince, but only the poppy helped. None of the purgatives and poultices he attempted seemed to do anything. Benen even considered bleeding the prince, knowing full well what the Moonsworn would do if they found out he'd violated their strictures against it.

In the end, Benen was reduced to simply taking notes on the poison's symptoms, on Arnulf's rising fever, and on the steadily increasing levels of the poison in his blood and, somehow, in his liver.

Just before dawn, the warrior's heart simply gave out from the strain.

CHAPTER TWO
Spirit Messages

Benen trudged up the stairs of the main semaphore tower, each step feeling like seven leagues.

The tower had long ago been built as a dovecote, but the doves had been moved to another part of Castle Morinth when the spirit semaphore had been built.

There were, in the spirit realm, certain stable currents that could last for years, decades, or even centuries, traversing tens or hundreds of leagues. There had been much debate about them over the years— the Moonsworn and Sunsworn merely thought them a curiosity of the spirit realm, a by-product of their twin goddesses' eternal revolutions. The Sei had thought them the exhalations of their stern god and judged attempts to interfere with them heresy. The Radhan's interest in them had only extended so far as distant hopes of using turbulence in the currents to predict storms. The Conclave Eidola, of course, had known them to be, like the rest of the spirit realm, the means by which the ancestors kept watch over their descendants.

The currents, however, proved slippery things, hard to affect and prone to slipping back into their previous states.

Then, nearly a century past, a Sunsworn noble, Vai en-Addem, had built the first semaphore in the tallest minaret of his manor house. The mad artist had intended it as a performance work, telling no one of his plans. When the current began filling with the turbulence of his semaphore, seers and scholars in the nearby city of On-Hagrad had panicked, starting a small riot among On-Hagrad's ziggurats that had baffled the local merchants and laborers. To this day, Hagradi townsfolk still joked about the learned being a superstitious, easily frightened lot.

The potential of Vai en-Addem's invention had quickly been seen, and within a decade, the first semaphore line was running between On-Hagrad and the nameless

Sunsworn holy city. From there, they'd spread all across the great southern continent of Oyansur. Despite Sunsworn efforts to keep the technology from spreading north across the isthmus, it made it to Teringia a few decades later, and soon the entirety of the small northern continent had been covered by semaphore lines.

Spirit semaphores were difficult and expensive to run. They had to be placed inside the spirit currents, in those rare places where they dipped near to the ground. Repeater stations had to be placed along the currents to pass along messages before they degraded too much. Every message had to be encoded into clusters of letters. Otherwise, they would take far too long to send. If you wished to keep the contents of a message secret, you had to encode them even further, since any seer could watch the messages being sent merely by watching the current. To make it even more frustrating, messages could only be sent in one direction— along the path of the current— which meant that many messages were sent on looping, circuitous routes from one current to another, often with many interruptions to be hand-carried between two semaphore towers.

That didn't even get into the sheer, absurd expense of building a spirit semaphore. The sophisticated clockwork mechanisms required rare gems, precisely blown pieces of glassware, and they had to be exactingly constructed by skilled workers on-site. The metals had to be carefully chosen and matched so that when they shifted size in different temperatures, it wouldn't force the machine out of alignment.

Still, for all their countless disadvantages, spirit semaphores had revolutionized society. Messages could cross Teringia in days, instead of weeks or months. They could travel all the way to the foreign, strange lands at the southern tip of Oyansur, if you had a mind to, and could guarantee that there was a recipient you shared a language with. Kings and emperors immediately saw the utility of the semaphores for war and governance. Merchants had been close behind— information was always essential to commerce.

The semaphore network had grown so important that entirely new towns and cities had arisen near convergences of multiple spirit currents.

It was still expensive to send information via the semaphore network, of course— the average craftsman or merchant couldn't afford it, let alone the average laborer.

Castle Morinth, by any standard, should have been Lothain's biggest hub in the semaphore network. There were literally dozens of nearby spirit currents capable of carrying messages, stretching across most of the nation.

There were only two problems with that. First, the fact that all the currents traveled away, not towards, Castle Morinth. Or, rather, they traveled away from the Mist Maze. Along with the strange monsters it spat out, it was a source of some of the longest spirit currents on the continent. Any messages to the castle had to be carried several dozen leagues by horseback.

The second problem, of course, was that there just weren't enough messages that needed to be sent by the castle, the prince, or the cattle herders of the villages below them.

So, the castle had just two semaphore towers— one atop the curtain wall's southwest tower that could send messages to the nearest military garrison, and one in the old dovecote that could send messages to Lothain's capital city of the same name.

Benen popped out his healer's eye, and instead he pushed in an amethyst sphere— after carefully and thoroughly cleaning both. Amethyst eyes were ideally suited to using the semaphore network. Despite how common amethyst crystals of sufficient size were, they'd skyrocketed in price over the last few decades, as the size of the network grew.

Most healers would have considered it below them to maintain a semaphore alongside their usual duties— semaphore seers were seen as mere drudges, the lowest rank of those who could see into the spirit realm. They only took a few months to train, once they'd developed the basic skills of seeing. Benen had often heard other seers claim that absolutely anyone could become a semaphore seer, unlike the more rarefied ranks of other seers.

Absolute nonsense, in Benen's opinion. Anyone could learn to be a seer, so long as they were hardworking, intelligent, and willing to sacrifice an eye.

Benen sighed as he reached the top of the semaphore tower, and took a moment to catch his breath before getting to work.

He started by removing the protective dust covers, setting the thin brass plates on the table to the side. Next, he undid a series of latches fastening down the semaphore arm, unfolding and extending them for readiness. Some of them were as long as six feet.

He fetched the crank out of its resting place in one of the empty boulins— the cubbies where the doves had once nested— and inserted it into the appropriate socket. He grunted and strained at the mechanism until he'd raised the semaphore up into the center of the current that traveled in through one tower window and out the other— the latter of which had been broken into the wall to stop it distorting messages. The thin wire meshes in the windows were enough to keep birds out of the tower without distorting the messages.

They did leave the tower viciously cold in the winter, though.

When he'd raised the semaphore to its appropriate height, he locked it into place, returning the crank to its cubby-hole. He then fetched several new gems from their boulins, replacing those on several of the semaphore's brass arms.

If this had been a full-size semaphore, that wouldn't be necessary, but Castle Morinth had only warranted smaller, cheaper semaphores— the kind an army might carry with them on the march.

Eventually, he'd finished making adjustments to the semaphore arms and strode over to the chain bench.

The chain bench was a long shelf set into the wall at chest height under a large group of boulins. Dozens of sizes and cuts of chain links could be found inside— some huge and smooth, others small and toothed, and others long and twisted.

It took nearly an hour for Benen to assemble the message chain. Not that it was particularly difficult— he was an old hand at the process; and he should have been able to assemble even the most heavily encoded long message in a third of the time at most.

No, the reason it took so long was writing the message itself. How did you tell a king that his son had been poisoned, and not only was the poison unknown, but the poisoner and their motives were as well?

As he worked, the healer kept glancing out the nearest window with his living eye at the courtyard below. Castle Morinth's Eidola priest worked below, carving the prince's name into the castle's monolith, so that Arnulf might join the ancestors, not the hateful ranks of the forgotten dead.

Finally, he finished clipping the message chain together, carried it gently to the semaphore, and fed the end of the chain in. The first few links were neutral-sized, and weren't strictly part of the message— they just marked the beginning of the message. The next few links detailed the recipient via a short identifier code. The links at the end were neutral-sized as well.

He hesitated for a moment, then clipped the ends of the chain together, forming a loop. He wanted to make sure this message made it through.

Benen fetched another crank from its boulin, inserting it into its aperture, and began to gently turn it. It turned easily, and the chain began to ratchet smoothly through the semaphore. As it did so, the arms of the spirit semaphore began to twist and spin, the cunning clockwork mechanisms responding to the different sizes and cuts of links in the chain. The spirit current began to twist and churn in recognizable patterns downstream of the semaphore, flowing gently away through the tower window.

He kept turning the cranks for as long as he could hear the sounds of the priest's hammer and chisel, repeating the looped message again and again.

Captain Oson fell ill that night, quickly followed by two other guards, three cooks, and a chambermaid.

Benen wept as he administered the last of the castle's poppy tincture, and was forced to move to skullcap, willow bark, catnip, and valerian to alleviate the pain. They might be suitable for relieving tooth-aches, sprains, and headaches, but they did little for the screaming victims.

Benen kept his hope that this was poison rather than contagion alive for days, as more and more of the castle fell ill, and he ran out of herbs to alleviate the pain. He filled his ears with wax to keep out the screaming echoing through the castle. He cursed the ban on the Moonsworn from all Lothain's fortresses. He tried not to think about the servants and soldiers deserting the castle, fleeing down the pass seeking safety.

Captain Oson was the first to come out of his delirium. He'd broken three fingers on his right hand, torn out half his hair, and pulled muscles across his body. His fingers and toes were blackened, with little feeling left to them.

The captain spoke in a broken whisper, his voice stolen by the screams of his illness. His bedsheets were stained with watery stool, and he ran a low fever still, but the screaming, writhing, delirium, and pain had passed.

In his broken, rasping whispers before he fell asleep, Oson spoke of a world robbed of color, of feeling as though his mind swam through mud. He spoke of lingering pains throughout his body, and of relief that his fingers and toes were spared that pain.

To Benen's peridot eye, the spirit turbulence of the poison had shifted. It still persisted throughout the body, but it seemed as though some key component had vanished from it, leaving it a shadow of its former virulence.

His hopes for poison over plague vanished as the screaming started in the village.

CHAPTER THREE
Mourning in Lothain

"One in seven?" the chirurgeon asked.

"At least," Carlan said, setting his copy of Healer Benen's most recent semaphore message on the table. "We don't know how many who fled the castle took sick afterwards, nor how many of those who fled the villages took sick. It could be as high as one in four. And of those who sickened, over half perished. None of the survivors have regained the use of their fingers or toes."

There was dismayed silence around the table, as the assorted seers, chirurgeons, herbalists, and alchemists all exchanged uncomfortable glances.

All avoided looking at the empty seats at either end of the table.

The great seat at the head of the table was distressing, to be sure— Sigis IV should have been there, but he had locked himself away in his chambers, mourning his beloved son. He had demanded a week of mourning from the capital— as much as a king or heir would receive, let alone a fifth son like Arnulf. At the moment, the king was likely getting his son's name tattooed onto him by a priest— an old practice that not many kept to these days, but the royal line of Lothain was nothing if not conservative and resistant to change.

The empty seat next to Carlan's at the foot of the table, however, was disquieting in a whole different way. The Moonsworn representative should have long since been here. Carlan, in all his years as the king's chief seer, had never seen the Moonsworn miss a meeting on medical matters. He'd summoned all the most prestigious medical experts in the city, all to advise on the matter of the mysterious illness that had felled Arnulf. The Moonsworn had been the first ones he'd invited.

The Moonsworn were, unquestionably, the foremost medical experts in the world— if they hadn't been, there would have been no chance that they would be allowed free reign of Lothain and the rest of Teringia, given the centuries-old conflict the Eidola had with the Moonsworn's sister religion, the Sunsworn.

"We're sure it's truly contagion?" one of the alchemists asked. "Healer Benen reported it as poison initially."

"What could poison that many people?" a seer asked, polishing his peridot eye.

"Foul vapours?" another seer asked.

Several people shot nervous glances at the empty Moonsworn seat at that. The Moonsworn had declared miasmic disease nonsense over a century ago, but ten years ago, an entire village in southern Galicanta had died, choking on foul vapours rising from a nearby lake. The Moonsworn had been largely silent on the matter, but it was common knowledge that there had been quite a bit of strife and debate inside the insular Moonsworn community after that. The Moonsworn had claimed they'd merely been volcanic gases.

Whatever they said publicly, it had been widely noticed that they'd not put much pressure on anyone discussing miasmic theory since then.

Carlan frowned, and got out of his chair, ignoring the creaking of his old bones.

"Vapours rolling downhill?" someone asked. Carlan didn't bother to look, instead heading for the window.

"It makes a certain amount of sense, doesn't it?" someone else replied. "That foul vapours would leak from the Maze of Mist?"

The door thudded open, and brisk footsteps entered the room.

"It's not," a familiar voice said, "a foul vapour."

Carlan sighed with relief internally, but he didn't turn around just yet. He stared out over the city, where all Lothain's pennants and banners had been replaced with mourning grey. The normally crowded, bustling evening streets seemed subdued, almost empty.

Arnulf had been reasonably well-loved by his people, but the rumors of plague likely had more to do with that.

"If it had been a foul vapuor," the familiar voice continued, "one would think it would have affected people more evenly."

"But Benen did say its presence increased over time in the body," another voice said. "That would make sense if he were breathing it in."

"Then explain," the familiar voice continued, "how, exactly, it was that Benen didn't find traces of the poison or contagion in the bodies of everyone else? There would be no escaping foul vapours for anyone in the pass."

Carlan rolled his eyes, then turned around.

"You're late, Yusef," he said.

Yusef on-Samn, the Lothain Moonsworn community's chief representative, frowned at that. "I was unavoidably delayed by internal Moonsworn affairs," the portly, bearded man said. He was darker-skinned than anyone else in the room by far, and he immediately stood out for it.

Carlan snorted at that.

"Forty years now we've known each other, Yusef," Carlan said, "and this is the first time you've ever been late to anything."

"Thirty-eight years," Yusef said, "and it's the second time. Fourteen years ago I…"

"Yusef…" Carlan said, warningly.

Yusef tapped his fingers, looking away from Carlan.

"It's the Ban," he finally admitted.

"Again, Yusef?" Carlan asked.

Yusef turned his gaze back on Carlan, frowning. "How many lives could have been saved if even a single Moonsworn had been there? You continually treat us as though we're spies, despite the sacred demands of our Goddess. She demands, above all else, that we care for others and not engage in the petty wars of man."

"Yet no man is perfect," Carlan said, the old arguments marshalling themselves once more. This argument popped up at least once a season, and never got anywhere. "The Ban has stood for generations, and…"

"Are my Sunsworn brethren likely to invade Lothain through the Mist Maze?" Yusef interrupted. "Do they have armies besieging Castle Morinth that have somehow skipped over the entirety of not only Lothain but Galicanta as well?"

Carlan blinked at that. Yusef interrupting him was hardly more common than Yusef being late.

"It's not just about Castle Morinth, Yusef," he said. "It's not just about the Moonsworn, either. It's as much about the rest of Teringia— there's not a ruler south of the Krannenbergs that doesn't hold to the Ban. If we were to lift it, they might take that as…"

"It *is* just about Castle Morinth," Yusef said. "There are people there suffering at this very moment, and there is a plague that risks spreading from there. I'm not demanding a lift of the Ban, merely a temporary exemption. Castle Morinth holds no strategic value against or to the Sunsworn, and sending in Moonsworn now could save lives."

"I…" Carlan stopped. "Give me a moment."

He turned back to the window, ignoring the murmuring voices behind him. Several people starting talking to Yusef at once, but Carlan left Yusef on his own to deal with the vultures.

Carlan stared pensively back out over the stone city.

Lothain had once been a city built largely of wood and clay. Located far out in the plains, there were no good quarries for half a hundred leagues. Two centuries ago, a great drought had struck Lothain, and the parched city had burnt to ash that summer. Oltaeg II, an otherwise largely undistinguished ruler, had ordered it rebuilt entirely of stone. Most of the varied types of stone were quarried in various locations in the Krannenbergs, and ferried down the Winterbranch River, which flowed out of the Mist Maze, down the pass Castle Morinth guarded, across the plains, and straight through the center of the capital. A half dozen small limestone quarries on the plain contributed as well, leaving the city a hodgepodge of different shades of stone.

Relations between the Teringian kingdoms and the Sunsworn had been better then, and the Moonsworn had been instrumental in redesigning the great city. A great sewer network had been built beneath the city, leading away from the Winterbranch, to artificial marshes a league away from the city and the river. Great settling ponds had been created to clean the muddy waters of the river so that the citizens might drink safely.

For all the thousands that had died in Lothain's Great Fire, Carlan couldn't help but wonder how many more lives had been saved from filth and disease after the city had been rebuilt. According to the Moonsworn, Lothain had fewer deaths from disease than any of the other Teringian great cities.

Though the Moonsworn never called them great cities. Lothain was one of the largest on Teringia, at half a million. Only the Galicantan capital Ladreis had more, yet even it was dwarfed by some of the cities on Oyansur— There were at least a dozen cities with twice Lothain's population or more on the southern continent. If a plague got loose here…

Carlan sighed before his thoughts could lead him down any other rambling tangents. He turned to face Yusef again.

"I can't simply grant an exemption without the king's permission," Carlan said, interrupting the conversation behind him. "I'll need to speak to him first."

Yusef simply nodded, then turned to face the others at the table.

It would hardly be easy to persuade the king, but, as shaken as he was from his son's death, he doubted Sigis would care much what he did. Carlan sighed, straightened his robes, ran his fingers through his beard, then set out to speak to a king in mourning.

Yusef strode through the torchlit streets of Lothain, already planning out the logistics of the mission to Castle Morinth, tallying out supplies, budgets, and timelines in his head.

He made a mental note to write it all down later. The other Elders hated it when he kept everything in his head and didn't produce records.

King Sigis hadn't actually confirmed the order, but Yusef had faith in Carlan. His friend was slow to change his mind, but when Carlan did, he'd throw his entire weight behind his decision. Yusef wanted the Moonsworn to be able to set out immediately when given permission.

As he strode down the cobbles, most of the laborers and lesser merchants and craftsmen nodded cheerfully to him, or at least bowed. The Moonsworn only ever charged what the patient could afford, and they offered healing free of charge when needed.

The nobles and wealthier merchants he passed, however, tended to eye him more suspiciously. Many of them would even refuse Moonsworn healing, afraid they might be Sunsworn in disguise, or some such nonsense.

There weren't many Moonsworn in the city of Lothain— just a community of a couple thousand or so. Only about one in five were healers— there was no shame in being a clerk or baker, if you did not feel the call to healing. So long, at least, as you kept the faith, lived by the sacred tenets, and kept to the rituals. Converts almost always became healers, but those born into the faith were much more diverse in their interests and professions. And of those one in five, a great many spent their time wandering about the plains, tending to villages.

Yusef waved greeting to a butcher he knew, whose daughter he'd once nursed through a childhood brush with mudpox. She was happily married now, and had children of her own.

Decades ago, when Yusef had first moved to Lothain, he would have crossed the street to avoid a butcher of furred animals. He'd thought the Lothaini to be barbarians, benighted and accursed folk to be pitied.

He still thought them barbarians, but he'd grown to love them for it. They were a straightforward, enthusiastic people, forward in their affection and their feuds. It was, to say the least, a refreshing change from the scheming, politics, and backstabbing of the Holy Cities— Sun or Moonsworn. He couldn't say he'd ever want to go back there.

Not that it would be wise of him to return to the Holy Cities. A memory as sharp as his... well, it had proven more a liability than a strength there, for some things were safer to forget.

It had taken a few years, but he'd started to adapt, even to thrive. He'd even managed to find a perverse sort of enjoyment out of Lothain's brutal winters— at least, out of staying indoors by the fire during them.

Yusef crossed one of the seven bridges across the muddy Winterbranch, pensively eying the sparse crowd. He would normally have loved the bridges to be this empty and uncongested. He hated having to hire a ferryman. Yusef was not cut out for traveling over even the gentlest currents. He'd much rather get jostled and shoved trying to cross one of the narrow bridges.

Tonight, though, everyone was hiding in their homes, mourning Prince Arnulf and fearing plague.

The old healer took a moment to watch the river, absently rubbing his eyepatch. He had only a simple glass sphere in there at the moment, to keep the socket open. As some seers aged, looking into the Sea of the Goddesses— what the Eidola of Teringia called the spirit realm— could begin to induce headaches. Glass on its own couldn't grant one vision into the Sea, removing easy temptation.

Carlan, of course, could still look into the Sea just fine, something he'd teased Yusef about on many occasions.

Crossing into the Moonsworn neighborhood was like entering another city entirely. Grey banners still hung about the streets, in mourning for Arnulf, and the mood was a little duller than it might have been, but it wasn't the oppressive quiet of the rest of the city. Arnulf hadn't been well known among the Moonsworn, and their greater numbers of healers, seers, and scholars were there to keep the people from panicking.

The differences went beyond mere mood, however. The cobbles were clean-swept, and the gutters and drains were kept clear of debris. There were more and larger windows, with tightly built shutters. A few of the wealthier Moonsworn healers and traders even had glass windows on their upper stories, though none were so rich as to put them on the ground floor and risk them being broken by playing children or opportunistic thieves— sturdy shutters were much safer.

Dogs and cats roamed the streets in far greater numbers than the rest of the city. All were well cared for by the community, and they often had two or three homes they'd wander between.

Most of the passersby nodded to him, a few even stopping to chat with him— though he made those conversations brief. His role as palace liaison and his position on the neighborhood's council of elders made him an important community member.

He'd certainly prefer to think it was because he was well-liked, but he knew most people saw him as rather stuffy and precise. Still, he could live with simply not being disliked.

His wife, Emala, was in the entry parlor when he arrived at home, tending to the household shrine. He kissed her on the cheek after he removed his boots, then climbed the stairs. He could hear the grandchildren arguing somewhere on the ground floor, likely displeased at having been ordered inside for the evening. He edged past two of his sons-in-law gossiping in the second-floor hall, then climbed to the third floor.

He strode all the way to the end of the hall, to the office he shared with his eldest daughter Nalda. She'd never married, having devoted herself to healing. Yusef suspected that she just didn't want to marry, considering that two of his other five daughters had also become healers, yet still had families of their own.

Both of them— and several of Yusef's largely forgettable sons-in-law— worked out of the home, making house-calls or working in one of the Moonsworn clinics around the city. Nalda, however, worked as his assistant. She'd done plenty of work in the city as well, but Yusef was grooming her to take his place in the community some day.

"Carlan said yes," Yusef said, not bothering with small talk.

"Did he say yes, or did he say that he was going to speak to the king about it?" Nalda asked dryly, not looking up from the ledger she was writing in.

"He said he was going to speak to the king, but that's the same thing as saying yes," Yusef said, rummaging in the cabinet between their desks.

"The king does have opinions of his own," Nalda said. "He might still reject the petition."

"Here we are," Yusef said, pulling a bottle of pear brandy out of the cabinet. "A celebratory glass is in order."

Nalda raised her eyebrow, but didn't protest when he poured her a glass as well.

"So who will lead the mission, then?" she asked.

"Who do you think?" Yusef said, sipping his brandy. It was a little on the harsh side, which was how he preferred it.

"Father, you're far too old to go haring off into the mountains to investigate a mysterious new illness," Nalda said.

"Too fat and lazy, too," Yusef said. "You'll be leading the mission."

Nalda started coughing at that, a bit of brandy apparently having gone down the wrong tube.

"You'll be up late tonight planning the logistics of the trip," Yusef said. "Supply estimates will have to be made for a whole range of possible missions— I'd like to send at least twenty healers, but the king might not be comfortable with that many. Plan for everything from the full twenty down to just yourself. I'll be double-checking your calculations."

He could have just given her his calculations, but he wanted her to be able to do his job someday.

His daughter finally caught her breath, then glared at him.

"You can't just put me in charge of the mission," she said. "There are far more qualified and experienced healers out there than me, and the council won't tolerate you abusing your position like this."

"I already cleared it with them," Yusef said. "There are more experienced healers— healers who have saved more patients, better chirurgeons, more perceptive seers, and more knowledgeable herbalists. At almost any single thing, you can find someone better than you. Not many, though. You rank near the top of all the healers in skill at nearly everything. You're one of the best-rounded healers in Lothain, and there's not a one of the Vowless that compares to you."

Nalda still looked skeptical.

"Not to mention," Yusef continued, "you're one of the few healers that both the Patient and the Dedicated still respect."

Nalda rolled her eyes at that, but seemed to relax a bit. The feuding between the two factions had grown steadily over the last few decades, with the Dedicated pushing for changes to doctrine more and more rapidly, and the Patient resisting the speed of those changes. It wasn't that the latter were opposed to change for its own sake— the core of the goddesses' teaching was that their children must come to learn and understand the world on their own. It was, instead, the Patient belief that the Moonsworn must be cautious when trying new techniques, for lives were at stake. It wasn't that the Dedicated were incautious or didn't care for the safety of their patients— though the Patient definitely accused them of such on a regular basis— it was that the sheer speed at which the Dedicated had been producing new treatments, ideas, and diagnoses was coming at a dangerously swift pace over the last few decades, as though the Moon herself had begun delivering them to the Dedicated in the holy city through dreams. Adapting to so many changes so quickly was challenging at best, and it was seldom at its best.

Yusef and Nalda had been two of the few to stay neutral between the factions in Lothain. Relations had been growing steadily more acrimonious, but there hadn't been any brawls or outright riots between the factions, like there had been in other cities.

"A list of your preferred healers for the mission is your top priority," Yusef said. He reached into his desk and pulled out a folder. "I've already done a good bit of groundwork already, so you should be able to get at least a little work done tonight."

Yusef sometimes remembered to write things down. Not always, but sometimes.

He handed her the folder and made to head back downstairs. He paused just before the door, however. "Oh, and allow me one little abuse of my position— no bringing your sisters along. One of my daughters in a plague zone is bad enough."

CHAPTER FOUR
The Rest Between

Nalda frowned as she rode towards Castle Morinth. The villages had been muted and quiet, with herds of cattle standing largely unattended. The few villagers wandering about seemed in shock, moving about like they had been broken and put back together haphazardly, with the tell-tale blackened fingers Benen had spoken about in his semaphore messages. Most of the healers from her party had split off already, to seek out and tend to the villagers, but she, along with two others, were heading straight to the castle.

In the end, the king had allowed them eight healers, including herself, as well as a military escort that Nalda suspected were there to watch the Moonsworn as much as they were there to protect them or reinforce Castle Morinth. They'd ridden hard, making the trip in two and a half weeks, instead of the usual three.

The castle gate was open, with only a couple of guards on duty. Both looked exhausted, but they lacked the signs of the disease they'd seen on the way in.

Nalda ignored the guards as her escort spoke to them, looking around her.

Castle Morinth was unusual, to say the least. It wasn't truly built for defense, though the royal family considered it their final redoubt in case of invasion. The castle walls were lower than many other forts, but the keep and its grounds were both immense, built to house the population of the villages below during the harsh winters of the Krannenberg Mountains. Not to mention the cattle and enough supplies for the whole winter. Unlike most castles, however, there was little in the way of a permanent population, save for the garrison and their support staff.

The River Morinth, a tributary of the Winterbranch ran directly under the castle walls and into the castle grounds, through a massive grate. The openings weren't just too small for a man to fit through, but too small for even a cat to fit. A normal castle would forego a vulnerability like a river running through it, relying on wells instead, but anyone attempting to breach the castle through the grate wouldn't do so well— the River Morinth ran out of the Mist Maze, and for all the successes Lothain had had keeping the pass clear of monsters, the river upstream of the castle was filled with hellish creatures. The grate kept them upstream of the castle, but no one went near the river there if they could help it.

Through the castle gate, Nalda could see huge scaffolds throughout the castle grounds from the annual summer maintenance. The storms that rolled out of the Krannenbergs were legendary in their fierceness, and the Mist Maze did nothing to alleviate them. Each summer brought new damage to repair from the winter storms.

Though the Moonsworn had been forbidden access to the castle since its construction, there were plenty of accounts easily accessible to scholars in the libraries of Lothain. She'd read several commanders' journals, a report summarizing its construction, and a decade's worth of expense reports.

Like so many political actions, Nalda suspected the ban was more symbolic than anything. That sort of thing struck her as utter foolishness. Though, in fairness, she knew she would make a terrible politician— she lacked certain virtues politics demanded.

Notably tact, patience with others, or the ability to conceal her irritation for longer than a minute.

For all its size, though, the castle was still dwarfed by the steep mountains to either side.

The scaffolds were empty of workers, however, as were the castle grounds, from what little she could see.

"Where is Healer Benen?" Nalda said, interrupting the conversation between the guards. "I would speak to him, if he hasn't died of your plague. We haven't received messages from him at any semaphore towers along the way for at least a week now."

The castle guard looked awkwardly at her. "The Wrack hit him, ma'am. He's awake now, but in bad shape still. His fingers can't work the semaphore chains anymore."

"I'd guessed he died, so that's an improvement above expectations. And the Wrack?" Nalda said. "Is that what you're calling it? Because it leaves you all twisted up, like something left on a beach by the tide?"

"I've never been to the ocean, ma'am," the perplexed guard said. "And I don't know where the name came from. Old Man Emmet was the first one I heard calling it that."

"Well, take me to him, then," Nalda said, impatiently.

"To Old Man Emmet?" the guard asked.

"No," Nalda snapped, "to Healer Benen! Why would I want to talk to Old Man Emmet?"

"He tells good stories," the guard muttered, but he led her through the castle gate.

Benen was still resting in bed when Nalda arrived, and she immediately pulled on leather gloves and began prodding his limbs.

"Introductions are generally customary," Benen whispered in a rasping tone.

"Healer Nalda," she said, inspecting his blackened fingers. "Your fingers don't look burnt, they look more… frostbitten."

"I said as much in my messages, didn't I?" Benen whispered, looking irritated.

Nalda shrugged. You really never could tell with Vowless healers. Some of them were almost good enough to be Moonsworn, but most were superstitious quacks, whose patients would likely be better off without them.

Nalda resumed poking and prodding at the middle-aged man, pausing every few minutes to take notes. Benen grunted on occasion, but seemed too exhausted to speak.

"You're not as badly injured as some of the other survivors you described," Nalda said.

Benen shrugged. "I'm not as young or as strong, am I? Too old and weak to break my own bones."

Nalda grunted.

"How far has it spread?" Benen asked, closing his eyes.

"It hasn't," Nalda said.

Benen cracked his eyes back open at that.

"At least, it hadn't a week ago," Nalda said. "That was the last time we visited a semaphore receiving station. Whatever this… Wrack is, it might have burnt itself out, Goddesses willing."

"Deserters should have reached other villages by now," Benen said.

"They did," Nalda said. "A couple of them were even struck down by the Wrack there, but no one from outside the pass has caught it yet."

Benen grunted at that. Nalda continued taking notes, waiting for Benen to respond. When no answer was forthcoming, she glanced up to see Benen's eyes closed and breath even.

Nalda blew air out of her nose in irritation and closed her journal. She might not have a particularly good bedside manner, but she was an otherwise excellent healer, and waking a patient just to settle one's own curiosity was hardly good for their recovery.

Besides, there were plenty of other survivors for her to study.

Nalda glared at her notes. "I have," she muttered to herself, "no idea what is going on."

It had been a week since she'd arrived, and the Wrack had proven utterly opaque.

Two-thirds of the residents of Castle Morinth had fallen ill with the disease. One in four of them had died. The residents were, however, largely soldiers or servants in the prime of their life.

In the villages, on the other hand, less than half of the residents had fallen ill, but one in two had died. Much of this, however, came from the fact that the villages had many more children and elderly than Castle Morinth.

Children stricken by the Wrack hardly ever died from it, and indeed, they suffered much less severely. The elderly, however, died in far greater numbers— almost all from their hearts giving out.

Heart failure wasn't the only cause of death, by any means. A few had died in the first moments of the convulsive attacks, frothing at the mouth. One blacksmith, in the throes of particularly violent convulsions, had managed to throw herself off her bed and break her own neck. The most common cause of death, outside of heart failure, was uncontrolled clenching of the throat muscles, leading to suffocation.

For how silly Nalda found Eidol superstitions, their funeral monoliths, engraved with the names of the dead, often made the Moonsworn's jobs much easier. Tracking the deaths caused by illnesses was an exercise in frustration and futility in most places. Your average Vowless hardly bothered to differentiate between dying of illness or dying of accident, let alone different types of illness. The Eidol, however, recorded causes of death quite compulsively in their death archives.

At least, if she could trust their records. Heart failure was easy enough for even an incompetent seer with a quartz eye to identify, but Benen was the only seer worth the name at the castle or the villages, and he'd attended relatively few of the ill. The Wrack had laid low over a thousand people, killing hundreds of them over the course of just two weeks.

To further complicate the numbers, they had woefully incomplete records of the fates of the deserters, or those who had fled the villages.

Many of the survivors complained of lethargy, memory loss, reduced color vision, and weakness in the limbs. Their blackened fingers and toes ranged from moderate stiffness to complete loss of mobility, with no signs of improvement. Dark urine was common, and the later stages of the Wrack involved days to weeks of diarrhea or loose stool. Many of their spouses complained of lack of... marital interest.

Nalda had never precisely understood most people's obsession with that sort of thing, but she at least knew not to underestimate said obsession, even if she'd never felt it herself.

The one village midwife that hadn't been struck down by the plague had proven herself invaluable. Not because she was particularly capable, intelligent, or even likable. No, in fact she was a gossipy, nosy, judgemental woman, whom Nalda would almost consider paying to stay away from her. Though, in fairness, Nalda would pay most people to stay away from her.

The midwife was so useful simply because she was so gossipy— she knew everything about almost everyone in the villages. Rather than painstakingly figuring out what each of the dead had done for a living, where they had lived, and who they'd had contact with, Nalda had been able to simply ask the midwife most of it.

Unfortunately, it meant she'd had to sort through endless piles of useless gossip as well.

Since she'd gotten to the castle, however, there had only been three cases of the Wrack in the villages. All three had died of heart failure, two of said deaths she'd been able to attend. Not a single case had been reported outside the pass, save for among deserters and refugees— at least, not according to the last messenger that had arrived, three days ago. If there had been an incoming semaphore as well, she could have had much more up to date information, but the nearest was two days' swift ride away. Few messengers were willing to risk plague to deliver messages to her, either.

Still, the next messenger should be arriving later today, with any luck.

The cases she'd attended had been… strange. She had a somewhat greater understanding of Benen's confused reports, now— the ripples the disease cast in the Goddess Sea were unlike those of any disease she'd ever seen before, and she fully understood how Benen had mistaken it for poisoning, at first. The ripples were larger and choppier than even those of horsepox or bride's blush.

On top of that, the sort of crude damage the Wrack did to the body far more closely resembled poison than contagion. Fevers rarely grew particularly hot, compared to most contagions. In most illnesses, delirium and convulsions went hand in hand with extremely high fevers, but not with the Wrack. Sailor's pox— the disease that Lothaini knew as Galicantan Pox, Galicantans knew as Sunsworn Pox, and Sunsworn knew as… well, every nation seemed to call it after someone they disliked— was one of the few exceptions, but its delirium happened years and years after infection, and was presaged by all sorts of sores and rashes. It also, well… definitely did not reduce marital interest in its victims.

The most baffling part was the contagion's disappearance. By now Nalda would have expected it to be halfway to Lothain, but it didn't seem to have spread at all. The Wrack's victims didn't cough or sneeze more than a healthy person. More victims than not had diarrhea, though almost never until after the delirium had ended. She wasn't even sure that was related to the Wrack, since others had reported watery stool as well.

Castle Morinth and its dependent villages were only a couple centuries old, constructed long after the Moonsworn had convinced the Teringian nations to follow their rules regarding building next to water. They weren't always the best at keeping to them, but it should have prevented waterborne illness from spreading this badly.

She could hear shouting outside the window of her temporary office, out in the castle courtyard, but she ignored it, focusing on her notes.

Senna, one of the other Moonsworn healers that had accompanied her, had suggested that the Wrack had a far longer dormancy period after spreading than most contagions, but Nalda doubted that, largely thanks to the cattle around here. She'd had to find out far more than she wanted to about cattle herding from the gossipy midwife to figure out the cattle herder's schedules. The hairy, long-horned mountain cattle had to be fattened up after a long winter. That meant that with the late springs in the mountains, they weren't herded down to the plains until the beginning of summer at the earliest, and usually later than that. The cattle herders in the villages had just started their cattle drives a couple days before Arnulf's death. By now, the cattle should have all been sold to lowland butchers and cattle merchants, with the herdsmen on their way back.

If, at least, the fear of the Wrack didn't keep them away.

Though… sailor's pox did go dormant for months, years, or even decades after the initial symptoms. The two diseases weren't much alike beyond the delirium, but perhaps some monster from the Mist had spread it among the town or village some time ago, and it only now had spread? Though it couldn't have been years ago, or soldiers that had been transferred away from their posts at Castle Morinth would have come down with it as well.

That was easy enough to check— she'd just need to know when the last troop transfer had been.

Though, on second thought, she rather imagined that the Lothaini would be suspicious of a Moonsworn asking about troop movements. Still, she'd inquire with Benen when she had a chance— he'd been nothing if not helpful, at least when he could stay awake.

There was just so much Nalda didn't know. Most importantly, she hadn't observed any victims in the post-delirium fevered stage. Benen had reported that the ripples— turbulence, the Vowless called them— had changed significantly after the delirium ended, but Nalda hadn't been able to see it for herself, and Benen hadn't been able to draw them. Being able to accurately draw the Sea was a skill only few could master— its subtle shadings and shifts lent themselves poorly to paper.

The door to her office burst open.

"Nalda!" Senna shouted, panting and out of breath.

Nalda gave the older healer an irritated look. She was unquestionably good as a healer and was considered something of an expert in unusual illnesses, but she was as excitable as a much younger woman and tended to burst in on her with some new idea at least twice a day.

"The courier's here!" Senna said. She took a deep breath. "It's the Wrack. It's spread."

Nalda was out of her seat and on her way down the courtyard before Senna could even blink.

CHAPTER FIVE

Monsters in Seibarrow

Annica had shuttered the windows of her room andd latched them. She'd taken the winter tapestries out from the loft, struggling to carry the thick cloth on her own, and had stretched and hung them over the windows. She'd torn up bits of cloth and shoved them into her ears. She'd wanted to melt wax into them, but Mama had stopped her— the only time either of her parents had taken notice of her at all in days. She'd bundled herself in as many blankets as she could, and rolled herself under the wooden frame of her bed. She'd pressed her ears between two pillows.

She could still hear the screaming.

Even as hot and stifling as it grew, even drenched with sweat, she kept herself wrapped up, trying to keep out the screams.

The servants had stopped coming days ago, soon after the screaming started. Mama said they were just afraid, but Annica knew she was lying.

The monsters had gotten them. Just like they were going to get Mama and Papa, and just like they were going to get her.

Dierdre paced across the house, counting her steps. Five across the wide entry hall. Ten through the parlor. Another four through the narrow, crowded back hall, maneuvering past the garderobe and the stairwell leading up to her and her husband's bedroom and their daughter Annica's bedroom. Five steps more if she entered her husband's office at the end of the back hall, or seven if she entered the kitchen, with its door leading to the alley behind.

It wasn't a big house, even compared to their old one, but they weren't sharing it with ten other family members over the family tailor's shop. It was finely built, as well, hardly letting in a draft during the winter, when all the winter tapestries were tacked up over the windows. It got a little warm in the summer, even with the windows open, but what house didn't?

Six back across the kitchen this time. She took a deep breath, shortening her stride again.

Four across the back hall.

Silas, the crotchety old miser who lived in the house sharing their north wall, had started screaming yesterday afternoon. It had broken something in Annica. The six year old had already been panicked and terrified, and when Silas started screaming, she'd hidden away in her room. Dierdre knew she should be with her daughter, but she couldn't hold still, couldn't stop moving.

Ten steps across the parlor.

Silas had stopped screaming after two hours. Dierdre didn't know whether he'd died or his voice had given out.

Three across the entry hall. She took a deep breath, pivoted, and made sure to take shorter strides on the way back.

She didn't even know if anyone had come to check on Silas or tend to him. She didn't even know if a priest had come to record Silas' name, if he had died, to make sure the ancestors could find him through the spirit realm.

Five across the entry hall.

She'd been so happy when they moved here. It wasn't far from the old place, but Thaniel's hard work, smart investing, and a windfall of good luck on a merchant caravan he'd joined had improved their lot far beyond anything Dierdre had ever expected. She'd considered moving in with Thaniel's family, crammed above their tailor's shop, far better fortune than a girl like her from the slums deserved.

Nine steps across the parlor.

Thaniel had braved the streets, despite her protests, to go check on his family. He should be back by now. The streets of Seibarrow were mostly empty— the townsfolk having all barricaded themselves inside or fled to the countryside.

Or were screaming and dying of the Wrack.

Three steps into the back hall, then into Thaniel's office.

They'd all heard the rumors from Castle Morinth. Everyone had been stockpiling food, and Thaniel's investments had been booming. Then the Wrack seemed to have just… vanished. They'd all breathed a sigh of relief, and Thaniel had even bought Dierdre a new necklace.

Then the town woke up a week ago to screaming in the night.

Five steps through her husband's office, past his desk and to the south wall of their home.

The old widows Asa and Sara lived there alone, claiming to be cousins, but everyone in the neighborhood knew they were no such thing, and that they considered themselves married. They were well-loved by all in the neighborhood, and this was hardly some rural village where even the rumor of such things would raise a mob. So long as they kept up the pretense, none would gainsay the women. Judgment belonged to the ancestors, not the living.

Four steps back across Thaniel's office.

There were just five screamers that first night, but Lord Arnulf— of the same name as the dead prince, may his name always be remembered— had been one of them. His sister, another. A palace cook. Two wealthy merchants that lived close to the Seibarrow castle.

A brief pause at the office door, then a turn to the left and five steps across the kitchen.

The second day, there were at least two dozen screamers.

She took a deep breath and evened her stride. Seven back across the kitchen.

The second night, there had to have been at least a hundred. Most of the remaining nobles in the city started dropping like flies. Wealthy merchants and well-to-do artisans. City guardsmen. Screams echoed all across the better parts of town.

Three across the back hall, pausing briefly at the stairs.

In the slums, where Dierdre had grown up, there hadn't been a single screamer. The Wrack had passed over them completely.

Halfway across the parlor, a particularly pained scream from down the street distracted her, and she lost count.

Dierdre thought of the cousins she hadn't spoken to in years, the monolith where her parents' names were recorded, and the narrow streets where she'd once played.

Three steps across the entry hall, then she turned and strode over to the shrine to the ancestors. She'd heard the heathen Sunsworn and Moonsworn had household shrines as well, to their murderous goddesses, as though in mockery of the truth of the Eidolon. Many of the poor spoke respectfully of the Moonsworn, but where had they been when her father was slowly dying after being run over by a cart? When her mother's neck had swelled up, and the growth had killed her over months? What little comfort either had gained came from their ancestors, not heathen goddesses.

Some of her fellow slum dwellers had mocked the Eidolon, but they were criminals and thieves. Most of the poor, though, kept to the faith. Even though many were foolish enough to praise the Moonsworn, they still honored the ancestors on fast days with gifts of food they could hardly afford, with gratitude for what little they had.

She turned without praying at the shrine, and took four unsteady steps back to the parlor.

When she was young, they mocked the rich folks, mocked the merchants who aped the nobles, for only caring about the ancestors when it was time for their names to be recorded. For griping about every gift to the ancestors on fast days.

Five steps to the middle of the parlor, then an abrupt stop.

She'd tried to be true to both her ancestors and Thaniels'. She'd never complained about the gifts to the ancestors, never turned aside the priests and acolytes on alms days, and tried to pray at the shrine every day. Had she done it enough, though? Were her ancestors still content with her offerings?

She turned and took four steps back to the entry hall. Three steps to the shrine. She started to kneel, then stopped.

Would her ancestors even be able to guide her, to help her? Had any of them ever known anything but poverty? But the slums? She had no idea. She didn't know where she came from. Shamefully, she didn't even know their names beyond her great-great-grandparents. She'd never even met her grandparents, for that matter.

Would Thaniel's ancestors know any more? They were honest working folk, but none of them had risen to the heights Thaniel had. And even if they had guidance, would they offer it to her, or just think her an unworthy upstart?

Dierdre pressed her first two fingers to her lips, then to the shrine, but she asked for no guidance.

Four steps back to the parlor.

On the third day, rumors had begun spreading wildly. That the Wrack was a plot by the Sunsworn, carried out by their Moonsworn agents. That it was a plot by the Galicantans, who wanted to try and unite the continent again.

Ten steps across the parlor.

That it was a plot by the northerners, with their beautiful songs and murderous ways, whose warlike ancestors demanded they raid and pillage the honest folk of Lothain.

That it was a plot by the jealous king of Geredain, who still believed he had a right to Lothain's throne.

Four steps through the cramped back hall, pausing briefly at the stairs.

That it was the revenge of the Sei ancestors, slain in battle centuries ago at the base of the low hill where the castle now rested. That their rage at being burned without recording their names had finally boiled over at a town that had the gall to name itself after their defeat.

Seven steps across the kitchen, where she rested her head against the locked and barred alley door.

That last rumor, for all its silliness, had haunted her dreams. The foolish Sei didn't honor their ancestors anyhow, worshipping some dour, joyless god that promised them nothing but more misery after their death. Something about it, though, had lodged under her skin.

Six steps back across the kitchen.

Four days into the screaming, the poor of Seibarrow had rioted. They'd seized the contents of the granaries, then barricaded themselves in the slums. For all the hundreds of screamers among the wealthy, among the crafters and merchants and nobles and artisans and guards, there'd only been perhaps a couple dozen victims among the poor and laborers by then.

Four steps to cross most of the kitchen, only to wince at another, particularly pained scream. This one bore the signs of a voice about to rupture, to give out.

Dierdre had never expected to learn what a screaming voice about to give out sounded like. She never expected to learn to drown out all but the worst screams. She never expected that as the number of screamers decreased— as they died, recovered, or simply tore their voices apart— that the quiet would scare her more than the screams. The city had hardly ever been quiet before. There was always something making noise. Even in the dead of night, guard patrols and nightsoil carts made their rounds. The only time she'd ever heard the city quiet before was in the silent hours after a blizzard had coated the city white.

In between the screams, little shards of that cold quiet were creeping in. Dierdre found herself shivering despite the heat.

Two more steps. Not towards the back door, but towards the fireplace, as though to warm herself.

There was worse than the screamers, though. Worse than the quiet. There were the moaners and the babblers.

The screamers were lost in some awful, mindless pit of pain. They only lasted a few hours at most until they stopped screaming. The moaners and the babblers, though… they just kept going, and going, and going. They were quieter than the screamers, and tended to be drowned out by them, but they kept lurking at the edge of hearing, as though waiting to come in.

Three steps to the back door, where she rested her hand on the bar.

Dierdre didn't know how long she stood there, thinking about opening the back door and walking into the back alley. She had no idea *why* she was thinking about opening the back door and walking out. She had no idea where she was planning on going, or if she just sought longer distances to pace, out in the back alley where the rats and other vermin lurked.

Before she could figure out the answers to those questions, a knock sounded at the front door.

Dierdre's mind went blank, and she could feel her stomach in her mouth.

The knock came again.

Nine small, slow steps across the kitchen.

She couldn't imagine Thaniel brought home good news. If his family had been fine, he would have been home hours ago. The Wrack must have hit them. Maybe one of his brothers. Maybe one of his sisters. Maybe his mother. Maybe his dissolute uncle, who only came home when he ran out of drinking money and needed a place to stay and work. Maybe his great-grandmother, a woman who everyone in the family joked about being so ornery and stubborn that the ancestors kept her alive just so they could have a little peace.

Six steps down the back hall.

Everything Dierdre had lacked, everything she'd craved out of a family, Thaniel's family had. They'd unquestioningly accepted a poor, illiterate, skittish girl from the slums, embracing her immediately. They'd taught her letters and numbers, and not one of them shamed her for her disreputable, slovenly, criminal cousins.

She loved them for it.

Fifteen steps across the parlor.

She couldn't even hear the screamers. She couldn't hear the moaners, or the babblers. She couldn't even hear that cold quiet in between them all.

She could only hear the intermittent knock, and the matching pounding in her ears.

Three steps into the entry hall. Three steps that took her halfway across, where she just stared at the heavy oak door.

She turned her head towards the family shrine, and a dreadful thought crept up on her.

When she'd prayed, how often had she prayed to her own ancestors, and how often had she prayed to Thaniel's? How many gifts had she offered her own ancestors, and how many had she offered Thaniel's?

Or, rather, how much more had she prayed to Thaniel's ancestors? How many more gifts of food had she offered Thaniel's ancestors on fast days?

And what would her lack of contact with her cousins look like to her ancestors?

How angry might her ancestors be?

The knock came again, and Dierdre swallowed.

Two determined steps and she opened the door to let Thaniel in.

Only it wasn't Thaniel.

It was his sister, Shalis, her eyes red-rimmed with tears.

Annica knew the monsters had gotten in when she heard the scream from downstairs. They'd come to torture Mama, then her. She bundled the blanket tighter around herself.

The screaming stopped, and footsteps thundered through the house and up the stairs. Annica's door burst open, and she screamed, knowing the monsters were there.

The monster in her room called her name, searching for her. She could hear another monster say something from downstairs but couldn't make it out.

Then the monster's hands were on her, and were pulling her out from under the bed.

She couldn't fight back, wrapped in the blanket, and she only succeeded in hitting her head on the frame, and everything went wobbly. The monster tore the blanket from her, and she weakly kicked at it, and realized it wore Mama's face.

The monster pulled her close to eat her, but the bite never came, and she realized the monster was Mama, and Mama was sobbing.

Then they were running down the stairs, past Auntie Shalis, who put a hand out to stop them, but Mama just kept running, and then they were out the door, and the screaming was loud and clear now.

Annica burrowed into Mama, trying to drown them out, but the bits of cloth in her ears didn't do anything to help now, and they slipped from her ears as Mama ran down the streets. Mama's tears kept falling on Annica's head.

They ran past her friend Jon's house, who she'd told Mama she was going to marry someday, and her friend Sara's house, who could sing really pretty, but her door was just sitting open now, and Annica knew the monsters had got her. They ran past the butcher's where Mama got their meat. He looked really scary but was actually really nice. His door was open too.

There was trash on the streets now, and rats hardly looked up from it as Mama ran past them. They ran past the cooper, the blacksmith, and then Annica didn't know where they were anymore. Mama kept running.

The houses were smaller and uglier and more run-down now, and there was a big pile of trash and chairs and tables in the street and there were people on top of the pile and they were yelling something— Annica didn't know what— and Mama was swaying and not looking at anything and her arms were all twitchy and then Annica was on the ground and Mama was on the ground and Mama was screaming and she didn't know where they were and Mama was thrashing about on the ground and Annica wanted her to get up because the monsters were coming.

But Mama kept screaming.

CHAPTER SIX
Precipice

Carlan was having an exceptionally bad day.

The king, panicking about the advancing plague, had ordered the palace sealed off from the rest of the city, and he had largely sealed off the capital itself from the rest of Lothain— save for shipments into the city. The rest of the king's council had supported the move, despite the opposition of Carlan, the medical council, and the Moonsworn. The only communication in and out of the palace now had to either be shouted down from the walls or carried by semaphore.

That's not to say that quarantining the palace and the city of Lothain from the rest of Lothain was necessarily a terrible idea solely considering the Wrack— they still had no idea how the disease was spreading, the quarantine might very well keep it out of the city. It's just that it was a terrible idea from nearly every other point of view.

The capital was the economic and administrative hub of the nation. Nearly landlocked Lothain had only one port and no great cities other than the capital. The provincial nobility was weak, and the populace held the throne in great esteem. Power in Lothain was centralized in a way that it wasn't in any of its neighbors— not even Geredain, so similar to Lothain otherwise.

With no less than four northern cities having been hit with the Wrack in the past two weeks, a good chunk of the country was already in chaos. Cutting off a huge chunk of trade, administration, and guard patrols around the nation would have disastrous consequences at the best of times, and this was *not* the best of times.

Of course, on the other hand, quarantining the city might do nothing. They still had no idea how the Wrack spread, and quite a few scholars, seers, and Moonsworn were convinced the disease had a truly absurd dormancy period— one of weeks or even months. If that were true, then the plague was most likely already inside the city.

They had no treatments, no cures. The only thing you could do for a victim was offer them something to dull the pain, and prices for poppy had skyrocketed— as had valerian, skullcap, catnip, willow bark, and any other herb that might offer victims the least relief from the pain. Healers and the wealthy around the city were stockpiling like mad.

To make it worse, the outbreaks in Seibarrow and the other northern cities nearest Castle Morinth had upended what they thought they knew about the disease. The nobles and city leadership had been laid low everywhere, with the wealthy and the merchants suffering almost as badly. In Seibarrow, the low-lying slums had been passed over almost entirely, while in two of the others, the poorer parts of the city suffered only lightly. In Frostford, the closest and smallest city to Morinth, the poor had been hit fairly hard, but they still got off far more lightly than the wealthy.

It was that fact, Carlan suspected, that had the leadership so panicked. Plagues of one form or another always worked people— rich or poor— into a panic, but this one was something else entirely. The wealthy couldn't buy their way out of disease entirely, but it was commonly accepted that they'd do far better than the poor. Having enough to eat, being able to afford healers, and not being packed together like rats in an alley all tended to let them shrug off the worst.

The poor only had the Moonsworn, who were overstretched and overworked. At least a half-dozen cities had already barred Moonsworn from entry or forced them out entirely, their rulers convinced the Wrack was a Sunsworn plot.

This only made the poor angrier and more panicked, as they didn't share the same resentments towards the cult of healers their betters did.

If only Yusef had been inside the palace when it was sealed, Carlan might not have such a headache now, but as it was, he had no other healers or seers he truly trusted or felt he could rely on.

Past that, the city itself drew close to a boil. The brutal, muggy heat of the plains in late summer and early fall should have had people lethargic, trying to do anything they could to keep cool, but fights were breaking out left and right in the city below, and there'd already been a half-dozen near-riots. The city guard was barely keeping a handle on things, and for that matter, they were close to rioting themselves.

Other nations were stirring as well. Galicanta and the Sunsworn Empire were both eyeing events in Lothain with interest, though the two powers were too focused on one another to take advantage. Sei raids from the mountains had picked up over the last few weeks, as the ill-tempered, humorless barbarians insisted the Wrack was sent by their dour god to punish Lothain. There might not be many Sei left, but they were an irritant, nonetheless. The two dozen or so small northern kingdoms beyond the Krannenbergs were shifting restlessly, clearly trying to decide whether to attempt an invasion with autumn and its fierce snows so close. Most concerningly, there were rumblings behind the Geredain border. Both nations always kept troops ready on their borders. Battles over contested territory were common, and the Geredain royal line had never abandoned their claim to the throne of Lothain— one which, Carlan admitted only in the privacy of his own mind, was a claim not entirely without merit. Their neighbors were still looking at the Wrack as more opportunity than threat, as it hadn't yet entered their lands.

No matter how much one hoped that trying times would bring the mighty to look past their own interests, disappointment would always be one's reward.

Their smaller neighbors to the west, at least, were paying them little attention other than cautious interest.

Trying to help govern a panicked kingdom with restless enemies, with limited communications and manpower, would have been headache-inducing enough for Carlan. Adding entitled nobles who kept demanding Carlan's time made it even worse. The fact that the palace had been sealed with only two thirds of its normal complement of servants, with a greater than usual number of nobles, was a miserable lump of uncooked flour in his bread.

Worse yet than all that, though, were the troubling reports of the names of the dead going unrecorded, that in some of the worst-struck cities, the priests were abandoning their duties, were simply unable to keep up with the dead due to sheer numbers, or had died off themselves. Carlan desperately hoped this was false, or at least exaggerated. Hopefully, families and neighbors were preserving the names of the dead, so that they might be transcribed into obelisks as soon as possible, lest the Wrack dead be prevented from joining their ancestors beyond the spirit realm.

None of that was the worst part, though. No, the worst part?

The worst part was that the idiot nobles were planning a masquerade. The other councilors and the king were fully behind it, in the interest of "preventing panic in the city". Carlan hardly saw how the nobility splurging on a wasteful feast and ball while their subjects suffered would do anything but enrage the populace, but he'd been overruled, and now party business was taking up valuable semaphore time, servant labor the palace could ill afford, palace clerks Carlan absolutely couldn't afford to spare, and simply getting in the way of everything. Nobles were constantly trying to send for food, wine, and costumes from the city, despite the castle being closed off, and somehow Carlan had been roped into denying them outside expeditions, despite not supporting the quarantine in the first place.

Carlan would never publicly voice an ill-word about the king, but the way his majesty had hurled himself into party planning was an obvious attempt to bury his grief at Arnulf's death.

This most recent bit of nonsense, however, was the absolute worst. He had Moonsworn summaries of the Wrack's spread to read, troop orders to send to the border, requisition forms to file, and a solid dozen petitioners to deal with, and the king had seen fit to send the royal seamstresses to measure Carlan for a costume for the masquerade.

He was, apparently, to be outfitted as a worried mother hen.

Yusef had gotten quite a laugh out of Carlan's semaphore messages describing the masquerade preparations— and his friend's most unwanted costume. He hadn't had many laughs, lately, so that one had been much appreciated.

The whole city was on edge, and there'd already been several attacks on Moonsworn in some of the wealthier neighborhoods they visited. Hardly any topic but the Wrack were on any lips, and everyone sought out those wiser or more knowledgeable with questions. Or, at least, they sought out those who best postured as wise.

The herbalists, chirurgeons, seers, and scholars, bombarded with questions from those below, in turn sought out others to ask— almost always members of the Moonsworn. Who, of course, turned to their elders, who turned to, of course, Yusef himself.

Yusef desperately wished he had someone to turn to with his own questions.

King Sigis IV— Sigis the Fat, Sigis the Useless Birdwatcher, Sigis the Easily Distracted, Sigis the Faint of Heart— had, in his infinite foolishness, ordered the semaphores closed to the Moonsworn, for fear that they'd inform the Sunsworn of Lothain's weakness. Yusef had had no communication with the nameless Moonsworn holy city, which lay widdershins about the holy mountain, for almost a week. He'd had no word from Nalda at Castle Morinth for nearly four days— it had taken messengers longer to reach the pass and close the semaphore to her.

Yusef was the only Moonsworn in the whole kingdom allowed access to the semaphores, and this only for the purposes of communicating with Carlan in the palace.

He still received reports on the spread of the Wrack, but they were all panicky, unrigorous, superstitious messes of rumors from Vowless healers. He had few reputable reports about the apparent changes to the Wrack as it spread— its special focus on the wealthy and the appearance of the so-called babblers and moaners.

He found the former far more interesting than the latter— based on what reports he did have, the babblers and moaners simply seemed to be victims who were suffering a less-extreme version of the first, most dangerous stage of the disease. They also suffered less blackening of the extremities than the screamers.

On top of that, in over half the cities struck by the Wrack, the plague didn't start small and grow over time— instead, dozens or hundreds of victims would start screaming in a terrifyingly short amount of time— often as little as hours. It was as if something were triggering it. In other cities, like Seibarrow, it spread a bit more normally, but that was hardly a consolation.

The bottle of brandy in the cabinet almost seemed to be calling to him, but Yusef resisted the urge to pour himself a drink. He dropped the latest useless report from a Vowless healer in Seibarrow, scooted back his chair, and strode out of his office, trying to ignore Nalda's empty desk.

Had he done the right thing in sending her into the heart of the Wrack? Would the standard Moonsworn precautions keep her safe, or would the Wrack claim her like it had claimed so many already? Even if she survived it, most of the surviving victims were shells of who they'd been, few able to move around much, broken physically and mentally, and living as though in a daze in a world drained of much of its color.

Who knew what the awful first stage actually felt like— few of the survivors had been able to offer any sort of cogent explanation.

Worries chased each other around Yusef's head as he trudged down the stairs, ignoring the worried whispering of his sons-in-law, trying not to wake the sleeping children. He reached the bottom floor, where Emala was tending to the shrine of the Goddesses, as she did so often these days.

He moved to kneel beside her when a knock came at the door.

Frowning, Yusef answered the door. On the other side stood Gilded Bensamen, the richest member of the Moonsworn community in Lothain. No one called him Gilded Ben to his face, but the fat, venal merchant's propensity for cloth of gold and expensive jewelry doomed him to the name.

"What?" Yusef demanded. It was late, and he had little interest in visitors.

"I, ah, that is," Bensamen said, "was merely in the, ah, neighborhood, and…"

Yusef gestured for the man to speed it up. Bensamen would quite happily take an hour to say something worth only a few heartbeats.

"I merely thought to stop by and show a…. a show of, ah, my support," Bensamen said, looking slightly affronted. "In these trying times, the, ah, pious must do all we can for the community and, ah, in service of the Goddesses, yes?"

The fat merchant pulled a jingling sack of coin from his robes, and offered it to Yusef. "To help, ah, support the healers' work."

Yusef raised a brow at that, but reached out and took the donation. Bensamen must be panicked about the Wrack indeed— he seldom showed more than the barest trace of piety, and he begrudged every penny tithed to the healers. Yusef knew for a fact that meat of furred animals crossed Bensamen's table more nights than not, that he kept no cats or dogs to hunt vermin, and that he had a household shrine to the Goddesses that was as gaudy as it was unused.

"I, ah, hope that we have enough tincture of the poppy for when it is needed," Bensamen said.

So that was why the merchant was making this donation. He'd failed to secure a supply for himself when it was still available, and he wanted to ensure he felt as little pain as possible if he caught the Wrack.

"We have ample supplies," Yusef said, "and they will be distributed in their rightful order, as the Verses of Impossible Choice lay out. You need not fear corruption or misuse by the healers."

He shut the door on Bensamen's greasy expression, ignoring anything else the man had to say, and turned to the shrine. He kissed the crown of Emala's head, and she smiled at him as he carefully lowered himself to his knees beside her, grunting.

Thankfully, though the Goddesses were quite strict on how one was supposed to pray, they didn't forbid the use of knee pillows, else Yusef might have been tempted to pray far less as he aged.

Yusef took a moment to simply stare at the candles in the shrine before he began his prayers. He felt like he was standing on a precipice, as though he were waiting for the tide to come in, a storm to strike, a tree to fall. A current was coming to seize them all, and he didn't know what else to do but pray.

CHAPTER SEVEN
A Visitor in the Clouds

Priestess Verna was picking her nose when someone burst into the village's Eidolon temple. It was one of the village children— a uniformly grubby, high-pitched, overstimulated bunch.

"Priestess!" the child yelled, blinking as their eyes adjusted from the bright daylight to the dim insides of the temple.

Before the child's eyes could finish adjusting, Verna removed her finger from her nose and quickly wiped her finger beneath the stool.

It was one of life's peculiar truths that no matter how many people picked their noses, they all treated it as something shameful and embarrassing, even in front of others whom they knew picked their noses as well. If every man and woman on Iopis picked their nose, they'd still all pretend not to. And, if Verna had to guess, they probably all did.

Verna's hair was more white than brown now, and she was, at the risk of praising herself too much, reasonably respectable and dignified in appearance and demeanor.

She still got the occasional recalcitrant booger, though. The human body didn't care in the slightest about one's dignity.

"Priestess Verna!" the child yelled again, running between the rows of obelisks, engraved with thousands of names.

Cloudholt was a village of fewer than two hundred souls, where everyone knew everyone. Half the villagers were Sei converts of questionable faith and morose demeanor, while the other half were Eidol born, but equally morose and lackluster in their faith. It would take millennia to fill all of the temple's obelisks with the names of the dead from

Cloudholt alone, but the obelisks weren't just for their dead— the Cloudholt Temple was a sacred Repository, filled with the copies of the names of the dead from a dozen towns and cities. If something happened to the obelisks on the plains, the ancestors' names would still be anchored here in Cloudholt, so they could watch their children through the medium of the spirit realm.

A priestess of Verna's education would hardly have been sent to such a small village otherwise.

"What is it, child?" Verna asked, picking up her chisel and mallet again.

"There's a visitor in the village!" the child said, in its high-pitched voice. "He's talking about sick people, and Granny told me to fetch you!"

Verna sighed, set down her tools, and stood up, her back creaking.

"Lead on, child," she said.

Her feet hurt the first few steps down the aisle— the soles of her feet always hurt after sitting or lying for any length of time these days. By the time she reached the temple doors, she was walking at a normal pace again, which was still far too slow for the impatient child.

Verna blinked as she stepped into the sun and looked around the village.

The temple was the highest structure in the village proper, and the view from its entrance looked down across the village, down the mountain, and far across the plains of Lothain. Cloudholt was a poor village, built just below the treeline on the shoulders of the Krannenbergs. It spent a good chunk of the year enveloped in clouds blowing against the mountain, but on a clear day like today, you could see forever.

Most of the villagers were simple herders, leading flocks of goats or a few stringy, badtempered sheep. There were a few woodcutters and craftsmen, a blacksmith, several carpenters, and a small number of miners— garnets could be found in the mountain's granite this high up, on rare occasion even ones large enough to sell to the seers, but it was backbreaking, unrewarding work.

It often seemed to Verna as though immediately upon hitting puberty, the villagers began aging three days for every one they lived. Their lives were hardscrabble and harsh, and there was little joy in them. Despite that— or perhaps because of it— they indulged their children more than the peasants down in the plains did, buying them toys and treats whenever peddlers came to town, or whittling crude wooden toys themselves, and hardly ever assigning any chores to them.

Verna rolled her stiff back a bit, then followed the child down into the village.

She really should try and learn some of the children's names.

The village didn't have any proper roads— the houses and goat paddocks were scattered almost at random in the bare dirt. Most of the sparse trees had been cleared from inside the village, but it was hard to tell the difference between it and the rest of the forest. There was hardly even a road up to the village— it was more like a game trail with a few stone markers alongside it.

Despite the poverty of the village, the houses were far from hovels. The villagers had as much good timber as they needed, from farther down the mountain, and more granite than they could ever hope to quarry. Most of the homes were built of stone and thatched with the long needles of the walking pines— called that because their trunks often didn't start until several feet off the ground, giving them the appearance of walking on their thick, protruding roots. There were plenty of wooden sheds, chicken coops, and the like. Not much in the way of livestock could survive up here— mostly just goats, sheep, and chickens. Pigs had been tried a few times, but the lowland breeds seldom thrived up here, and there weren't any highland breeds close enough for the villagers to purchase.

They had no lord to prevent them from logging the forests below them for firewood, yet they never pushed the forest too far— the villagers had a strict logging schedule, fine-tuned over generations, and they never took too much from any one spot. It tended to be enforced with social shaming and penalties paid in home-brewed beer— though if a family was having a particularly rough year, everyone would just look the other way.

Down at the bottom of the village, where the rough trail arrived, Verna could see a crowd gathered around someone. She frowned. Unexpected peddlers were rare, but hardly unknown, yet Verna saw no mules carrying goods. The sheep were sheared in summer this high up, but that was long done with now, and autumn fast approached. Miners took their garnets down into the foothills, and gem traders didn't come up this high themselves.

The child, seeing she was on her way towards the stranger, took off, clambering up a rain cistern for a better view. The village's well didn't provide enough water on its own, so the village made up the gap however they could— there were always water barrels lying around in the summer, hauled hours up the mountains from the nearest stream, if need be. In the winter, there was plenty of snow to melt.

She began hearing an unfamiliar male voice as she walked through the crowd, the villagers making way respectfully enough for her. Not as quickly as they might in the lowlands, but…

When she got to the center of the crowd, she found herself looking at a tall, slender, middle-aged man. He wore well-worn but well-kept finery, carried a stout walking stick, and a leather knapsack rested at his feet. Over one eye, he had an eyepatch that marked him as a seer.

Something about him screamed trouble to Verna.

She had absolutely no idea why her instincts were screaming trouble about the man. If Verna was honest with herself, she'd been sent to tend to the Repository not just for her faith in the ancestors, but due to her… difficulties with people.

She lived inside her own heart more than in the world around her, communing with the ancestors and tending to the obelisks that kept the names of the dead. Verna was a poor hand at politics, and she understood matters spiritual far better than matters worldly. It had come to a shock to her when she realized that, rather than being a position to be competed over, many priests in the Eidol ranks considered being sent to tend one of the remote Repositories by a Hierarch a punishment.

She supposed most of the priests she knew thought her naive to actually believe the teachings and consider it a great spiritual honor.

To put it simply, Verna hardly had a scheming or suspicious bone in her body, and if she weren't a priestess, she was quite sure she would have been taken for everything she had years ago by some grifter or other.

So the fact that her instincts were going off now, while the villagers around her just seemed excited and interested in the man, was quite worrying to Verna, and she couldn't help but think that perhaps the ancestors were trying to warn her of something.

"A half-dozen cities now," the man said, in a deep, rich, voice, like butter across fresh bread. "It's killing nine of every ten, and rendering the tenth speechless, broken, empty husks. No shadow of their former selves left, to the point their own ancestors don't recognize them."

There were gasps and murmurs from the crowd as the man spoke. As he turned, his eyes fell on Verna, and a flicker of surprise ran through them— it seemed he wasn't expecting a full Eidolon priestess in a little mountain village like this.

Several villagers called out questions about the Wrack, but the man waved them off.

"We're safe up here for now," he said. "It's been a long trip, and I'd wet my throat and rest my feet. I can share news with the whole village later."

Verna just watched as the villagers bustled about, preparing a place to stay for the man— likely a spare mat in front of someone's fireplace, as Cloudholt was too small for an inn.

Though some would call it too small for a Repository, for that matter, or even a name. Verna had been in plenty of larger villages that had lacked them.

Still, as small and out of the way as Cloudholt was, they'd heard the news of the Wrack, of its brutal ways and the screams of its victims. It hadn't sounded so bad as their visitor made it out to be, but… perhaps the Wrack's dangers were what the ancestors were warning her of.

Verna said nothing as the crowd dispersed.

"We were told the last days would come many millennia hence," the man, Olefs, said. "We were told they would come when the ancestors outnumbered the living so many times over that even with their minuscule hunger in the spirit realm, we could not feed them on fast days. They would eat the world out of house and home, and the living would starve. They would die with their names unrecorded by any, and be lost in crossing the spirit realm, while the ancestors would be left maddened by hunger for eternity."

Verna leaned forwards towards the fire pit a little more, watching him from over the flames in the afternoon light.

"We were wrong," Olefs said. "The end times come swiftly, and they come now. The Wrack will break all of mankind's cities, all of mankind's kingdoms, and even the heretics will fall like wildfire."

There were gasps and murmurs from the collected villagers, and a babe in arms started fussing.

Verna felt as though she should stand, yell that Olefs was a heretic, but doubt stayed her voice. The teachings on the Last Days, the Hungry Days, were the strangest in the Lays of the Eidolon. The Book of Hungry Days was arrhythmic and jarring, unlike the flowing verse of the other books, and it went on and on with no allowance for breath in a way that simply seemed to demand it be spoken faster and faster without end or pause. It lacked the clarity of the rest of the Lays, and theological arguments about it were more common than agreements— though most preferred to avoid speaking of it entirely.

Olefs spoke for hours then, of the nightmares he had seen in the lowlands, of the way the fingers and toes of those struck down by the Wrack simply rotted and fell off, and how their screams would render their loved ones deaf, their eardrums burst. He spoke of the way the Eidolon priests and priestesses abandoned their duties and left the victims to be lost forever in the spirit realm.

Verna once more almost shouted, but doubt grew in her again as the villagers around her shot her suspicious, angry, and scared looks, as though *she* were the one to have abandoned her duties.

Olefs spoke of the dawn of the Hungry Days and of a winter that no matter how mild, would kill more than any winter before, and of a spring that would stay hungry no matter how warm it grew.

He spoke until it grew dark, long after most of the villagers would normally have retired for the night. It grew chilly as the day's heat vanished, but the villagers only clustered closer to the fire and to one another. It seemed they felt not the chill of a late summer night atop the mountain, but instead the chill of winter.

And then— only then— did he spring his trap and offer a way out. Verna didn't even speak out against it at first, wrestling so mightily with doubt in her heart as she did. He spoke of a vision brought to him by the ancestors, of a way that some faithful might be saved.

The Conclave Eidola taught that they were all prophets, to some extent— the ancestors spoke to all of them, and they had but to learn to listen. True prophets, however, were rare— there had only been nine and twenty of them ever recorded. True prophets were spoken to not just by their own ancestors, but by the ancestors of an entire city, or an entire kingdom. Some said the last prophet would bear a message from *all* the ancestors someday, though that was mere folk superstition, to Verna's mind.

Olefs spoke humbly, and that stayed Verna's hand until it was too late. He claimed only a vision from the ancestors of Frostford, where an impassable stretch of river froze over every summer. He claimed that they'd sent him here in a vision, and that they'd told him how he— and a few of the true faithful of Cloudholt— might yet be saved.

Part of her knew Olefs must be lying, knew he was a conman, knew that this is what the ancestors had tried to warn her of, but her fear and her doubts put a crack in her faith, and Olefs' words had crept into her and stayed her tongue too long.

Olefs told the villagers how the lowlanders had lost their faith, and he talked of how they paid only lip service to the ancestors, and offered them only rotten offerings of food on fast days. He spoke of the mountain folk's steadfast virtue and strength against temptation, and the villagers all nodded, because he said what they already knew.

Verna said nothing, though she knew those allegations untrue.

Olefs told the villagers they must seal off the trail, and to lay snares for those unfaithful of the lowlands who would try to force the Wrack upon them as well.

Verna said nothing, though innocent peddlers might be hurt by the snares.

Olefs pulled back his eyepatch, revealing a sphere of opal, and he spoke of its powers to see into the hearts of men and see their faith— powers known only and revealed only to him alone by the ancestors.

Verna said nothing, though she knew opal to be nothing more than a pretty stone, no more spiritual than glass.

Olefs told them that they must carve their own names in the living trees around the village, that the ancestors know these living might still be faithful.

Verna, at last, found her voice. She cried out against the heresy of carving the names of the living for the ancestors, of lying to them, of trying to cheat one's way into their arms.

Her pleas fell on deaf ears, for she'd been silent too long.

The villagers did everything Olefs said over the next few days, and hardly even looked at Verna. They tolerated her presence, but no more. The once ample tithe of food the villagers gave her became a thin, paltry thing indeed, and no one set foot in the Repository to pray or ask wisdom of the ancestors.

No one spoke up against Olefs, for fear he'd see weakness or evil in their hearts with his glimmering eye of a dozen colors, that glittering sphere of frozen fire. Most seemed not to want to speak up at all. None saw aught wrong with Olefs getting the first share of food, a tithe of garnets, or moving in unwed with the pretty young widow who lived near the bottom of Cloudholt.

At least that last kept him away from Verna. She'd been halfway convinced he'd try to steal the Repository from her as well.

Olefs made no moves at all against her, in fact. When asked, he merely told others that her heart was still faithful, even though she couldn't hear the ancestors, and resisted their truth.

Verna felt only shame at that, for while the ancestors had spoken to her, it was true she'd resisted their truth when they'd tried to warn her about Olefs.

Autumn arrived like a landslide, and the first snows arrived just eight days after Olefs' arrival. Calling it autumn was, in truth, a little disingenuous— up in the mountains, there were essentially only two seasons— a short summer, then winter the rest of the year.

She tended to her obelisks. She prayed. She watched the clouds drift through the village, and she waited for another message from the ancestors. An omen. Anything.

She was not expecting it to come in the form of screams. To come as the Wrack.

The villagers had already formed a mob around the widow's house when she arrived, Olefs' screams echoing out of it. They held torches and axes and mining picks, and they nervously shuffled around, steeling themselves for the next step.

When Verna set foot among them, none of them would meet her eyes, save for the young widow and her two children, who stared at her pleadingly.

Verna stood by the door and listened to the screaming inside and felt doubt again. She felt anger. She felt hurt by Olefs and betrayed by the village. She felt a profound and shameful relief at Olefs being stricken down. Most of all, though, she felt fear. Fear that Olefs had been right about the Hungry Days coming, and that they'd arrived at Cloudholt.

She rested her hand on the stout door, closed her eyes, and prayed.

And the ancestors responded, and this time, she doubted them not.

"Go home, everyone," Verna said.

No one said anything or moved, just shuffled awkwardly behind her.

Verna turned and faced the crowd.

"Go home. There's nothing else to be done here."

She gestured to the widow and her children. "Take yourselves up to the temple until it is done. You may rest in my quarters."

The widow looked at her nervously, then nodded and guided her children out of the crowd and upward toward the Repository.

"You and you," Verna said. "Go fetch an extra barrel of water and gather what herbs for pain you can. You two big fellows, you stay here with me. I'll need you to hold him down— if the tales of victims hurting themselves are true. The rest of you, go home."

"Ma'am," one of the villagers said, "he's got the Wrack. He brought it with him. His heart's impure!"

"Of course his heart's impure!" Verna snapped at the unlucky man. "He conned all you fools into thinking he was a prophet, didn't he?"

Several of the villagers looked angry at that, others ashamed, but none spoke.

"I gave orders, didn't I?" Verna snapped, and stepped forwards.

Always before, Verna had been the retiring priestess. Always before, she'd sought the ancestors' company over the living. Always before, she'd been the kindly adviser, the patient listener.

When she stepped forward now, she could feel the ancestors step forward with her, and the whole village took a step back.

"His heart might be impure, but that's no excuse for ours to be as well," Verna said. "We must be better than those who hurt and lie to us. Only time will tell if the Hungry Days are upon us or not, but even if they are, we shall not fail our duties to our ancestors. And I promise you this: If they are upon us, not one of you will go with your name uncarved in my obelisks. If the Wrack breaks this whole village, not one of you will go with your name uncarved. The ancestors will protect me long enough to make sure you join them."

Verna turned away from the crowd and opened the door.

"What about you, Priestess?" a child's voice said. "Who will carve your name?"

Verna looked back at the crowd.

"I have a sick man to tend to," she said, raising her voice to be heard over the screams let loose when she opened the door. "And I gave you all orders."

Verna turned back and stepped into the house.

CHAPTER EIGHT
More Tales Of This Night Than Any Other

Carlan picked uncomfortably at his costume, glaring out at the ball. The king had followed through on his threat of making Carlan wear a hen costume. It was tasteful and reserved, of course— a feathered white silk half-mask over his eyes, and a yellow silk beak over his nose. White and red robes with feathers sewn in. Bright yellow boots.

He honestly wouldn't take a clipped copper about the costume either way. It was annoying, but it paled next to the sheer amount of work he had to do tonight. It was just a matter of time until he could get to it— he need only wait until Sigis was well and truly drunk, then he could slip back to the mountain of paperwork building up in his office. It felt like everything that could possibly go wrong was going wrong. Thanks to the reduced number of patrols, hunters, and shepherds, even the wolves had moved down out of the mountains and forests early this year.

Carlan pretended to sip at his wine and strode through the party.

The palace staff had built a great fountain in the center of the ballroom in a matter of days, with a waist-high basin stretching twenty paces across, with living fish swimming about in it. Catfish from the palace grounds' fishing pond, it looked like— hardly the most ornamental fish, like you'd find in the ponds of Galicanta, but ornamental fish did badly in Lothain's harsh winters. The fountain's structure was water-sealed wood, not stone or metal, and it was meant to be taken back down again after the party. The actual fountain mechanism was a great clockwork thing, and there was a chamber hidden within it where a servant continually worked the pump that sent water spraying up from the brass pipes.

The king's adviser would wager money there would be drunk nobles swimming in it before the night was up.

Potted plants had been dug from the grounds and moved into the ballroom in huge numbers, giving the whole room the appearance of a manicured jungle. This late in the year, most of the ornamentals had to be dug up and moved into the king's glasshouses, lest the oncoming cold kill them. Those glasshouses were a monumental expense. Glass was not cheap, even for kings. Carlan distinctly remembered one of the only times the dead Prince Arnulf had gotten in real trouble as a child, when he broke one of the great glass panes.

He'd been too busy to ever really take the time to mourn the dead prince. He'd known Arnulf the prince's whole life, and had been quite fond of him. Everyone had been fond of Arnulf. He just had so much life to him. Carlan had never had children of his own, but had never regretted it save when spending time with the king's children, instructing them in the ways of governance. They'd been a good lot, by and by, but Arnulf had been the most lively and good-humored of them all. And though he was far from the cleverest, he'd still been Carlan's favorite.

Carlan sighed, and turned to look at one of the plants.

A mulberry tree imported all the way from the south of the continent of Oyansur. Radhan ships had sailed it— and many other plants— from the mysterious empires of the far south, past the domains of the Sunsworn Emperor, past the Galicantan Empress's ports that were both fortresses and works of art, and all the way to Swalben, the grim, stormy port that was Lothain's one access to the sea.

They'd made a tidy profit off it, too, like they always did. No one had faster or more reliable ships than the Radhan.

Carlan made another mental wager that more than a few plants would be knocked over, watered with wine, or even pissed in. Quite a few of them wouldn't be making it to the glasshouses this year.

If he actually had someone to wager against, he'd be raking in a lot of coin, but having the king's chief adviser and seer making cynical bets tended to upset people, for some reason.

Bored, and needing to stay where the king could see him in attendance, Carlan dodged around a crowd of useless gossiping second and third sons and strode over to the fountain. He pulled his mask up onto his balding head, then carefully popped out his glass eye. He pulled his little belt pouch from his robes and put the glass sphere into its slot, then felt the various compartments. Garnet? No, the fountain was wood and metal. Obviously not amethyst or peridot…

Citrine.

He pulled the yellow-orange sphere from its individual pocket, carefully shined it on his robes, then popped it into his socket and pulled his chicken mask back down.

Almost before the mask was back down, he'd dropped into the spirit world. He didn't even need to close his good eye, like many lesser seers did. The reference marks on his eyes were fewer than most other mages, and of his own design. They were harder to use, but if you could handle them, they allowed far swifter focusing.

Carlan often thought that all this administration business was a waste of his talents, and that he should have stayed a seer.

Citrine was commonly known as the architect's left eye — the companion to garnet, the architect's right eye. The deep amber currents he found himself floating in seemed to react more strongly when they passed through metal or, to a lesser extent, wood. Or, more accurately, the citrine brought out those particular patterns of turbulence more clearly than other gems did.

There was endless debate about whether it was the color or internal structure of a gem that affected one's vision into the spirit realm, or an admixture of the two. Perhaps its composition as well. The clarity of a gem, at least, had proven to have nothing to do with it— nephrite jade was completely opaque, yet was more useful to a ship's seer than any other gem, allowing them to perceive rocks and fish below the waves, as well as the very shapes of the sea currents themselves. Scholars had spent countless hours trying to figure out precisely what combination of traits affected the uses of a gem, even to the point where there were paintings of the amusing scene where one seer spent hours staring at another seer's eyes from inches away as they worked.

Carlan ignored the turbulence in the corners of his eyes from where the spirit currents passed through his mask, and focused in on the fountain. He rapidly made himself ignore most of the noise— turbulence carried along the currents from interacting with materials before what one chose to look at. He quickly parsed out the borders of the fountain and began resolving the outlines of its clockwork innards purely from the ripples in the yellow-orange spirit currents.

From his other eye, he simply watched the water rain down from the fountain into the pool. The images didn't blur or blend. Rather, they somehow… overlapped, one image present atop another.

However seers saw— Carlan, subscribed to none of the overblown theories touted by philosophers, and was content to admit he didn't know— they weren't truly seeing like they would from an eye. They weren't perceiving light.

It made perfect sense to Carlan that the vision from his two eyes wouldn't blend, since he was perceiving two different worlds: the physical and the spiritual. That said, seers who had replaced both eyes with gems apparently didn't have any visual blending between two different gems either, which was somewhat puzzling. It did occur when they used two gems of the same kind, though.

That didn't even get into the truly strange seers, those who had learned to hear or smell the spirit realm at the cost of those senses. There was nothing that wasn't puzzling about them.

It took less than a minute for him to fully resolve the internal structure of the fountain— and even to parse out the servant working the fountain's pump, which largely just consisted of the servant walking in a circle and pushing the wheel inside his chamber. Citrine wasn't great at seeing, but it made out bone just fine.

Carlan spent a few minutes watching the servant walk in circles before a drunken noblewoman wearing a dress that was supposed to resemble armor interrupted him, clearly wanting some sort of reassurance that the Wrack wouldn't be arriving in Lothain anytime soon.

He offered her a few meaningless platitudes, but his heart wasn't in it. Anyone with half a brain could tell the Wrack would be arriving soon— it had been slowly creeping south across the plain towards the capital, in its jerky, stop-and-go pattern. They still had no idea how it spread, but it hadn't missed Carlan's attention— or that of many others— that it moved at the speed a man might walk across the countryside, if he were in no hurry.

It would be in Lothain in weeks at most, if not sooner. Much sooner.

Some patterns were holding true, at least— it struck the nobility soonest and hardest, often decapitating the leadership of cities. Your odds of death rose with your personal wealth, at least in the first wave. A second wave of the disease usually struck around two to four weeks later, and that one usually hit the poorest members of society, though its victims were seemingly chosen much more at random than the first wave.

It was, perhaps, ironic, that as the noblewoman left, relieved, Carlan thought that the king might actually be saving his own skin by sealing himself into the castle. They'd been locked up here for weeks— well past even the extraordinarily long dormancy period between catching the Wrack and it breaking you that the Moonsworn claimed it had. That, despite all the inconvenience and disastrous consequence for Lothain as a whole, Sigis' cowardice might actually have worked.

Then the screaming started.

The instant the screams began, Carlan knew them for what they were. It wasn't a scream of terror or surprise, but of pain, and he'd only heard its like in battlefield medical tents before. More screams started immediately after, but they were obvious as screams of panic.

Carlan tossed his cup into the nearest potted plant, winning his bet with himself, and strode off towards the screaming.

Drunken nobles rushed past him in terror, disrupting spirit flows and sending distracting ripples across the yellow-orange currents. One nearly shoved Carlan into the fountain pool, but he caught himself just in time. Another noble actually did trip and fall into the pool, startling the fish away from him.

Part of Carlan had expected to find the king writhing on the ground— the Wrack seemed to have a sort of poetic viciousness to it, and striking down the king first in Lothain, like it had his son in Castle Morinth, would have been exactly the sort of thing the Wrack would delight in.

But no. The king was cowering on his throne, curled up in its corner as though it would protect him. The screamer was a sweaty count by the name of… Heinrich, Carlan believed. He was a sycophant of little standing— the type Carlan avoided as much as possible. Were the situation less urgent, he was sure he could think of the man's titles and descent, but he didn't bother now.

"You and you!" Carlan shouted. "Get over here and help me!"

The two Carlan had pointed to— a foppish looking nobleman and a guard— hesitated for a moment, then rushed over and helped pin down the thrashing Heinrich.

As the two men held down Heinrich, Carlan quickly checked to see whether it was indeed the Wrack, not that he had much doubt.

Mild fever, screaming, delirium, muscle spasms— they were all there.

Rather than scramble and try and switch to his peridot eye, Carlan tried looking at Heinrich through his citrine eye.

He couldn't make out much at first, but it didn't take him long to find the distinctive patterns Benen and the few other healers they had reports from described. They looked odd, through a citrine eye, though that didn't mean much when using the wrong gem.

Heinrich spasmed hard enough to throw the two off him, shuddered, and went still. Carlan bent down to feel for a pulse.

"That was fast," he muttered. "I'd wager his heart was pushing failure to start with."

The nobleman gave him a shocked look, but then scrunched up his nose and scrambled back.

Carlan rolled his eyes at that. Bowel release was a normal part of death, though this was a little on the fast side. He…

Carlan paused and glared at the man's jewel-silk pants. The obnoxiously expensive fabric was the one material a seer couldn't see through, and for some ridiculous reason, Heinrich's only genuine article of jewel-silk were his pants. He cursed, then began undoing Heinrich's belt.

"What are you doing?" the king demanded from his throne.

Carlan pulled down the fat corpse's pants.

"His stool is solid, sire," he said.

"What does that matter?" the king asked, his voice hysterical.

"Doesn't it seem strange to you that diarrhea only seems to develop in the victims of the Wrack after all the screaming and writhing ends?" Carlan asked.

"Are you trying to say this was the Wrack?" the King asked.

"Of course it was," Carlan replied, looking over the stool in the spirit realm. "What else could it have been? Do you know many illnesses that just show up uninvited out of the night and make people do that?"

"We need to flee!" the king shouted. "We need to ride, to get out of the city."

"If we've been infected with the Wrack," Carlan said, "we were infected a week and a half to three weeks ago, or somewhere thereabouts. There's nothing we can do."

Carlan took off his hateful chicken mask and threw it off to the side. He pulled out his citrine eye, cleaned it off, and exchanged it for his peridot eye. Taking care to clean it— haste led to infection— he popped it in, and forced himself into the spirit realm.

He frowned as he looked at the peculiar turbulence patterns of the Wrack in the green currents flowing through Heinrich's corpse. They were by far the strongest in his liver, just as described.

Carlan would wager that Heinrich wouldn't be the only screa...

Before he could finish that wager in his head, someone else in the ballroom collapsed and started screaming.

The king whimpered, curling up smaller in his throne.

Carlan ignored the new screamer, and turned his eye on the crowd.

"You there," he said. "Fetch the palace healers, if they're not on their way already. You, dressed as a tree, run to the cloakroom— I left a medical satchel there, just in case. Fetch it for me."

He carefully ran his eye across the room, looking for any unusual turbulence coming from the base of anyone's ribs. The liver was one of the largest organs, so he didn't need to strain himself too hard.

"You," he said, pointing to the woman dressed as a falcon or some such nonsense. "Lay down on the ground, now. Someone fetch something to tie her wrists with."

"What?" she said, looking confused.

"Better than hurting yourself falling. You've got the Wrack too," Carlan said.

The turbulence had started up in the currents flowing through her a few seconds ago, and she...

She was running away. Lovely.

Before she could get far, one of the guards grabbed her arm and pulled her back. Good man. Tough keeping your head in situations like this.

Carlan spent the next minute or so watching her torso from just a few inches away as the guard held the woman.

"I feel fine," she said. "You must be mistaken. I demand you let me go immediately!"

"It came out of nowhere," Carlan muttered. "There was no sign of it in you just a couple minutes ago at all, and it just showed up. Not to mention how unusually close together it is with Heinrich and the other victims. Could something be triggering it? Something in the air? A stress response due to the screams?"

Carlan stepped back as the woman started screaming. She thrashed so hard that she yanked out of the guard's grip, giving him a broken nose in the process. Carlan could visibly see the Wrack flowing out of the woman's liver in huge amounts into her body.

Carlan stepped away from the two, and looked around for the next victim, only to spot trace ripples of the Wrack in the spirit current floating in front of him. He looked down at his own torso and frowned.

"Bollocks", Carlan said in a dignified tone of voice. He frantically pulled his journal and a stick of graphite from his side pouch and began writing down his observations.

"Someone needs to make sure this note gets to Yusef the Moonsworn!" he shouted.

He kept his peridot eye focused on his liver, watching the Wrack grow more intense.

A terrible thought occurred to him, and he frantically jotted it down, then ripped the pages he'd just written out of his journal.

"I need someone to transmit this via semaphore!" he shouted.

He felt oddly warm, moreso than the weak fever at the beginning stages of the Wrack could account for.

The guard with the broken nose stepped forwards and accepted the note and took off at a run.

Carlan sighed, then carefully lay down on the ground. He noticed that the fountain had stopped.

He had time for three deep breaths before the pain hit in a wave.

In Lothain City, a siege was happening in reverse.

In front of the palace gates, the city guards had spent much of the evening holding off a restless, irritable mob, angry at the sounds of music and festivities coming from the palace. It had come close to violence several times, and tensions between the guards and the mob had been high.

The guards, most of them, hadn't even wanted to be there. They hadn't been allowed into the palace; they'd just been ordered there by their commanders earlier in the day to prevent trouble. There were usually a few angry souls outside the palace gates these days, but everyone was expecting trouble— somehow, despite a complete lack of movement in and out of the palace, the word of the masquerade had spread through the city like wildfire— most likely through the semaphore links between the palace and the city.

Much of the mob had dissolved away immediately when the music ended and the screaming started, but some fast-thinking member of the crowd had shouted to bar the gates.

The guards had joined right in.

They piled carts, trash, and construction materials in front of the gates in huge mounds. The palace guards on the walls shouted at them to stop, but when they fired an arrow at the crowds, the city guards responded in kind, and the palace guards, already disheartened by the screaming from inside the palace, quickly withdrew.

Perhaps if Sigis IV had maintained the palace siege engines, or had bothered to keep cauldrons of oil and firepits ready by the murder holes over the gate, they could have done something. As it was, when a crowd of desperate servants and nobles poured out of the palace and tried to unbar and push the gates open, they found them lodged shut.

The gate was built to open outward, for a normal siege, where attackers meant to force it open. Now that worked against the residents of the palace, for the mob could easily keep the gates shut. With their access to the walltops, the nobles and palace guards normally would have easily cleared the palace gate of the mob and city guard.

These were hardly normal circumstances, and within a couple of hours, their attempts to escape had ended, and the only sounds coming out were screams.

The king sent a long series of angry semaphore messages, trying to force the city guard to open the gates, but those messages ceased before dawn, and what could have turned into a battle in the streets of Lothain simply... fizzled out.

The Moonsworn didn't even attempt to get access to the palace to help the stricken— only a small handful of them were let in even at the best of times, and the nobility's suspicion of them had climbed ever higher as the Wrack advanced.

Besides, they knew their efforts would be needed out in the city streets soon.

Within a day, the screams weren't just inside the palace.

CHAPTER NINE

Every Name That Ever Was

Rupert and Ida followed Priest Otto through Swalben, and Ida prayed.

Swalben was never quiet. The seabirds called from sunup to sundown. The wind blew, never ceasing, only shifting directions. The waves crashed against the rocks and piers, tide in, tide out, tide in, tide out.

Once there were a thousand human noises to go along with those. The shouts of dockworkers and the laughs of drunken sailors. The bells that rang the hour every hour. The voices of eighty thousand souls who prayed and blasphemed on the steep and narrow streets of Swalben. But now there was only the one human sound in these grey, drizzling days, and it screamed, and it moaned, and it babbled, and the Wrack owned Swalben.

And Ida prayed to the ancestors over and over and over again in her head, desperate to hear from them, but not because she needed advice or guidance or even comfort. She prayed just in the hope that they might speak to her, and their voices might drown out the screaming, even for a few moments.

And the three of them, the last priest and the last two acolytes of the Church Eidola in the once-great port of Swalben in the once-great kingdom of Lothain, went house to house, street to street, racing to find the names of the dead.

They found a house packed with a family who would rather die together than flee, and who wept with joy when Otto knocked on their door holding his book with the names of the dead.

They found a sailor dead on the street, not even of the Wrack, but with a knife wound in his back, and no one knew him, but in the way of sailors, they found his name tattooed on his chest, surrounded by tattooed vines and wires, that the ancestors not think he was committing blasphemy. It was a false superstition, for nothing could keep tattooing the name of someone living from being blasphemy, but Otto didn't even frown at the tattoo, only wrote it down.

They found a beggar with blackened fingers and clenched muscles lying atop a drain, and none would admit to knowing him. Ida and Rupert both wept at the poor man's lost name, and even Otto had to take a few deep breaths.

They went house to house, street to street, and the names crept into Otto's book one by one.

They found a whole family, dead in their home, and it took them an hour to find someone in the neighborhood who could identify them all. No one else in that neighborhood had died.

They found a corpse so bloated in her own home that they didn't even know if she'd died of the Wrack, or how long she'd been there. They searched her house until they found some record of her name, and Ida felt like a filthy thief as she pawed through drawers and cupboards, and she wept in anger and didn't look at Rupert or Otto.

They stood on the steps of a house that reeked of death for what felt like hours, as Otto pleaded with the man on the other side to let them in— or at least tell them the names of the dead, but the man only shouted back awful blasphemies in his rage and grief, and he would not let them in nor tell them the names of the dead. And Ida shook to hear those blasphemies and felt an awful shame when part of her hoped this awful man would have his name unrecorded too, and when they walked away, she saw that Rupert looked as angry as she did, but Otto just looked sad.

They went house to house, street to street, and the names crept into Otto's book three by three.

They walked among the whores and slatterns and graceful men of the Winding Alley by the docks, which was as wide as any street and longer than most in Swalben. And Ida, who'd grown up among respectable merchant folk at the top of the city, felt shame and disgust at coming to this place her family had always warned her about. And at the end of a day spent in the Winding Alley, she felt shame and disgust only at herself, for the whores and slatterns and graceful men had taken them into the warmth of one of their brothels and set them up at a table and lined up patiently, giving them the names of their dead one by one, and they fed the priest and his acolytes, showing one another kindness that Ida hadn't seen in the city since the Wrack had come. And Ida saw how gracious and kind Otto was to each and every one of them, as though they were kings and queens and scholars of note, and she promised herself she'd be as holy as him someday.

They went from pier to pier, between the few ships that hadn't fled Swalben, who had lost too many sailors to the Wrack to sail the stormy autumn seas, and Ida pressed in close to Rupert and Otto, afraid of these rough men, but Otto went honestly and patiently to each of the ships. He laughed and joked and shared drinks with the men, and Ida didn't understand until she realized that this was how they mourned. She saw how they would all pretend not to see when tears came to the eyes of one of their number, and how even the roughest and vilest of them seemed afraid to go more than a few feet from the others. And she never forgot how Otto held a flask of vile sailor's brew to a man's lips whose fingers had been burnt by the Wrack and couldn't grasp any longer.

They walked among the great trading houses, where the wealthy and their clerks had once counted every single coin that flowed through Swalben like water until a man could drown in them like the fiercest river— and many men had. Now, though, the houses were empty and abandoned, and coins simply lay scattered about, untouched, as though they were as valueless as seawater. And they found many a body lying where they had fallen, untouched, and none of them bore their names in their pockets or on their chests, and Otto's face grew darker and sadder, until they found the madman, pockets bulging with gold coins that dripped out with every step, and the madman was able to tell them the names of every single corpse and how much every single corpse owed him. Otto thanked him and graciously tipped the man a gold coin that he picked up off the ground, and the madman put it in his pocket and it immediately fell out, but he didn't even notice as he just walked away tallying up his ledgers out loud. And Otto told Ida and Rupert that he knew the madman, that he was a cruel man, a miser, a man of little faith who treated his workers like slaves despite being one of the richest merchants in the city, but that today he'd more than atoned for all the ill he'd done in his life. And Otto caressed his book of names sadly, and looked away.

They went house to house, street to street, and the names crept into Otto's book ten by ten.

They visited the poorest slums where only one in twenty had even gotten the Wrack and fewer died, and Ida watched as Otto inscribed those few names into his book with as much care as any other.

They visited the richest mansions where all had fled or died and the book filled faster and faster, and however tight Otto's eyes got or however white his knuckles grew, he never took less care with any name.

They visited a street of blacksmiths and coopers and carpenters and ropemakers and when Rupert spoke of splitting up to cover more ground, Otto took one look at Ida, then said they'd stick together, for no-one should be left alone when the Wrack might strike them down at any time. And Ida felt relief, but also shame and terror that names might be lost because of her fear.

They went house to house, street to street, and the names filled up Otto's book to the end, and he turned the pages, but there were no more pages. Then he turned back and back and back through the book looking for open space, empty margins, or pages he might have skipped. And he began to weep and curse himself for wasting his time with neat calligraphy.

And he threw the book then against the wall of a house, and he began to run past houses and streets and out of sight, wailing and ranting and shouting blasphemies until he was out of earshot too, and then Ida only heard the seabirds and the wind and the rain and the screaming and the moaning and the babbling.

Ida gently picked Otto's book off the wet ground. She picked up the three pages that had fallen out, and slid them back into the book. She told Rupert to follow her back to the temple, but he shook his head and told her he'd wait for her here. And Ida walked back to the temple. And with every street she passed, she thought of the names they'd collected on those streets, and the thin little book began to feel heavier and heavier with the weight of all the countless souls it held. And all the confusion and anger and betrayal at Otto was the first thing to go, as the weight of that little book bore down on her and exhausted her and forced her to abandon everything but the book.

And by the time she finally dragged herself up the stairs into the temple, and stored the little book in a box meant for all the names to be transferred to the obelisk, she thought she understood why Otto had run, and all that anger and betrayal was outweighed by the memories of all the kindnesses and dignities he'd offered to everyone he spoke to and his tears at every lost name.

And Ida rummaged around the temple until she found a dead priest's journal, half filled with complaints about the temple's cooking and musings about hierarch politics. She carefully tore those pages out of the book and set them gently on the dead man's desk, because the book would soon be heavy enough without the dead man's thoughts, and she grabbed more graphite and a pouch big enough for the book.

And when she returned to the street where she'd left Rupert, and found him missing, she didn't panic. She simply waited and listened for a moment, then followed the sound of gentle sobbing until she found him in a nearby house, where his arm dripped and bled from where he'd begun carving the names of the dead into it.

And Ida gently washed his arm and wrote the names revealed when the blood was washed away into her book. And then she washed his arm again and bound it in strips of silk that must have been so valuable once and now were only valuable for their cleanliness. And the two of them left that house with its dead whose names had been preserved.

And they went house to house, street to street, and the names crept into Ida's book one by one.

CHAPTER TEN
Time Marked Only By Wind

Yusef vomited out his window again, then rubbed his temples. The headaches had been incessant for weeks, now. He was too old to be diving into the Goddess Sea, but he'd been using his gemstone eyes for hours every day.

He slowly trudged back to his desk and picked up his quill.

One hundred and seventy-four of the faithful dead so far.

Five in the riots on the day after the Masquerade, when the autumn winds began to blow.

Four more in the fires that followed. Surprising how much there is to burn in a city of stone.

One simply of slipping on cobbles in the first autumn rains.

Three healers mugged for their pain-killing herbs. Two still had their coinpurses left on their belts.

Ninety-four dead in riots eleven days after the Masquerade. Mob of nobles, merchants, and impressionable laborers blamed us for the Wrack. Fought them off with help from city guard.

Yusef stopped at that last one and had to take several deep breaths before continuing.

Out of pain-killing herbs day thirteen.

Day fifteen, Gilded Bensamen struck down with Wrack. Dies before sunset.

Day sixteen, twelve cases of Wrack among faithful. Four dead of Wrack, and one killed by his own dog gone mad, terrified by its owner's screams.

Day seventeen, nine cases of Wrack among faithful. Seven dead.

Yusef continued writing down the dreadful litany, not even caring about efficiency at this point. You were supposed to keep semaphore messages as short as possible, so as not to clog up the semaphore currents, but few messages went out at this point anyhow.

Yusef finished the message, and trudged over to the window to dry heave.

He slowly, gingerly collected his things, and trudged down the stairs.

No busybody sons-in-law gossiped in the stairs or halls now. One had died in the riot. The others stood guard at the barriers around the neighborhood, or escorted the healers about the city to tend to the ill.

Halfway to the ground floor, Yusef paused to catch his breath, and sat down on the stairs. One of the household cats, a bedraggled ginger tom, clambered up the stairs and settled in his lap, purring.

Yusef smiled wanly and scratched the tom's round face. Most of the countless cats in Lothain's Moonsworn quarter were hiding under beds and in alleys, terrified by the screamers. The dogs wouldn't stop howling, and many of them had been turned into nervous wrecks.

Yusef had actually seen rats on the streets. He'd never seen rats in the Moonsworn quarter before.

A few of the cats, though, seemed entirely unconcerned by all of it, like this tom. It was not the cleverest or the prettiest animal, and certainly not the best smelling, but it was one of the most affectionate.

His head eased up a little on the pounding after a few minutes petting the tom, and muscles he hadn't even realized were tensed relaxed a bit in his shoulders. He gently pushed the cat off his lap and slowly plodded down the stairs.

The cat gave a disgruntled chirp, then padded off, probably to cuddle with one of Yusef's grandchildren, who hadn't played or left the house in days.

That so few of the Moonsworn had died thus far spoke to the faith with which most of the community followed the laws of the Moon Goddess, who had given them those laws for their own protection.

That none of the dead Moonsworn had numbered among their ranks of the children was nothing less than a blessing from both Goddesses.

Yusef paused at the shrine to say a quick prayer, trying not to think about how empty it seemed. Trying not to think of the day when the mob came for the Moonsworn.

The Moonsworn Quarter was quiet, or as quiet as any place pierced by screams, moaning, and babbling could be. Even after reading all the reports, even after spending so long preparing himself, he'd been unready for the Wrack. He'd been unready for its noise.

All the reports spoke of the horrendous din of the screams, but what numbers had been offered spoke of the fact that there simply couldn't be that many screamers at one time, save in the initial fierce burst some towns had. Most of the screamers tore their vocal cords within a few hours, and none lasted longer than a day.

Yusef passed a young couple holding each other for comfort, and he looked away.

He knew now that it wasn't simply the measure of the screams on their own the semaphore reports had spoken of. It was their *weight*. The sheer grating force of them. It was like being forced to stare unblinking into a stranger's eyes for hours on hours, to have their soul forced upon you unfiltered by the rituals, lies, and walls of civilization. To not be able to hold yourself apart and keep your innermost self a place of peace.

Somehow, the moaners and babblers were even worse. There were far fewer of them, but their voices never gave out, and they seemed to almost understand what was going on around them. Those that recovered seemed to remember the pain and delirium better than the screamers, and Yusef didn't envy them that.

As he drew closer to the barricades, Moonsworn began approaching him, asking him for the truth of rumors.

Geredain had closed the borders.

The port of Swalben had fallen into the sea.

Geredain had already invaded.

No, the forces of the Galicantan Empress had invaded.

Galicanta had closed its borders.

Monsters had overrun Castle Morinth, and were running rampant across the plains.

Swalben had closed itself off from the world.

Swalben was blockaded by Galicanta to keep the Wrack from traveling by sea.

Swalben was blockaded by the Citrine Isles, to keep the Wrack from their shores.

The Galicantan Empress and the Sunsworn Emperor rode to war once more.

The Fractured Duchies had united at last.

Geredain and Galicanta were at war.

The Sei had invaded the plains.

That last, at least, Yusef could dismiss. The Sei had been broken a generation ago, when Geredain and Lothain had, in a rare instance of cooperation, invaded the Krannenbergs to smash the Sei raiders once and for all, to punish them for their alliances with the singing Northerners. Despite the Singers being Eidol Vowless as well, they were ill-loved by the nations south of the Krannenbergs. The Sei weren't gone, but he doubted there were more than a few thousand of them left, up in the mountains worshipping their hungry, bitter god of dust. The best they could launch were ineffectual raids. Irritants, no more.

As Yusef reached the barricades, a couple of the Moonsworn guards detached themselves and escorted him through the narrow aisle leading out. Without saying a word, they fell into step with him as he trudged through Lothain.

He could immediately feel the difference. There were more screamers here. The streets were even dirtier and felt more hopeless.

A few of them looked his way, and some of them waved, but Yusef ignored them.

Rats roamed the streets, and Yusef forced himself to look at the piles of trash, to count how many of them wore clothes and should be walking and laughing and…

Some ugly part of Yusef smiled deep within his chest at the thought that those piles of trash wouldn't be forming any more mobs.

The stench was like a wall he was trying to force his way through.

What should have been a walk of a few minutes seemed to take hours until they reached the river, where the bridges had once stood. The mobs and guards had pulled them all down, in an effort to keep the Wrack on the other side with the Palace.

Carlan's last, hasty message ran around his head again, and he wondered at it.

Yusef looked to the river and saw a child drinking its water, but rather than pull it away or scold it as he once would have, he simply looked away. He kept walking.

They came to the semaphore tower by the river, and the city guards watching it just nodded and let him pass. The king was dead, and the nobles had betrayed the people. They didn't give a damn about orders forbidding the Moonsworn from using the semaphores.

Yusef trudged up the stairs, and though the tower was only three stories tall, he climbed for seven times seven years, like Ehairon from the children's story, and his head pounded and ached. He focused on Carlan's message and not the hole inside him, for the message was horror enough.

Carlan's conjecture that something in the air, stress, or even the screams themselves were what kicked off the first, deadliest wave in each Wrack outbreak— at least, during the ones that erupted like wildfires, rather than the slower sort. It made a dire sort of sense to Yusef and his healers and scholars. Being an external trigger was unlikely, for outbreaks had erupted in such different conditions across Lothain. The only plausible external trigger the Moonsworn had thought of had been that perhaps cooling temperatures triggered the outbreaks, but Yusef doubted that. The initial outbreak at Castle Morinth had been during the heat of the summer— which, admittedly, was much cooler in the mountains than on the plains, but even then, many of the first outbreaks on the plains had been during the heat of late summer and early fall as well.

No, the initial outbreaks being a stress response was more likely. Or a response to the screaming.

Yusef climbed to the top of the stairs, where a Moonsworn seer, amethyst eye glinting in the wan sunlight, slowly cranked the handle of the semaphore, the arms slowly ratcheting and revolving. The looped message chain he'd crafted three days ago, detailing their findings about the Wrack, clattered and twisted. Clattered and twisted. Another seer watched at the window, waiting for anymore messages.

One of Yusef's guards silently took over from the seer at the semaphore, and Yusef strode over to a nearby desk to begin assembling a new message chain.

As he pulled the links from the many drawers resting atop the desk, to begin assembling the message he'd written, he tried not to think of Carlan's other bit of conjecture, and once again he failed.

The tides of the Goddess Sea and the currents that flowed through it, trended south across Lothain from the Mist Maze. You could track currents in the Sea almost precisely along the path of the Wrack.

The Wrack couldn't be floating in the Goddess Sea.

Not without the Goddesses putting it there, and plagues were not the tools of the Goddesses, but of their sister who they had chained inside the earth, who would not just go nameless like the Goddesses, but not even be allowed a title.

Of course, if it were some venom released by the nameless sister— for toxin lay in her domain as much as disease did— that might explain why the Wrack could be seen by citrine.

Yusef desperately tried to shake the thought from his mind. For their nameless sister to have loosened her chains that much, to have touched the Sea, would mean…

Well, it would mean the end of times, when she broke apart the world itself, to escape its prison and resume her battle with her sisters until they overwhelmed her and built a new world to imprison her— as they had a thousand thousand times before, and would a thousand thousand times again.

A particularly piercing scream reached the tower. Yusef dropped a link, and he had to laboriously lean down to pick it off the floor again.

As he slowly finished the chain, his thoughts turned to Nalda. He'd received no messages from her since the ban. No word. The outbreak at Castle Morinth had died down before the outbreaks on the plains even began.

Perhaps the soldiers at the castle were merely keeping to the king's orders.

It was, he knew, a bit of an overblown worry on his part. No word from Castle Morinth had reached them at all in weeks, for that matter, but that was no surprise— the semaphore network had started falling apart soon after the Wrack hit the plains. He doubted there were any occupied semaphore towers left in the north of Lothain. What few messages they'd received from Swalben had been routed south through the Fractured Duchies and Galicanta, then back north into Lothain.

Yusef prayed every day that Nalda was safe.

He finished assembling the message chain and carefully carried it over to the semaphore looped over his arm. He crouched down, and as the old message was feeding through, he unhitched its loop, hooked in the new message, and carefully guided the new, extra-long chain over a series of pulleys to keep it from tangling.

The Moonsworn turning the crank didn't even have to stop, let alone slow down. Yusef wasn't as skilled as a semaphore seer, but he was more than skilled enough to loop in an additional length of chain mid-message.

The momentary flit of pride faded, and Yusef stood with a groan. He didn't even bother to check the outgoing message, leaving it to the semaphore seers.

Yusef began padding down the stairs, brooding over whether there were enough active semaphore towers to the south to get the message to any other Moonsworn community. Despite Galicanta's ban on the Moonsworn, a few small communities had been allowed to stay. However, even in the best of times, many of their messages were intercepted and censored.

His guards followed behind him, returning the operation of the semaphore crank to the seers. Normally, the seers would have assistants to work the cranks, but in these times...

Yusef's brain took to uselessly revolving the thousand complaints and pleas he'd gotten from his healers. Most notable, of course, was their continual resistance to recording the names and death details of the Vowless. It was a small chore, even in the worst of times, and already something most healers did for their records, but many of the Moonsworn hated having to participate in pagan Vowless nonsense.

For years, Yusef had refused all protests, and commanded Lothain's Moonsworn to continue. Not just because it was a smart move politically— one that kept the Vowless from distrusting the Moonsworn entirely.

No, simply because it was a kindness that cost them nothing but a little ink and a few words, and the world could always use a little more kindness.

Now, though, that dull, aching hole inside of him was whispering that even that little bit of ink and those few words were too much for those hateful Vowless.

His anger grew and grew as he descended the stairs, and he finally found himself listening to what he'd been trying to avoid inside himself, dwelling on what he had no time to dwell on.

When he exited the tower, he didn't even look at the city guards at the door, he just marched straight on.

Yusef didn't know what he was thinking when he saw the child again. If you asked him, he might say he hadn't been thinking at all.

That would have been a lie. He was thinking of Emala, and the mob, and letting those thoughts feed the angry hole in his heart as he clenched his fists and stalked straight towards the idiot Vowless child drinking from the river.

He was thinking about kicking the child into the river, and the thought made him happy.

When he reached the child, he stood over it for long seconds, shaking with rage, and grief, and every pent up resentment he'd ever formed against the heathen Vowless, who treated them as objects of constant suspicion, who kept watch on them as though they were spies, just for not praying as they did. He thought of a daughter who might be weeks dead without him knowing, because of a stupid, cowardly king's order to keep his people from using the semaphores. He thought of a son-in-law who he'd always dismissed as useless who'd died a hero driving off the mob, trying to protect Emala, and he had deserved better from Yusef. He thought of a thousand tiny slights from Vowless, and even his damn headache, and it all fed into the hole inside him, which just kept growing and growing and never getting filled.

And he found himself starting, in his head, a warrior's prayer, a prayer to the Sun Goddess, a prayer for strength and a prayer for will and a prayer he'd never expected to say even in the privacy of his own head.

Then he caught sight of the child's blackened, clumsy fingers, and the way the filthy river water just ran right out from between the cupped fingers that didn't work right anymore, and the way the child was reduced to lapping up a few droplets from its palms. He saw how skinny the child was, and how its muscles kept twitching the way all survivors of the Wrack did.

Then the child looked up at him, and he was looking at a little girl who looked even emptier than the hole inside him, and his anger just…

Flowed out of him like the water between the little girl's fingers.

And shame filled the hole and washed away the half-finished prayer, and it felt a hundred times heavier than anger, and he almost broke under its weight.

But he didn't.

He leaned down and gently picked up the girl, who hardly seemed to weigh anything at all, and he carried her all the way home through the bitter autumn wind without saying a word, and though his head and his stomach and his back and his knees hurt as badly as ever, they didn't seem to matter so much anymore.

And he let his tears fall freely, not caring who would see them.

And he started another prayer, but it wasn't to the Sun.

CHAPTER ELEVEN
Adrift on Land, Home at Sea

Captain Mathias of the *Unfortunately Inquisitive Wren* was, despite everything, having a good day.

His ship had a damaged keel and rudder, a temporarily patched hull, was badly overcrowded, running low on food, and had been anchored off a barren rock at the edge of the Citrine Isles for weeks. They hadn't seen another Radhan vessel for even longer. The miners, fishermen, and shepherds of the windblown, rainy isles had closed off their borders entirely in an effort to keep the Wrack out. His crew was going stir crazy, and the one rocky beach they had access to on the island was covered in seabird shit and was filled with their relentless squawking from their cliff nests, so it hardly made a good place to escape seeing the same faces day in and day out. And there had been quite a few sprained ankles from trips to fetch water from the freshwater spring emptying onto the beach.

Mathias, however, could quite easily and happily overlook all that.

There hadn't been a single case of the Wrack onboard. Not one.

So despite the cold and the spray Mathias was resting, quite comfortably, in a hammock in the ship's rigging, with one of the ship's cats purring on his chest.

It was, to be sure, not the wisest decision, and he'd have spent quite a lot of time yelling at any of his crewmembers who did the same outside a breakwater, but they were in the lee of the rock they were anchored next to.

"Captain," someone said from just a few feet away.

Mathias kept his eyes closed.

"Captain," the voice said, "if you don't stop pretending to be asleep, I will flip your hammock with the next wave and send you straight into the water."

Mathias groaned. "Rank insubordination. Besides, you'd drown the cat."

"Insubordination? Really? I hadn't realized," his first mate said.

Mathias opened his eyes and glared at his cousin, Ann. Most of the crew was related to him one way or another—Radhan vessels were family affairs, and most Radhan spent more time at sea than on land. They had enclaves in quite a few larger port cities across the continents of Teringia and Oyansur.

Which was, of course, part of their problem. They'd been part of the Radhan fleet evacuating their enclaves from the west coast of Teringia. The *Unfortunately Inquisitive Wren* was carrying a third of the population of the Swalben enclave, while the other two thirds had boarded the much larger *Dawn Eagle*. The *Dawn Eagle* had made it out of the Swalben Harbor just fine, but the *Wren* had left almost two hours later at low tide, and in their haste to escape before the Wrack arrived, they had steered too close to the

Swalben breakwater, and a freak gust of wind had slammed them into it.

Mathias was quite happy to go before any board of inquiry once they rejoined the fleet, for they'd made it out of Swalben in time, and escaped the Wrack.

"We're running out of food," Ann said.

"Interestingly, I'm aware of that," Mathias said, shifting in his hammock. "Anyhow, haven't we started fishing already?"

"They're hardly biting," Ann said. "It's not even enough to make for a mouthful apiece divided between everyone."

Unlike the *Dawn Eagle,* they hadn't had time to load supplies before leaving. They'd simply packed people in with anything they'd carried, then when they'd filled up, they tossed any of their cargo that couldn't be eaten onto the docks and packed more people in. They'd barely gotten everyone on board in time even then.

"How many more days' worth of food do we have?" Mathias asked, already knowing the answer to that question.

"Five days, maybe? We can stretch it out a little further if we reduce rations again, but..." Ann said.

Mathias grimaced. They'd already done that twice.

"Still no sign of the fleet?" Mathias asked.

Ann shook her head. "With our luck, they've probably already sailed to Rendezvous."

The greater Radhan fleet was based out of Rendezvous— a massive archipelago a third of the way around the world from southern Oyansur. It had massive forests of good shipbuilding timber, rare trade goods that couldn't be found anywhere else, and, most importantly, it was completely uninhabited by any people other than the Radhan. The Radhan had discovered it nearly two hundred years ago, and they had managed to keep it a complete secret from the rest of the world. Some nations surely suspected its existence, but suspicion wasn't proof.

Not that it was difficult to keep the secret— most ships and sailors on Iopis were miserable in comparison to the

Radhan, and offered no true competition. Iopan sailing had
improved in recent decades as the numbers of nephrite-
bearing seers increased, but still, most Iopan ships wouldn't
even leave sight of the shore. The fishermen and merchants
of the Citrine Isles were a little more courageous than that,
but it was scant praise— it was less than two day's sailing
from Western Teringia to the Citrine Isles.

Rendezvous also had one of the great Mist Mazes in the
sheltered sea between its islands, far larger than the little
one in the Krannenbergs the Lothaini feared so much. The
Radhan, at least, understood the value of the mazes, and
some of their best ships could safely sail it and return.
Safely being a relative term, of course— more Radhan ships
were lost in that maze, and the lesser one to the southeast of
Oyansur, than to all the storms on Iopis.

"Has Nesem had any luck with the semaphore?" Mathias
asked.

Ann shook her head.

Ships were too unstable for the clockwork semaphores,
and holding still enough for a semaphore stay put and
work in the aetheric currents— what the Eidola foolishly
referred to as the spirit realm and the Sworn referred to as
the Goddess Sea— was nearly impossible. It could
sometimes be done in still enough waters, and they'd
anchored right below a major aetheric current, but Nesem,
their ship's chief seer, had been trying with no luck to get it
to work since they'd anchored here.

Mathias glanced down from his hammock and spotted
Nesem in the prow, where he was staring upwards—
presumably at the aetheric currents. The currents made for
a navigation tool almost as reliable as the stars, though
none of the landbound peoples had yet figured out all their
tricks as of yet. The Singers were close, but not enough to
worry over just yet.

"We're going to have to try and climb the cliffs, Captain,"
Ann said.

Mathias shook his head. "Absolutely not. Those cliffs are
a crumbly mess of shale most of the way up, and there's

that huge overhang at the top where it transitions to sandstone."

"It would solve all of our problems, Captain. Seabirds and eggs for food, and Nesem is convinced that there are stable aetheric currents up there that could be used to reach out to the Seawatch," Ann said.

Mathias didn't doubt Nesem on that— he'd transferred to the *Wren* two years ago from another Radhan ship that largely traded in the southern shores of Oyansur. He'd proven to be quite nearly the most skilled seer Mathias had ever worked with, in forty-some years of sailing.

"It would solve all our problems, yes, save for the fact that the cliffs are too dangerous to climb."

"We'd only have to climb it once," Ann said, "and carry some rope up."

Mathias groaned. "We've surveyed every inch of the cliffs over the beach, and there's no viable route to the top."

If they'd managed to stay with the *Dawn Eagle*, they wouldn't have had this problem. The larger ship's crew had rather more… versatility in how they addressed their problems. Of course, that versatility came at the cost of quite a lot of wildly expensive Quae jewel-silk, but…

Mathias cleared his thoughts of what-ifs and if-onlys and focused back on the problem at hand.

"If there was a route I was convinced was even possible— forget even being safe— I'd allow it," he said.

Ann gave him an uncomfortable look.

"What?" he asked, suspicious.

"You're not going to like this," Ann said.

"There's a lot I don't like," he said.

"I mean, you're going to like this even less than most things," Ann said, flicking the rigging lines in the way she did when she was nervous.

"Just spit it out already," Mathis said.

"One of our crewmembers believes they've found a way up," she said.

Mathias just stared at his first mate for a long moment.

"By the fact you haven't said their name, I suspect I know precisely which crewmember you mean," he said.

Ann just shrugged.

"Of course I'm not going to like her idea, I don't like any of her ideas," Mathias said. "All of her ideas are terrible, and they always seem to end in someone getting hurt. Usually her, but it somehow ends up being me nearly as often."

Ann just nodded.

"Do you remember her "improved" block and tackle?" Mathias demanded. "How expensive it was to fix the dock?"

Ann nodded again.

"Or her new space-saving cargo storing scheme? The ship nearly toppled over!" Mathias said, starting to work up into a well-worn litany of complaints.

Ann looked like she wanted to argue that one, but didn't.

"Or her shortcut through the Moon's Horns? We had gouges in the hull to port *and* starboard," Mathias said.

Ann gave him a sheepish look as she nodded.

"Or when she decided to become a seer without telling anyone, and comes back to the ship short an eye?" Mathias demanded.

"I remember all of those things— and a hell of a lot more," Ann said. "But… I also remember that the dock was already rotten, that we still use her new cargo storing method and just take more care redistributing the weight, that the shortcut *worked*, and we got the cargo into port at Ladreis just in time, and, well… she might be an even better seer than Nesem now."

"She's reckless, impulsive, and can't stay focused on any task once she's mastered it," Mathias snapped. "She's got a lad or lass in literally every port, has almost missed departure half a dozen times, and has broken up at least three marriages that I know of. If it weren't for a very small number of *extremely* lucky successes, she would have long since been thrown off the ship."

"It's not that small of a number of successes," Ann said, "and it's definitely not just luck. She fixes more problems than she causes, and there's no braver soul on deck."

Mathias sighed. "I'm going to hate this idea, I just know it. I don't know where she gets it from."

Ann chuckled. "She is your daughter."

Mathias snorted and closed his hammock over the cat and himself. His voice came out muffled from inside his canvas cocoon. "I blame my husband. Tell Eissa yes, but I don't want to hear a word of what her plan is, and I'm not leaving my hammock until it's done."

"This plan is so, so much worse than you described it," Ann said.

"Are you implying that I misled you?" Eissa said, a wide grin on her face as she finished stripping off her clothes, save for her leather pouch full of eyes strapped to her left bicep.

"I don't think I'm implying it," Ann said. "I am, in fact, directly saying you misled me."

Eissa winked at the older woman with her nephrite eye. Eissa had never much seen the point of wearing an eyepatch— they were just there to make others more comfortable, and that was no fun at all.

Ann opened her mouth to object, but Eissa just smiled and hopped out of the dinghy.

The water this far north was what most people would describe as bitterly cold, but as far as Eissa was concerned, it was merely bracing.

She swam around to the back of the boat, where her invention floated. Unlike many sailors, all the Radhan could swim, but hardly any could come close to Eissa. She'd come in third overall among all the Radhan fleets in the great games at Rendezvous three years ago. She had actually won the two day race, where competitors had to make an uninterrupted swim between islands. The winner of that one was always a woman, but she'd also placed highly in the short distance swimming sprints, where the men tended to dominate.

Eissa excelled at anything she put her mind to, and she saw absolutely no reason to be humble about it. She certainly wasn't humble about her newest invention.

Well, it wasn't precisely her invention, if she was to be honest. She'd gotten the idea from the Nemennemak islanders, who had been using them for generations to navigate the sea caves beneath their islands. They used the devices to help harvest the luminescent silk from their cave worms, which was traded to the Quae Empire, who in turn wove it into jewel-silk. Since the Quae blockaded the Nemen islands to maintain their monopoly on jewel-silk—and executed anyone who tried to sneak into the islands— well…

Eissa felt entirely justified in not telling anyone she'd swum out to the islands by the cover of night and spent a few days with the Nemennemak, who really couldn't give a damn about the Quae Empire's laws one way or another. They'd been happy to show her around the islands. She didn't share a single word with them, but she'd been working on replicating their curious mode of transit they used to maneuver through the tight tunnels that lead to the silkworm caves ever since.

"So… your brilliant invention is just a plank," Ann said.

"This is hardly a plank," Eissa said, indignant. "I spent weeks carving this out of a single chunk of wood, then carefully waxing the wood until it wouldn't absorb water."

Ann gave her a flat look. "Alright, it's a weirdly-shaped waxed plank."

Eissa just sighed and climbed atop the board. She had no idea what the Nemennemak called them, but Eissa had been calling it her wave rider.

The wave rider was about eight feet long and roughly oval shaped, coming to a point at either end. It had a small keel on the bottom near the back. She didn't know what wood the islanders carved theirs out of, but she'd chosen teak, on the general principle that if it was good enough for ship building, it was good enough for her wave rider. Their wave riders were only about five feet long, so they could maneuver in the narrow caves at high tide, which was the only time the silk was accessible. The cave ceilings were too low for actual canoes, but the islanders could fit through floating on their wave riders. Eissa's was designed for use out in the open, hence its greater size.

She found teak a hassle and a half to work with, but the board had turned out decently. Despite lacking metal tools, the Nemennemak boards had been considerably more elegant. She wasn't sure how they pulled that one off.

Ann handed Eissa her waterproof canvas satchel first, which Eissa slung over her back. It contained dry clothes, her canteen, rope, and iron pitons to anchor the rope from the top when she got there. Next Ann handed over her double ended paddle, the blades set at right angles to one another. The Nemennemak only used single ended paddles, but they were going for maneuverability and compactness, not speed.

Eissa untied the rope from the little hole she'd carved in the back of the wave rider, then turned towards the front and kneeled.

"Good luck," Ann called.

Eissa took a deep breath and started paddling away from Ann and the dinghy.

They'd rowed the dinghy into the lee of a rock spire jutting from the sea. Before Eissa paddled the wave-rider out of that same lee, she gently patted her arm pouch to check that her eyes were still there. Of her nearly two dozen eyes, she'd only brought three, plus the nephrite in her socket— her little arm pouch couldn't hold any more.

She didn't bother to swim her mind into the aether currents, because she'd never left them. Other seers only dove down into their unreal depths when they needed to look into things, but Eissa stayed in them even when sleeping.

From her living left eye, Eissa saw the crashing spray, rocks jutting from the sea, and off in the distance, the imposing seacliff that was her target.

From her right eye, Eissa saw so much more.

Nephrite was by far her favorite eye. In its domain, it gave clarity unmatched by any other gem in their own domains, save perhaps emerald, and nephrite's domain was the sea. Once she'd learned to interpret the ripples and waves in the aetheric currents, the sea became her domain as well. She could see every current, every undertow, every wash. She could see fish swimming about below, and rock spines lurking so close beneath the surface they would gut even a dinghy.

And from both eyes, she saw the massive waves rolling in a steady, relentless line, crashing a solid dozen feet up against the cliff.

For whatever strange reason, during this world's creation, the shale hadn't been made to rise as far here as over the rocky beach on the other side of the island. Over there, the sandstone was a good eighty feet in the air. The sandstone cap of the island sat at an odd angle atop the shale, though, and on this side, the sandstone was far lower.

Just about a foot or two above where the waves crested against the cliff, in fact.

If she'd been trying to climb anyhow, the shale was still too crumbly and awful to ascend. And the sandstone leaned far over it, creating a lip as wide as fifteen feet in places. In one spot, though— one narrow spot— a great chunk of the sandstone had crumbled, leaving a narrow chimney leading upwards.

Climbing the shale wouldn't work, but riding a wave over it straight to the sandstone chimney?

Probably still wouldn't work, but it wasn't impossible. Though, in fairness, any reasonable person— and most madmen— would call it an insane death-trap.

Eissa laughed, and paddled straight into it.

Eissa's back muscles were already straining a little by the time she approached the cliff. She could swim all day or row a dinghy without getting tired, but paddling her wave rider was quite different than either.

For most of the approach, she'd been just building up speed, dodging rock spires, and trying not to capsize on the huge swells.

Then she finally caught a wave of the right size, and it had just been a mad sprint to stay on the wave and stay positioned just right.

The spray kept splashing her live eye, and rather than blink it clear, she had shut it entirely, depending solely on the milky green aetheric currents to guide her.

It was strange, paddling madly atop the wave and hearing crashing foam around her, while merely seeing the peaceful green currents dancing around. She could interpret them well enough to know what was around her, but it looked absolutely nothing like the physical waves and rocks.

Rapidly growing closer to her was a field of aether where the ripples water cast in the currents simply stopped, and were replaced with the incredibly faint ripples that were all nephrite could see of what rocks cast into the aether.

Eissa took a deep breath, threw aside her paddle, and stood up on the wave rider.

Then, as the wave drew towards the cliff, she leapt.

For a moment Eissa felt like she was flying, and then she threw her arms out to either side of her as she slammed into the cliff and was drenched in the spray. She felt shale crumbling at her feet and thought she'd failed for a moment, and then she realized that her arms were wedged into the sides of the sandstone chimney.

The first few moments were the hardest. The chimney was widest at the bottom, and her weight was resting on her arms and shoulders. She thankfully hadn't misjudged the width of the chimney, so her arms weren't at full extension. If they had been, she wasn't sure she would have been able to pull herself up.

She ached from paddling and from slamming against the stone, but she couldn't take time to rest, lest her arms give out.

She carefully, slowly, swung her left foot up, she and managed to get that foot wedged into the sandstone chimney.

By this time, she'd blinked her living eye free of the saltwater and could look around her.

Above her and to her right was a little outcropping of sandstone. If she grabbed it, she could pull herself up a little and get her right leg into the rock chimney. She'd have most of her weight on the right side of the chimney then, and if the little outcrop broke, she'd fall to the waves below, and she wasn't sure if even a swimmer as strong as her could survive in that.

Another wave crashed below her, splashing her with droplets of saltwater. She took another deep breath and *pushed* with her left leg while shooting her right upwards. Her fingers barely — oh so barely — wrapped around the outcrop.

And it held.

Eissa breathed out a sigh of relief, and pulled her right leg up, bracing it against the chimney.

She still didn't rest yet, instead pulling herself a few more steps and handholds up the chimney. It wasn't as bad as she'd feared — the rockfall was still recent, so the waves hadn't had time to smooth the base of the chimney out too much. And this sandstone was fairly durable compared to a lot of sandstones she'd encountered — and just as easy to climb.

The chimney constricted a bit, until Eissa could comfortably rest her weight on her legs and give her arms a little break. She sighed in relief, then opened one of the eye pockets on her arm pouch. She then reached up and carefully popped out her nephrite eye. She felt her shoulders tense automatically as half her world went dark. Careful not to drop it in the brutal surf below, she slid it into the open slot, and buttoned it closed again. She then popped open the next pouch, and pulled out her garnet eye, slotting it into her empty socket.

She felt a sting of salt water in her socket that had gotten on the garnet, but within two blinks, her mind was swimming the aetheric currents again, the stinging inhibiting it not at all, and her shoulders relaxed again.

Garnet was especially unusual among gemstones— it was attuned to stone, but perhaps too attuned. The ripples and waves in the aetheric currents were so thick as to be almost opaque. Though that made the currents far more visible than those of other gems, almost becoming a detriment, they came so thick and close together.

When you first looked at stone through a garnet seer's eye, it looked almost black. Save, curiously, for garnet, spinel, and a few other uncommon minerals— those didn't show up at all in the garnet currents. Spinel was the only one of those used often other than garnet, and its uses were very different. Curiously, garnet and other spinels didn't show up to spinel eyes either.

A mystery indeed, and one she intended to solve someday, but not one Eissa had time for at the moment. She rested weight on her arms again and began clambering upwards.

It took some training before you could learn to see between the thick garnet ripples, but once you could, it let you see the innards of the stones themselves. It might seem frivolous to those who didn't know better, for stone was just an undifferentiated mass to the ignorant, but stone had a grain, like wood, and it had flaws and cracks that any mason, architect, or sculptor must know.

Or, in this case, a madwoman climbing a cliff.

Garnet guided Eissa's hands and feet to secure cracks and strong outcroppings, warning her when a seemingly innocuous patch of sandstone was unstable and at risk of breaking.

She could have levered her back against one wall of the chimney and shimmied up it, but that would be a disadvantageous position when she reached the top, and one that— somewhat illogically, she knew— felt like it gave her less control, even if it was easier on her muscles.

As she approached the roof of the chimney, where the top of the tall, narrow wedge of rock had fallen out, she edged farther and farther back, until her hands and feet almost touched the edges of the chimney. Then she took a moment to peer upwards through the rock above her head for handholds. Locating a likely one, she reached up and back with her left hand and inserted her hand into the crack. She did the same with the right hand, grabbing onto a small but stable nub of rock.

Then, slowly and cautiously, her back muscles straining, she leaned back until her head and torso were coming out from under the chimney's roof, and began slowly edging her feet farther up the sides of the chimney. She eyed the structure of the rock above her, then lifted her right hand up, leaving most of her weight on her left hand at this angle. She crossed her right hand over her left, then grabbed onto another crack.

Her shoulders groaned and complained of the awkward angle, but she edged her feet higher. Her butt was jutting out now, and even less weight rested on her feet.

As much as this position hurt, Eissa took her time planning out her next move. She took a series of deep, fast breaths, then let go with her left hand and leapt upwards.

For a moment that felt like an eternity, Eissa's right hand was the only part of her touching the cliff. She felt as though her heart was going to explode out of her chest and her stomach fall out of her mouth.

And then her left hand sunk into the particularly deep crack she'd been aiming for, and her left foot landed on a nub of sandstone, and she was kissing the cliff face, her heart pounding.

Afterward, Eissa could never have told how long she spent clambering up the cliff. It felt like an eternity, and when she reached the top, she collapsed onto the ground, panting.

She was covered in scrapes, bruises, and cuts, like she always was after a climb. She had a truly massive bruise on one leg that she somehow hadn't noticed until she reached the top— if she had to guess, her wave-rider had slammed into her thigh as she leapt to the chimney. Her muscles all burned and ached, and she doubted she'd be able to move much at all the next day.

And yet...

Her mind rested quiet, without the constant churn of ideas and impulses that often kept her awake far into the night and kept her from holding still during the day. She treasured moments like this, when she wore herself out from physical exertion, mental exertion, or a bout of lovemaking. Moments when she could just rest at peace for a moment, and forget about the expectations of her fathers and her people. Forget about her constant hunger for new experiences and new ideas. Forget her frustration and disappointment at how slow and dull most people were, and forget about plagues and idiot empires following the idiot commands of idiot leaders.

She just stared at the blustery sky that couldn't decide whether it wanted clouds or sun and felt at peace.

Until, of course, a perplexed gull pecked her in the forehead.

"I'm going to enjoy eating you," Eissa muttered.

The bird cocked its head at her and squawked.

CHAPTER TWELVE
Defeat Without Ever Fighting A Battle

In some lives the regrets pile up young.

Opportunities not taken. Dances not danced. Words said in haste and anger.

In other lives they stretch out.

Apologies never made. Ambitions unrealized. Years wasted in stubbornness.

For a precious few lives, those lives most interesting to the poets whose hearts love the tragic, the regrets pile up right at the end.

Knight-Marshall Ulric of Westfen, commander of the Royal Army of Geredain, cousin of His Majesty King Albrecht the Resolute, ninth of that name and title, rightful ruler of Geredain and the rebel territory of Lothain, was one of those people.

Honestly, his cousin, Albrecht, really should have been one of those lives as well, but Ulric had not once in his life ever seen Albrecht regret anything. He'd seen Albrecht *blame* others for failures, but to regret failures would be to admit that Albrecht was anything less than perfect, and so far as Albrecht was concerned, that was the next best thing to treason.

Though, Ulric contemplated, as he was led up to the gallows behind his cousin, there were surely poets who would write about Albrecht anyway. Perhaps give him a stirring gallows speech, instead of spitting, cursing, and demanding to be set free.

And crying. Can't forget the crying.

Ulric's title of Knight-Marshall was, to say the least, bunk. Nonsense. Pointless. A complete farce.

It wasn't that he was a bad knight or soldier, by any means. He was up training at dawn every day, with sword and lance and bow. There were few more accomplished riders in all of Geredain. He should know, he had a permanent offer of a purse of silver for anyone who could beat him in a horse race. He'd paid it out seven times, but compared to the number of contests he'd had?

Well, Ulric felt he deserved a little bragging.

His accomplishments didn't just lie in the realm of the physical, either. Ulric spoke five languages, could recite over a hundred poems by heart, and had a singing voice that, while hardly the most beautiful, was perfectly suited to any song of the sort that people would laugh at and clap along to. He'd read more books than any other knight in Geredain— and most of the nobles. He'd memorized every map of Teringia— and quite a few of northern Oyansur. He'd studied the memoirs of all the great generals, spending hours interviewing every single officer who'd commanded a battle or skirmish for Geredain.

Ulric was quite aware of how many men held military posts merely for their blood, and he was determined to prove his worth by deed as well. Not that he'd say that out loud— he didn't want to offend his ancestors. Still, he'd always wanted to be counted as among the worthiest of his family's dead someday.

That last would be unlikely to happen now.

The reason his post as commander of the armies of Geredain was meaningless was, of course, Albrecht. His cousin, as sure as he ever was of his own brilliance and valor, personally took over the command of every last ancestor-forsworn skirmish he could, and he demanded Ulric's presence at his side at all times in battle.

Ulric had never decided whether that made him a glorified attendant, a trained speaking crow, or just a theater prop.

He rather liked crows, and the thought of relieving himself on his cousin like a poorly trained bird had, shamefully enough, crossed his mind on one or two occasions over the years.

Well, rather more occasions than that.

Ulric had never written poetry, but he'd tried to live his life so the poets might write about him. He'd prepared himself so that when the day the Usurper in Lothain showed weakness, when it was time for the royal line of the Resolute to retake their long-stolen throne, he would be there as the tip of Geredain's spear. No poet would need struggle to fit him into their epic retellings of Geredain's battles.

No poet would likely even try to fit him into one of their works, now, for Geredain had fought no epic battles here.

Geredain had the greatest population of Moonsworn on Teringia. You'd have to go south past Galicanta to the Sunsworn Empire on Oyansur to rival it. Some of the most brilliant minds of all Iopis came to dwell in Geredain, in great part thanks to the Geredain's Eye of the King— one of the few emerald eyes that had ever been made, and one of only three on Teringia. And, rarer yet, the Geredain kings were among the few who would lend its use to scholars from other nations— save, of course, for scholars of of Lothain or Galicanta. There were countless brilliant minds and peerless healers in the king's court, yet Albrecht listened to none of them while planning his invasion of Lothain.

The healers and seers, Moonsworn and otherwise, advised closing off the border immediately, to keep plague out. Albrecht began sending scouts across it instead.

They advised keeping the semaphore lines open so that news of the Wrack might arrive, and the Moonsworn might coordinate a response. Albrecht instead cut off all outgoing semaphore messages and began sending raiding parties to destroy Lothain's semaphores.

They advised warning the populace to not drink the water of the Rhost River, which flowed through two Lothaini cities and alongside countless villages, in case the Wrack was transmitted by water. Instead, Albrecht began the construction of massive siege barges to be poled up the gentle river.

The first few weeks of the invasion had gone swimmingly. They'd taken village after village, city after city, and none had offered even token resistance or even real complaint at having their crops and livestock seized. Albrecht's ego had grown to even greater proportions than usual, and he'd seemed almost disappointed at having no battle to offer them.

Ulric's doubts had only grown and grown.

He'd felt no honor or glory in pushing around the dazed survivors of the Wrack, just a growing sense of shame. The living victims of the contagion moved as though fighting against a powerful river current, their fingers and toes burnt until they were nearly useless. Those who had avoided infection entirely weren't much better, and they spent their time either tending to the victims or frantically preparing for winter.

He'd always held visions of battling other noblemen in glorious combat, but the nobility of Lothain had been reaped like the harvest by the plague. That fact left many of the Geredaini nobility nervous and twitchy, to say the least, but Albrecht proclaimed it merely proved that the ancestors were on their side, and the Lothaini nobles were being punished for siding with the Usurper's family.

The first time Ulric encountered screamers had left him badly shaken. They were few in number, though— the Wrack had already mostly burnt itself out in Lothain.

By the time the winds of winter had started blowing, they'd seized most of eastern Lothain. Albrecht, of course, took the occasion to make a speech claiming the Wrack was on their side, insisting they'd retake his ancestral throne by the Midwinter fast.

A poet would have had the first Geredaini screamers interrupt the speech, or better yet have Albrecht be its first victim, but the Wrack broke out in their camp two days later, among the soldiers, leaving the nobility nearly untouched, reversing its usual pattern.

The army had just… crumbled. The soldiers, already wildly on edge, had fled in huge numbers, leaving only a small, loyal core. The King's Eye, which Albrecht had foolishly brought with him into Lothain, went missing along with the deserting troops.

The raging king had insisted that they press on, that the Wrack had already conquered Lothain for them.

News reached them that the Wrack had broken out in Geredain over a week ago. It had broken out all along the border with Lothain, and had followed the Rhost deep into the heart of the kingdom. On top of that, the kingdoms to Geredain's east had closed off their borders entirely.

More soldiers, and even some nobles, deserted.

They'd pressed on towards the capital, only to meet with a Lothaini army. It was a battered, mismatched thing, of city guards, the house guards of the nobility, and massed civilians, but it had dwarfed their demoralized remnant of an army.

Albrecht had demanded they attack. His army, Ulric included, had simply surrendered on the spot.

Ulric stood in the snow and watched the Resolute Line of Kings of Geredain come to an end. It wasn't a good end, and it wasn't the sort of end he'd ever anticipated for Albrecht or himself.

At least the Lothaini had promised to preserve their names, that they might not be lost from the ancestors. Ulric took a little comfort from that kindness.

As his guards walked him to the gallows, he idly turned his head to one of the guards.

"I should have been a poet," Ulric said.

The guard chuckled at that.

CHAPTER THIRTEEN

A Galicantan Propensity for Polite Lies

The polite lie was considered something of an art form in Galicanta, at least amongst the nobility. The Galicantan commoners were considerably blunter, and Raquella was far more comfortable among them than the nobility.

The key to the whole endeavor of the polite lie was ensuring the other party knew it was a lie, which Raquella had always thought defeated the whole point of lying. They'd developed ninescore and more subtle tells and rituals to ensure the other party knew it was a lie as well.

The fact that there were significant numbers of Moonsworn in Galicanta, despite the supposed ban, was one such polite lie. The nobility— and the Empress— merely referred to Galicanta's Moonsworn as "southern provincials", which not only served the lie that the ban was total but also bore the barb of claiming they'd conquer the Sunsworn Empire someday.

The Galicantan nobles were ever fond of layering their meanings. They were obsessed with elegance, subtlety, and delicate maneuverings, and Raquella had to admit, despite herself, that they excelled at all three. Their art and music were sublime, their architecture was ornate and daring, and their poetry was comparable to the best of what was on offer in the Sunsworn Empire.

It was just too damn bad that the Galicantans were also the most bloody-minded, vicious people on the Teringian continent.

They had a few rivals for that title on Oyansur, though— Raquella was loyal enough to her Sunsworn kin, but she knew that there were quite a few Sunsworn nearly as bad as the Galicantans. The current emperor was as belligerent as they came, and far less fond of learning, culture, and beauty than the Galicantan Empress.

Raquella had high hopes that the Emperor's heir, Amazahd, might be a man of rather more refinement.

For all her frequent irritation with the Galicantan polite lie, she'd learned to live with it over her nearly forty years living in the Galicantan capital of Ladreis, and it seldom roused her ire anymore. She'd come here not yet twenty, and oh, it had infuriated her at first, but while tempers burned fiercely in Galicanta, the weather was too hot to let them burn long.

Today, however, was an exception. Today, she was quite willing to sustain her temper over the trouble the polite lie could cause.

"How long ago?" Raquella demanded.

"At least three weeks," one of her healers gathered in her office said.

"So it could already be in Ladreis for all we know," Raquella said. "And just because they wanted to preserve their pride or some such nonsense, the Galicantans hid it from us. Or more likely don't want it getting back to the Sunsworn through us. And now we're going to have to scramble to prepare for the Wrack's arrival."

"I mean, there aren't any rivers running from the Lothaini border to here," another healer offered.

Raquella glared at him. "It's not waterborne, idiot."

"It followed the Rhost in Geredain, though!" he offered weakly.

Raquella sighed. "Fine. It might be partially waterborne, if the month-old reports we've been getting through an elaborate chain of semaphore relays running from Geredain over the Krannenbergs, through Singer territories, then carried by ship to the Fractured Duchies, and then via poorly hidden and encoded semaphore messages to our Vowless contacts here in Ladreis are correct— which is entirely too long a chain of relays for me to trust without a hefty serving of skepticism alongside it. Based on the reports we have from the Lothaini Moonsworn, only a small part of the Wrack spread along the path of Lothain's rivers. In addition, even if the Wrack did spread along the

Rhost, who knows— perhaps it was actually spread by boatmen on the river."

She grimaced, saying the harsh word *Wrack*. Daugthan, the language of Lothain and Geredain, was a guttural, rough tongue— nothing like the more graceful languages spoken in Galicanta or the Sunsworn Empire.

There was a direct translation of the word in Galicantan, but it was almost too graceful to use to describe the plague. And she still didn't understand why the plague was named after washed-up seaweed.

"What if the Masquerade theory is correct?" one of the younger healers asked nervously.

Raquella just ignored the question. The Goddesses would not allow a disease like the Wrack to spread through their Sea. The nameless third sister simply could not be that close to freedom.

"What are the odds the Empress will let us use her emerald?" another healer asked.

Raquella sighed. "Practically nonexistent," she admitted. "She'd need to acknowledge that we exist first, and she's never even spoken directly to any of us southern provincials."

A few of the assembled healers let out bitter laughs at that.

The rest of the meeting was taken up by Raquella ordering the preparations for her healers and the small Moonsworn community in Ladreis— mostly scholars and seers. There was always the risk the Empress would turn against them at little provocation, so the Moonsworn allowed relatively few families here, compared to their larger communities in the other Teringian nations.

The Moon had commanded they heal the sick and tend to the wounded of all peoples, but that certainly didn't mean all peoples wanted their help, nor did the Goddess go out of their way to ease their task. All lands had their challenges.

The Eidola nations south of the Krannenbergs all feared they were Sunsworn spies, and greatly distrusted them.

The Eidola nations north of the Krannenbergs, the fearsome peoples known as the Singers, greatly respected the Moonsworn, but they didn't hesitate to exile or execute them if they violated any one of the Singers' twelve-score and twelve laws. Though the Singers may be violent and warlike, none loved law the way they did. But then, nowhere else were the laws things of beauty, sung by judges and guards.

The Sei hated everyone who didn't worship their mournful, bad-tempered god of cold and silence.

The Radhan were, quite possibly, friendlier to the Moonsworn than any other people— often remarking they felt a kinship to the Moonsworn— but even they never allowed any Moonsworn to stay on their ship more than a few months. It was rumored that there was some sort of secret Radhan homeland, outside their enclaves throughout Teringia and Oyansur, but none knew for sure. The Radhan also regularly tried to seduce unwed— and sometimes even wed— Moonsworn, which had caused more than its share of problems.

The kingdoms and empires to the south, well… that was another story. The Sunsworn Empire was mighty, but there were those it walked lightly around. Still, by and large, their attitudes tended towards benign dismissal of the Moonsworn, which they could certainly deal with.

In recent years, one of the most troublesome kingdoms had, surprisingly, been the Sunsworn Empire itself. The current Emperor was making complaints bordering on that old heresy claiming that it was wrong for the Moonsworn to treat the enemies of the Sunsworn Empire. But, of course, when the Emperor says something, it is a truly brave— and truly foolish— person who accuses him of heresy.

In Galicanta, the problem was straightforward. There were no fiercer enemies than Galicanta and the Sunsworn Empire, constantly battling over the narrow isthmus between the two continents and launching fleets to battle in the seas to either side of it. The Galicantans had long distrusted the Moonsworn, considering them spies of the Sunsworn. And, of course, there wasn't a people more violent and prone to challenge you to a duel or a war than the Galicantans.

They weren't, Raquella reflected, always wrong to do so. The Sunsworn regularly tried to slip spies into the Moonsworn ranks these days. A few decades ago, under the reign of the current Emperor's father, that would have been unthinkable, but…

She turned her thoughts away from those cynical thoughts, and finished giving out orders. Her last one was that Blind Sherra be briefed on everything they knew of the Wrack. She'd likely turned her interest to the plague already, but Raquella needed to be sure.

When the others had all left, Raquella idly pushed through the reports on her desk. Several had blocky, unsightly letters, each the same as the last. Raquella hated the new… printing press, they called it. It was hideous, ungraceful, and far slower than writing, save for if you wish to make dozens of copies of something.

Some of the younger Moonsworn scholars claimed it would change the world, but a report of supply shortages bore the same details in proper handwriting or in that blocky nonsense.

Raquella sighed, and stood up, her knees creaking only a little. She was old, yes, but her family aged gracefully, and she took far better care of herself than many did. Plus, not only was Galicantan cuisine delicious, Raquella was entirely convinced that it was excellent for one's health— at least, minus all the meat of furred beasts the Galicantans ate. That the Eidola ate the meat of furred beasts was truly vile, but she'd learned to live with it. Raquella was quite happy sticking to the region's lighter fare. The Galicantans could do absolute wonders with fish and vegetables and olives.

She poured herself a glass of pale wine, made from grapes grown just a day's ride outside Ladreis, and strode over to the open balcony.

The day was drawing to a close, and Raquella made a point of watching the sunset from her office whenever she could.

She could see the brilliant, sapphire-blue ocean from her window, so high up on one of Ladreis' countless hills. There were few steeper cities in the world, hence the old joke that even the elderly and children in Ladreis had the legs of warriors. Ladreis sloped down the steep hills down to the seashore, through countless winding alleyways and twisting narrow stairwells. Between them were numerous terraced plazas and fountains. The whole city was built of the local sandstone, ranging from purest white to bright yellow to a deep sunset orange. The rooftop gardens were shocking bursts of green, with flowers of nearly as many colors as the Galicantans wore on their persons. The Galicantans had more names for colors than any people she'd ever known.

In the distance, she could hear the faint crash of waves in the harbor below, and above it, the voices of a city of a million souls, all laughing, arguing, fighting, and singing. In the little plaza with the fountain directly below her, children yelled and screamed as they chased a ball around, while their mothers gossiped around the fountain. She could smell a thousand heavily spiced dinners being cooked by the fathers and grandfathers of the city, and she knew from experience that if she spent a few hours walking through the city, the scent would slowly shift and change, for every neighborhood and family in the city had its own spice blends, culinary traditions, and secret recipes that the men of the city had been known to literally kill to protect.

Even now, in the depths of winter, Ladreis never knew frost, and even its coldest nights only compared to a cool autumn night in Lothain.

As the sun slowly sank in the sky, the city came ablaze with the fires of twilight, and the night lanterns would be lit throughout the city, until someone looking down upon the city would gain the impression of standing above the stars themselves.

Though this was the city of those who proclaimed themselves her enemies, she had spent her life tending to them. She was no seer, but she followed the path of the healer nonetheless. She had no children, no family. She'd dedicated her life to Ladreis instead. Raquella loved this city, and she prayed to the Moon to spare it in the weeks to come.

CHAPTER FOURTEEN
A Duel at Sea

The day dawned clear and bright, and the fishermen of Apiela had sailed as far as they dared, until land was but a speck on the horizon. They were brave sailors and would take their knives to any who suggested otherwise, but they were no Radhan, to sail beyond the gaze of the ancestors.

The priests said that the ancestors saw everywhere, but the sailors knew this to be the posturing of uncallused hands that it was. The land was the domain of the ancestors, and if a man or woman were to die at sea out of the sight of the land, the ancestors would be unable to guide them to their arms, even with their name recorded. The sea kept what it took.

It was Illana who saw the Radhan ship coming into sight over the horizon first. Illana of the fierce smile, Illana of the hair like beaten copper, Illana the sharp-witted and sharper tongued, Illana who every fisherman and many of the fisherwomen secretly or not so secretly loved, Illana of the green eyes that could see farther than any of them.

The fishermen of Apiela cheered, for it was always a good day when the Radhan came to trade. They laughed, joked, and insisted that they would be chaste, and stand firm against the advances of the sea traders, whose appetites were famous. And all laughed at their outrageous lies, for the Radhan were nearly so charming as Galicantans themselves, not to mention less likely to take offense and a knife to them as another Galicantan would, and few there would turn down their advances if offered.

Pietro the quiet— that lean and thoughtful lad who so few noticed, that straight-backed uncomplaining worker, when it was his turn to boast, only smiled faintly.

"I might resist if I had reason," Pietro said.

And the sailors saw that he smiled at Illana the fierce, who should have been born a noble, so she might earn her spurs and fight against the heathens, for any life less was a waste of fire. Illana made a rude gesture, and fingered her belt knife ostentatiously, but Pietro's smile stayed, and as the sailors jeered, only Pietro— Pietro the thoughtful, Pietro who walked like a dancer— saw the faint blush come to her cheeks.

It was again Illana who called out to the fishing fleet some time later— Illana of the voice like a babbling brook, Illana of the voice like a shepherd's flute. Illana who let them know that there was something wrong with the Radhan ship.

And as the fishermen watched, they too saw that something was wrong with the great Radhan ship. It listed to one side, ropes lay tangled, and sails hung a-tatter off its tall masts.

Finally, the oldest of them, the fleetmother, old Enanda the salt-scarred, declared the ship lost to them, for it was caught in the great southerly current.

And the sailors all touched their lips and then their hearts in prayer as the word was passed between the fishing boats, and they were all quiet for a moment.

Until Illana the brave— Illana the foolhardy— spoke.

"We should sail out to it."

At those words, a great hue and cry went up, each man and woman more ready than the last to call foolishness, to protest, for none of them save old Enanda had ever sailed out that far. Yet all knew it was fear that stayed them, and the protests were weak from shame.

"I agree with Illana," a voice called out.

And the sailors looked, and saw that it was Pietro whose arms bore beautiful inked birds.

"Of course you want to sail out beyond the ancestor's gaze, you fool. You want to sleep with Illana," a sailor called out.

Pietro turned to face the sailor— Alphonse, of the ready fists and the crude temper. Alphonse the giant of a man, who in Apiela, only the blacksmith stood over.

And Pietro, whose gaze always met your eyes, said, in a quiet voice that carried across the fishing ship in the sudden silence, "Does that not make me brave?"

And Alphonse the brute snarled. "Sailing out past the gaze of the ancestors makes you foolish, not brave."

That little half-smile came onto Pietro's face then, which was not a beautiful face as the faces in a painting might be, but one which lingered in your memory nonetheless.

"It was not sailing out to sea which I claimed made me brave," Pietro said.

And Illana, so swift to take offense and so swift to give challenge, pealed out laughter like bells, and suddenly the whole crew was laughing, and the other fishermen on the other boats all strained to hear.

And with that laughter, it was decided, and they sailed out to the Radhan ship.

And the rest of the fishing fleet, so as not to show themselves cowards, followed.

And for the first time in all their lives, save that of old Enanda, they sailed out past the sight of land, and past the watchful gaze of their ancestors.

The Radhan ship was battered worse than they had seen from afar, as though it had sailed through a storm untended. As they drew close, none hailed them, and they smelled the stench of death, and they knew it for a ghost ship.

The fishermen would have fled, but Illana who feared nothing, Illana who lived life only by full measure— leapt from the prow, and seizing a dangling rope, she scrambled to the deck of the Radhan ship, which bore the name *Dawn Eagle*.

Behind her followed Pietro, who could swim the harbor three times over, and Alphonse of the jealous and cruel gaze.

And the rest of the sailors followed, so as not to be shown cowards.

Aboard the *Dawn Eagle*, they found far more bodies than should be on a ship this size, all bearing blackened fingers and toes, and everywhere rats nibbled on the corpses, and showed no fear of the fisherfolk. The ship's boats were all gone, taken by any survivors. And the sailors of Apiela knew the Wrack had been to this ship, and the sailors quailed, for they rightfully feared the awful plague that their village had thus been spared. There was no shame in fearing the Wrack.

But Illana, who never hesitated to reach for what she desired, laughed at those cowardly enough to flee.

"Surely," Illana said, "there are no cowards here."

And behold, there were not.

"This ship is adrift, and salvage," Illana said. "The sea has given this ship to us, which surely has many fine things aboard. We should not spurn the gift of the sea, for the sea is even quicker to take offense than I."

And the eyes of the sailors brightened with greed, but another voice stayed them.

"No," was all it said, and all the sailors turned, and there they saw Pietro, who never spoke an unneeded word.

"No," he said again. "Though Galicantan they were not, all sailors are our brothers and sisters, and I say we should honor their dead in their way, by sinking the *Dawn Eagle* and giving them to the sea. For our ancestors' home is of the land, but the ancestors of the Radhan belong to the sea, and I would give them to their ancestors."

And the men and women all looked at Pietro, who had never spoken so many words at once, and then at Illana. And those with a bit of wisdom might have seen a flash of shame across Illana's face— Illana who had oft before been led astray by her passions.

And those wise might suspect that the flood of anger on her face then was at herself, for letting her greed overcome her, but the rest, those men and women who loved and drank and laughed without needing the curse of wisdom, saw only the anger, not the shame, and they knew it to be aimed at Pietro.

"Pretty words," Illana said, glaring at Pietro, "from a coward."

And the sailors went silent, for all knew what came after that.

Old Enanda, who bore her share of knife scars and more, stepped forwards, having just made it to the deck of the *Dawn Eagle*.

"We lie out of sight of the land," she said. "If you must fight, let it wait until land."

And Pietro, who did bear the curse of wisdom, but perhaps was not yet ready for its burdens, shook his head.

"And let Illana dishonor our salt-kin?" he said. "That I shall not stand for."

For he was right, that they must not steal from the dead of the sea, but like so many of the young, he let being right go to his head.

And Old Enanda, who bore the greatest curse of wisdom in Apiela, sighed, for she knew there was no stopping this now. There might have been once— divide the two on different ships, let tempers cool, and perhaps an apology might be forthcoming. She would have forbid the looting of the ship herself, had she boarded soon enough to stop this foolishness. Perhaps both might have survived the duel, because in truth, few duels were to the death these days. At the very least, the duel would be on land, where the ancestors might guide the loser home.

But now one party stood accused of cowardice, and one of dishonor, and Old Enanda knew better than to fight the tide.

And on that deck, filled with corpses and neglect, circled Illana the beautiful and Pietro the quiet, and part of each regretted every word that had been said, and part of each desperately hoped that something might stop this, but both of them knew nothing would, and that chain of pride they'd thrown around one another drew tighter and tighter, until two knives flashed.

And Pietro lay on the deck and bled, and Illana would bear a new scar across her collarbone, and not an eye in the crowd was dry.

For the men and women of Apiela were not afraid to show their hearts, and something beautiful had been stillborn this day.

And Illana wept quietly for Pietro, who she might have let steal her heart someday. She wept quietly for Pietro, who had fallen to her pride.

And for the first time in Illana's life, in the depths of her heart, she cursed her pride.

And a crack formed in that pride, and the seed of the curse of wisdom was planted inside it that day.

Old Enanda stepped forward then, and looked carefully at Pietro the quiet, whose quiet came not by choice now.

"He's not dead yet," she said simply and bent to look closer.

For a moment none spoke, and hope began to rise in many hearts.

Enanda sighed then, and dashed those hopes against the rocks. "But it won't be long," she said. "He'll make it not to sight of land."

And Illana's quiet tears turned to loud sobs, and among the shriveled corpses of the Wrack, she embraced Pietro, who was soon to join them.

And the sailors all touched their lips, and then their hearts, for Pietro's soul was soon to be lost, here out of sight of land.

And they turned towards their boats, to sail back to their own waters.

But a sound stayed their feet, and they all turned back.

For Illana, whose wit was so swift, had slung Pietro over her shoulder, and begun to climb the rigging. And for a moment none understood.

And then, like a crack of thunder, understanding spread between them, and they began to cheer and shout, and the *Dawn Eagle* knew joy for the first time in many weeks.

And Illana the swift flew up that rigging like none had ever seen anyone climb rigging before, not even unencumbered by any burdens, and they were amazed.

For Illana was encumbered by not just by Pietro the dying, but by her own pride, for pride does not die in a day, and hers was a heavy burden indeed.

And perhaps the burden of pride was too much, for a rope broke, and Illana slipped.

And the sailors gasped, for Illana now hung from the broken rope with one hand, and held Pietro's wrist with the other.

And they knew she wouldn't make it in time.

But another hand reached out and seized Pietro's other wrist, and together, Illana and Alphonse carried Pietro upwards.

For even a brute like Alphonse may still have honor, and weep at such a tragedy.

And together they brought Pietro to the crow's nest, on the top of the tallest mast, atop a truly great ship indeed.

And Illana gently kissed the crown of Pietro's head as they settled him into the crow's nest.

And that mast was just tall enough that when Pietro opened his eyes for the final time, he could see, at the far edges of his dying vision, just barely cresting the horizon, the smallest speck of land.

CHAPTER FIFTEEN
Her Dedication Lacking

"She's not even a seer!" Yersina insisted.

"No, but she's still a widely respected scholar with years of field experience who has studied under some of the greatest Moonsworn administrators, city planners, and healers," Yakob replied.

"How are you supposed to even properly understand healing with two living eyes?" Yersina continued.

"Weren't you literally just complaining yesterday about how the Patient vastly overemphasize scrying when diagnosing illness?" Sariah asked.

"Only when it's at the unnecessary expense of other clues!" Yersina said. "Scrying is still by far the most effective tool. If we didn't have seers, the healing arts would be literally impossible to practice. It's dishonest to ever count a non-seer as a true healer."

"That's a bold claim," Sariah said.

"I think she's right about that, even if her other complaints about Raquella are unfounded," Yakob said.

"Look," Yersina said. "I genuinely think that Raquella is a terrible choice to lead Ladreis' Moonsworn during a plague. She's fine as an administrator in normal times, but with the Wrack approaching?"

"You're saying that having her in charge will lead to more deaths in the city when the Wrack arrives," Haim said.

"She's not a seer, which fundamentally limits her understanding of medicine," Yersina said. "She's more concerned with not irritating the Empress and her court than actually saving lives. And she's a hard-line believer in Patient methods, which have utterly failed to stop the Wrack so far. We need to attempt Dedicated methods now. This is no time to be conservative and avoid risks— that, in and of itself, is an unnecessary risk."

"So, what then?" Yakob asked. "We try to get her replaced?"

Yersina shook her head. "Even if we could get a message to the holy city in time— which we can't, thanks to the prohibitions on us sending messages south via semaphore— they almost certainly wouldn't see things our way."

"So, what then?" Haim asked. "Are you suggesting we convince Ladreis' Moonsworn to mutiny against Raquella just weeks before a plague arrives?"

Yersina shook her head. "You know what I'm suggesting," she said.

No one spoke for a moment. The fifth person in the room, however, had to struggle not to curse out loud as she realized what was being proposed.

Of course, the reason she was staying quiet mostly had to do with the fact that she was spying on the four young Moonsworn healers from the rafters.

Joanna was in a state of borderline panic as she listened to the four young Moonsworn argue fiercely below here.

The Galicantan throne had a surprising number of spies monitoring the Ladreis Moonsworn population. The Empress and her ancestors, though they'd publicly forbidden the presence of the Moonsworn, fully understood the need for the healing cult. While Eidola healers had improved drastically over the years, they were still far from the skill and knowledge of the Moonsworn. If you needed anything more complex than a bone set, it was foolish to go to anyone other than one of the Moonsworn healers. Not to mention, having Moonsworn around kept cities remarkably healthier— and actually listening to them about city design cut down on death by disease to an absurd extent.

It had been claimed that living in a city that forbid Moonsworn entirely took a decade off your life, and Joanna suspected there was a lot of truth to that.

There were also definite dangers to having Moonsworn around. For all the Moonsworn denials otherwise, Sunsworn did sneak into the Moonsworn ranks— usually as spies among the non-healer Moonsworn, but on occasion as an actual healer. That last was terrifying, given the possibilities of healers acting as assassins.

There was another downside to having Moonsworn about, and it all revolved around a very particular passage from their holy book, which commanded them to 'slay the false healer to save the innocent life'. Compared to some passages from the Sunsworn holy book, that was incredibly tame, but the Moonsworn could be distressingly creative with who they chose to apply the label 'false healer' to. They'd assassinated bureaucrats simply for interfering with their duties before, referring to that as false healing through a chain of theological contortions. Terrifyingly, the Moonsworn had absolutely no compunctions about honor or killing cleanly. Poison was their preferred method, and it was seldom a gentle poison.

Some of the Empress's spies had noticed these four sneaking about, and Joanna had been assigned to follow them, because there was absolutely no worse possible time for there to be a Sunsworn infiltration. In the midst of open warfare would be better than this.

Members of the Dedicated sect of the Moonsworn plotting to kill the leader of the Ladreis Moonsworn community, who happened to be a member of the Patient?

That would almost certainly erupt into further violence among the Moonsworn, something all of Galicanta could ill afford right now.

Joanna badly wished that Galicanta understood the schism between the Patient and Dedicated better. The Dedicated had simply arrived seemingly out of nowhere a few decades ago, pushing a number of new treatments and diagnoses. Moonsworn schisms usually ended violently, but this one had remained mostly stable for decades, with few murders and assaults— largely due to the fact that neither side could reasonably label the other false healers.

The easiest solution here would be to have the four conspirators killed, but Joanna desperately wanted to avoid that if possible, and she suspected the Empress's secretive, anonymous spymaster would agree. Even ignoring the fact that they wanted as many healers alive as possible for the Wrack's arrival— which was closer than the public realized— there were often unintended consequences for killing Moonsworn.

For one, the Moonsworn could not be underestimated. They were excellent at figuring out who had killed one of their members, at least in the general sort of way, and there were certainly awkward political pressures they could apply, even as marginalized as the Empress kept them. For another, Moonsworn being murdered tended to embolden anti-Sunsworn zealots, and often led to further Moonsworn being murdered.

And, of course, there was always the risk that the Moonsworn would decide whoever was killing them were acting as false healers.

Anti-Sunsworn zealots striking at the Moonsworn was a major risk right now, especially if word got out about the incredibly low rates of Wrack infection among the Moonsworn. All their intelligence so far implied that the Wrack had nothing to do with the Moonsworn, at least. They were hardly only the benevolent healers they presented themselves as, but for all their scheming and questionable loyalties, they would never deliberately spread a contagion.

Haim glanced upwards as he stretched in his seat, but Joanna barely even tensed. She was well-concealed among the rafters, and she had no worries about the seer spotting her with his gemstone eye— she was entirely concealed in Quae jewel-silk, even having a veil of it over her eyes.

Quae jewel-silk was known for four things: its unparalleled ability to take dye, its unusual strength, its extreme comfort, and, most importantly, the fact that it couldn't be seen in the spirit realm. Seer-sight seemed to simply slip right over it. It didn't show up as an absence or void in the spirit realm, either— seers were simply unable to perceive it. In addition, the undyed silk was a curious dark grey, rather than the white of other silks. It was unknown why that grey didn't interfere with jewel-silk's ability to take dye.

But, as a curious consequence of that series of facts, the undyed silk was far more expensive than the dyed silk. The silk itself might not be visible in the spirit realm, but the dye was, and the bright colors made sneaking impossible to the naked eye. Quae was more than aware of those uses, and as a consequence, the only undyed jewel-silk to be found had to be purchased for exorbitant prices on the black market.

Haim looked back down to the others as they argued, but the tension didn't leave Joanna's shoulders as she contemplated the risk the four young healers posed to the stability of Ladreis.

Something needed to be done.

Raquella tried not to gawk around her as she and the other Moonsworn were led through the Imperial court. In all her decades in Ladreis, she'd never once seriously imagined coming here. She didn't know of any Moonsworn who'd ever been openly invited into the palace. Whenever a noble wanted to consult with a Moonsworn, it almost always happened outside the palace. In emergencies, Moonsworn healers were sometimes smuggled in at night, but they never got to see more than a few servant's hallways.

She was fairly sure she was gawking as much as any peasant. The Imperial Palace was *magnificent*.

The palace, unlike so many of the larger Galicantan constructions, was not built for war. It was an immense, graceful expanse of minarets, cupolas, archways, raised bridges, and balconies, all fashioned from a delicate-looking pink marble quarried half a hundred leagues away. The ceilings were high, breezy affairs, and the whole palace was meant to keep its occupants cool in the often brutal heat of Ladreis.

Inside the palace, there was not a single inch of undecorated space. The walls, floor, and ceiling were filled with mosaics, murals, tapestries, and paintings. All of them depicted scenes from life— everything from lavish masquerades to scenes of war, from fishermen at sea to farmers in their fields, from market scenes to merchants crossing the great deserts. Many of the murals and mosaics looked as though they dated back all those centuries ago to when Galicanta had ruled all of Teringia, and much of northern Oyansur. Their great empire had declined immensely over the centuries, but it had never fallen.

To her shock, she realized that the eyes of seers in many of the scenes were actually filled with tiny gem chips. Gem prices dropped monumentally once they were too small to use for eyes, but that hardly made them worthless.

The other Moonsworn behind her were whispering in amazement, nudging each other and pointing out particularly noteworthy scenes. To Raquella's relief, the Patient and Dedicated were quite cheerfully interacting with one another, their usual animosity forgotten, even if momentarily.

Raquella was still slightly in shock from the revelations the envoy from the court had delivered to her. She'd known the tensions between the two factions were growing, but not to the point where violence was being contemplated. The envoy hadn't told her who was involved, so as to prevent Raquella from responding violently herself. Part of her honestly suspected that had been a wise move on their part. She knew she had quite the temper— in that way, she was almost Galicantan herself.

Fury hadn't been her only response, however. She'd also felt immediate guilt, because she knew quite well she'd backed the Ladreis Dedicated into a corner. Raquella had spent years shooting down the overwhelming majority of their proposals and denying them the choicest assignments. Not out of any personal animosity, but because she genuinely thought that the Dedicated were far, far too hasty in their experimentation and shifts of doctrine. It hadn't been her intention to make them this desperate, however. That had been a severe oversight, to say the least.

The last thing she expected, however, had been for the Imperial court to be acting to try and preserve harmony among the Moonsworn. Just as shocking had been the invitation to the court, which wasn't addressed to the 'southern provincials', but instead to the Moonsworn by name. That was as good as official recognition from the Empress, which could radically change the Moonsworn's situation in Galicanta in the future.

Raquella had, when choosing the Moonsworn to accompany her, been quite careful to select them half and half from the Patient and the Dedicated. She hadn't, however, informed them of the biggest piece of news the envoy had shared with her.

To Raquella's surprise, they were led deeper and higher into the palace. The carvings and hangings and mosaics grew more opulent, and crowds of nobles watched them intently as they passed, gossiping quietly among themselves.

Raquella had been expecting to be led to a minor audience hall somewhere, not deep into the heart of the palace. As the clothing of the courtiers, provincial nobles, and military officers grew more and more decadent— fine linens and silks being replaced by jewel-silk and cloth of gold— part of Raquella grew hopeful, while a greater part grew nervous.

Finally, their escorts passed through a truly massive marble archway, with an ornate set of stairs leading upwards beyond it. You could march an entire village up the staircase side by side and it wouldn't feel cramped.

As they reached the top, it took a moment for Raquella to catch her breath and understand what she was seeing.

The audience room they found themselves in was mind-bogglingly immense— larger than all but the greatest plazas in the city below. Immense windows filled the walls, overlooking the city and the sea below. Huge fluted columns supported the roof, taller than trees. Unlike the rest of the palace, there were no carvings, murals, or art of any kind, save for a great shimmering web of wire hanging taut below the ceiling.

The instant Raquella saw the web, she knew where she was.

The grand throne room of Galicanta, the Voice of the Empire. Raquella had never seen it before, but she'd read a thousand descriptions of the room, built at the absolute height of the Galicantan Empire, when it ruled all of Teringia and even down into Oyansur.

The Voice of the Empire, a room only used for the most important occasions, and seldom more than a few times in an Emperor or Empress's reign.

Most often, for going to war.

The walk across the grand hall seemed to last hours. The crowd of nobles was immense, yet was still dwarfed by the Voice of the Empire.

At the far end was the throne of Galicanta, the heart of the Voice.

The throne was unlike any other in the world. It was suspended on a small forest of wires, which stretched taut up to the ceiling, to the walls to either side, down to the floor, and to the wall behind it. The floor curved in a great bowl below the throne. The seat itself was fairly small compared to most thrones, but loomed high above the floor in its web of glimmering wire. It was fashioned of some secret alloy of metals that was redder than silver, paler than copper. The alloy wasn't forged for its strength, though it was strong. It wasn't forged for its beauty, though it was beautiful. No, the alloy was forged for two reasons.

First, that it was more ductile than any other known metal, allowing the drawing of immensely long, sturdy wires with ease. And second, that it carried sound to an incredible degree.

It had taken hundreds of seers working for decades to design and build the Voice of the Empire, and it was a feat of engineering that beggared any other that Raquella had ever heard of.

The Empress sat utterly still upon the seat of the Voice and stared expressionlessly at the Moonsworn as they approached. There were no steps leading up to the metal seat— Raquella had read that there was a cunning sling on pulleys used to lift the Empress up to the throne when needed.

The Empress was an ancient, tiny woman, who seemed to be mostly wrinkles by weight. She was garbed entirely in flowing robes of jewel-silk, but otherwise, she bore little adornment, save a thin diadem of the same mysterious metal alloy as the throne. Her hair was wispy and white, and her skeletally thin wrists looked as though they would break at the slightest touch.

Her eyes, though, bored like augurs into Raquella as she approached. Empress Phillipa Sammatrask was three years shy of a century, and she had ruled Galicanta with an iron fist for all but fourteen of those years. Her father had died in battle when Phillipa was just a girl, leaving her the sole heir to the throne. No one had expected her to hold it long, for the succession in Galicanta could be a brutal thing. One of the royal cousins or aunts or uncles was sure to take the throne for themselves.

But they didn't. Phillipa had ruthlessly destroyed every threat to her rule. The first attempt on her throne had been at her coronation, in this very hall. She'd supposedly had her guards seat the offending cousin upon the throne, to be left there without food and water until he either starved or fell. The cousin, apparently, had chosen to fall and be cut to pieces by the countless wires suspending the throne. Curiously, the interruption seemed to have changed Phillipa's mind about taking a new name upon ascension— the first Galicantan Emperor or Empress ever to not do so.

Given that, according to the Church Eidolon, monarchs were the only people who could ever take a new name without being lost to the ancestors, this was a decision much discussed even to this day among the Vowless.

Some claimed she'd executed fully half of her close relatives before the rest had fallen in line. She'd dealt with every single threat to her rule swiftly and harshly. She had outlived five Sunsworn Emperors, four Lothaini kings, six Geredaini kings, and countless other rulers across the world. She had outlived half a dozen husbands, and was noted for her complete lack of humor or mercy. She had borne more than a dozen children, and outlived all but two of them, one of whom was doddering and senile now. She had a small army of grandchildren who all lived in terror of her. She'd declared no less than eight wars during her reign, and she had conquered quite a few of the Fractured Duchies before an alliance of Lothain, Geredain, Dannagrad, and Roske forced her back, in concert with a Sunsworn assault on the Choke.

Empress Phillipa was a proud, cruel, and ruthless woman, and her enemies universally offered her both respect and fear in great measure.

The collected Moonsworn delegation all stopped a few feet ahead of the wires descending from the base of the throne, and bowed as a group. It was slightly ragged and unsynchronized, as they were unused to the rituals of court.

Raquella's knees were happy that they were in Galicanta and not Quae— she had heard tales of the Quae Imperial Court, where supplicants were forced to prostrate themselves before their Emperor.

The Empress didn't appear to have blinked once as she glared down at the Moonsworn. The silence seemed to drag on and on before the ancient monarch finally spoke.

"For decades now, I've tolerated your little Moonsworn infestation in my city," Empress Phillipa said.

Her voice rang out along the wires attached to her throne, and echoed down the wires spanning the ceiling of the room. Her voice came out sounding bell-like and inhuman, but it could be heard clearly throughout the entire massive hall. Its distorted echoes could be heard down in the city as well, and though the Empress's words could not be made out in Ladreis' streets, all knew that events of great import were happening in the palace.

The throne and its wires, the Voice of the Empire, carried and amplified sound perfectly, and even a whisper would echo louder than any man could shout.

The Voice of the Empire was, unquestionably, one of the greatest wonders on Iopis.

And, given its occupant, one of the most terrifying.

"I've done nothing to interfere with your work," the Empress continued, her face like an iron mask. "Though, I must admit, I've often wondered if I was not making a mistake. That even if you truly did not spy for my Sunsworn foes, whether your very presence might count as an insult to Galicanta."

Raquella struggled not to tremble at those words, because they were not what she'd been expecting. Truth be told, she'd expected to be met by some minor functionary in a minor audience hall, not here in the beating heart of Galicanta by the Empress herself. And she'd certainly not expected a speech like this. Doubt came over her, and she wondered whether the envoy had spoken truth to her or not.

The Empress let the silence drag out, as the last ringing echoes of her voice drained from the wires. Her eyes seemed to pierce Raquella through.

Finally, she spoke again. "Today, I am glad I did not wipe you out, for the Wrack is coming. Its cries have been heard only a few days ride out."

Even over the draining echoes of the Empress's voice, Raquella could hear the gasps and curses of the courtiers and nobles. Surely many if not most of them had known, but for the Empress to state it so baldly, in the very home of the Galicantan polite lie, was a shock to them.

Raquella too had known the Wrack was close, but not that it was that close. That almost certainly meant that the

Wrack was already in Ladreis, given its long dormancy period.

The Empress gestured, and a palace servant darted forwards, a plain cedar box clutched between his hands. He bowed to the Empress, then turned to Raquella and opened the box.

Inside, nestled in jewel-silk, lay a single seer's eye.

The Empress's Pride, a perfect, polished, spherical emerald. One of only three on the Teringian continent, and one of only a handful in the world. The King's Eye of Geredain was said to have been lost during their failed invasion of Lothain. The Singer's Truth, the third emerald, never left the great Eidolon cathedral where the Singers elected their Highest, who would command and direct all of their great Choruses.

Raquella exhaled raggedly in relief. This is what the envoy had promised.

"I offer to you my greatest treasure," the Empress said, "so that you might fight this plague. It is yours until the day the Wrack is defeated. Raquella of the Moonsworn, I place the responsibility for my emerald eye on you, and those you see fit to use it. Guard it well."

There were, of course, countless strings attached to that statement, as the imperial envoy had made clear. The great jewel would never go unescorted by the elite palace guards, and were it lost, well… the Empress most certainly valued the emerald more than any number of Moonsworn lives.

Raquella bowed in thanks to the Empress, not saying anything, for you were only to speak to the Empress if she demanded it. That wasn't a Galicantan custom, merely Phillipa's own.

As Raquella gently closed the cedar box, latched it, and accepted it, her mind was already racing with plans for it. She intended to allow its use to a small number of the most skilled Moonsworn scholars, divided evenly among the Patient and the Dedicated. And, to bridge the growing divide, she'd offer it to the Dedicated first.

They'd also try to fit Sherra into the rotation, and for all the animosity between the Moonsworn factions, she doubted either would object to that. Be nervous? Most likely. But not object to it.

Even if that precedence wasn't enough to settle the anger of the Dedicated, however, they'd never dare assassinate her now, for all healers would value access to the Empress's Pride more than any dispute amongst themselves. The clarity an emerald eye offered to a seer examining a human body was truly legendary.

Many of the Moonsworn suspected that the Wrack was simply too small to see with a peridot eye before the screaming began, that it was some strange form of contagion far smaller than any they'd seen before. That what they could see with peridot eyes just before the screaming began was the disease… changing form, growing, or clumping. That with the emerald eye, they might be able to finally spot it before it shifted form. Perhaps even see it in the water, if that was how it was truly spreading.

The Empress's voice interrupted her. "That is not all."

Raquella's eyes shot back up to the Empress.

Phillipa let the echoes drain away again and the tension build again before she spoke.

"There are no prouder people on Iopis than my subjects, and none who deserve that pride more than my subjects. It is our greatest strength, but also our greatest flaw. And, in the face of the oncoming plague, it is no strength."

Raquella could actually hear the shocked whispers of the court over the draining echoes from the wires.

"Seldom in my life have I ever asked for anything," Empress Phillipa said. "But now I must ask for something from you that I cannot command."

The Empress said nothing for some time, and Raquella wondered if she intended to speak further.

"I would ask that the Moonsworn step forwards in the coming days. I would ask that you, Raquella of the

Moonsworn, take command of all healers not only in Ladreis, but in all of Galicanta."

As the room erupted into shouts, confusion, and protests, Raquella could only gape at the Empress.

CHAPTER SIXTEEN
A Fragmentary Message

Ivrahim was a coward. He knew he was a coward. His family knew he was a coward. Everyone in his home village knew he was a coward.

He was too afraid to fight another man. Too afraid to go to war. Too afraid, even, to venture out alone into the night.

Most of all, he was afraid that his name might go unrecorded, as the names of cowards sometimes did, and he might be lost to the ancestors.

And so Ivrahim fled his hometown and became a seer.

Once that would not have been so easy. Once only the third sons of the wealthy and promising priests could become seers, but now, now there was much demand for them, for the semaphore network always needed more seers. So long as you were clever enough of mind, you could earn your way as a seer.

So Ivrahim had his eye plucked out, learned to see through amethyst, and learned to work the clockwork semaphores.

For once Ivrahim felt proud— for though he'd been afraid to lose his eye, it hadn't stopped him.

And when he received his assignment, he was uncomplaining about it. For though it lay far out in the desert at the heart of Galicanta, far from the great cities, it was honorable work, and he need not be ashamed of it.

When he arrived at that dusty, rocky place, with no structures visible in any direction save for a single well and a tall, rickety wooden semaphore tower, Ivrahim felt fear again. Not of the isolation, for in his shame he sought not the company of others, but of the great height and shoddy construction.

Yet he climbed the stairs inside the tower nonetheless. Past the storeroom and the little kitchen at the base. Past the mess where they would eat. Past the bunkroom where he and the other three seers would sleep, which only had three beds, for at least one seer must be on duty at all times. Up and up, higher than he had ever been. Though that said little, for Ivrahim had always had many fears, and height ranked chiefest among them. He had only once climbed a tree as a child, and his father had to climb up to get him out, since Ivrahim had been too cowardly to climb down.

And as Ivrahim reached the creaking top of the tower, where the great clockwork machine of brass and gears and chains rested, he looked out over the edge, and the world seemed to twist and breathe and pull at him, and he stumbled back away from the railing, fighting to not let the vertigo overwhelm him.

Ivrahim spent little time with the other three seers.

He had little in common with them, after all. They'd all had great scholarly ambitions, had all read more books than Ivrahim had ever seen, and all bore great bitterness at their paltry assignment.

Ivrahim's only ambition was for a quiet life, to serve well and honorably, and to have his name recorded so that he might join his ancestors and have them be not ashamed for him.

He bore his fellow seers no ill-will, nor they him. They simply had nothing in common.

If anything, they thought well of him, for he willingly took upon himself the shift that ran from late night to dawn. If they were ever curious about the lash scars covering Ivrahim's back, where his father had punished him for his cowardice, they said nothing. They thought him a good fellow— one who simply enjoyed solitude— and they weren't wrong.

They weren't right either, though. Ivrahim chose that shift because, in the dark, the vertigo's hold over him was weakest. It was bad during the day, but it was at its worst at twilight, when the air below him began to call him, to physically pull him, until he could hardly stand without clutching the railing.

Dawn was a little easier, but he was always happiest when his replacement arrived, and he could leave the open semaphore room at the top of the rickety wooden tower.

He did not go up to the top save for his shift, so the other seers might not know him a coward.

His shifts were easy enough. Few messages were sent at night, so there were few to pass on. He merely had to watch the spirit current that hung alongside the tower. A few leagues after this tower, it shot high into the sky, out of sight of any seer. When messages came through them, he need merely transcribe them onto paper, assemble them into a message chain, then send them on their way through the other spirit current, which ran through the semaphore room and all the way to Ladreis.

He had a brazier to keep him warm in the cold desert nights, and a little lantern for assembling message chains, but he preferred as little light as he could, and he sat on the floor, so he might not see the ground below, and he watched the spirit realm and the spirit current from one eye, and the stars with the other.

His days were quiet ones. He went to sleep after dawn and awoke in the early afternoon. He ate a quiet breakfast, exchanging greetings with any of the other seers about, and then he took a stick of graphite, a drawing board, and a small stack of paper, and he walked out into the desert.

Ivrahim had never tried his hand at drawing or drafting before he was taught to be a seer. He had, to his surprise, turned out to have quite a deft hand at it, and he suspected that was what had earned him his spot as a seer. When his left eye was plucked out, he had to relearn much of it, for losing an eye hurts one's drawing immensely, but it recovered quickly.

More than just being good at it, Ivrahim found that he enjoyed it. He found a peace in it he got nowhere else.

So he spent his days drawing. There was no worry about using up paper, as their weekly supply runs brought more every time, for it would be ill fortune for a semaphore tower to run out of paper. Since it had been built, huge piles of paper had accumulated in the corners of the storeroom, each sheaf bound in waxed cloth to keep rodents from eating it.

At first the other seers teased him gently, saying he would swiftly grow bored of the empty wasteland around them, with only a single tower and a single well to draw. But when drawings started to accumulate around the tower, pinned to the wooden walls, resting on tables, and drifting under beds, the teasing quickly ended.

This made Ivrahim happy indeed, for even though he knew the teasing gentle, it still made a part of him flinch— that cowardly organ deep inside of him. For Ivrahim had been on the receiving end of cruelty for the sin of his cowardice often enough that a part of him could no longer tell a gentle jest from a cruel barb.

It also made him happy, for he knew his art was good.

He drew the tower, yes, and he drew the well, but he drew so, so much more.

Ivrahim drew the skulls of cattle that had died in the great cattle drives across the desert, from Lothain to the great cities of Galicanta. He drew the green and brown striped lizards that sunned themselves in the dirt, and the grey lizards with the blue necks that sunned themselves on the rocks. He drew the shy little desert mice hunting seeds and bugs, and he drew the wispy dry plants that grew those seeds and the little bugs that ran about the rocks. He drew the long brown snakes and the tiny grey ones that lived under rocks.

Ivrahim drew the sunsnakes, those bright blue vipers who alone among the ground-dwelling animals did not conceal themselves— for anything they bit died, and anything that bit them died likewise, for their flesh was as deadly as their venom. Though the other seers thought him mad, he was not worried, for the sunsnakes feared nothing, and they hardly stirred themselves when he drew close.

Ivrahim drew all five types of scorpions, from the tiny brown ones whose sting could not penetrate his skin to the immense, dull white giants the size of his hand, who Ivrahim knew to keep a very respectful distance from. They would not kill him, but they would make him very sick indeed. He drew the great desert tortoises with their ancient eyes, which grew so large the tops of their shells came above his waist.

Ivrahim drew the skittish desert antelope, who would only come close enough to draw after many weeks of sitting quietly near a salt lick until they grew to trust his presence. He also drew the wild desert goats, who once they were canny enough to realize he carried no weapons, simply walked right up to him, sometimes even trying to nibble his paper. His fellow seers asked him to kill one to add to their larder, but Ivrahim merely smiled and shook his head. He would show them the newest drawing, and they never had the heart to ask again.

Ivrahim drew the hardy desert trees with their little waxy leaves, the fierce hawks that patrolled the skies, and the vultures that circled even above the hawks.

The rains were what Ivrahim dreaded the most, for they came unpredictably, and when they did, he would often be trapped in the tower for days by the rain, the mud, and the fierce floods that flowed like hammers through the little gulches of the desert.

But the rains were also what Ivrahim anticipated the most, for afterward, the desert would erupt into color. Countless flowers and green plants erupted from the ground. Little ponds dotted the desert, each filled with tiny colorful fish, which came from he knew not where. Frogs and toads of a dozen sizes clambered from the ground and filled the air with their songs. Birds sang, and countless buzzing insects filled the air. There were even tiny, fingernail-sized freshwater crabs that appeared in the pools, only to bury themselves away like everything else when the pools dried.

And Ivrahim did his best to draw them all.

Years passed, and other seers came and went, but Ivrahim never left his little tower. He worked his midnight shifts, drew, and accumulated back pay. He drafted an improved map of the local spirit realm currents, which the Ladreis Collegium actually commended him for.

When the first rumors of the Wrack arrived at the tower, Ivrahim gave them little attention. The other seers spoke of little else, but few unencoded messages about it were sent at night, so Ivrahim paid it no mind.

Then, for a brief period, traffic exploded, and they were all suddenly working themselves to the bone. They began doubling up for shifts, and Ivrahim found no more time for drawing.

And then the message traffic began dying away. Not slowly, and not evenly. Huge chunks of the message traffic would just end all at once.

They all knew what was causing it. Semaphore towers were being abandoned to the Wrack.

One by one, the semaphore towers north of them began to fail. Some sent messages informing them of their closure. A few kept going intermittently with only a single seer working when they could. Most just… stopped.

Ivrahim found time for his drawing again, but part of his mind was always dwelling on the north, now.

As the towers north of them began to fail, and the reports of the Wrack spreading into Galicanta and Geredain began arriving, the other seers grew more and more nervous, often arguing amongst themselves.

Ivrahim kept himself out of the conversations.

Soon the messages from the north, from Lothain and northern Galicanta, began to dry up entirely. Entire days would go by without any messages. Ivrahim was sure parts of the semaphore network must still be in operation, but it wouldn't take that many failures to the immediate north to cut their lonely wooden tower off from the rest of Teringia.

The other seers began to argue that they should leave. They weren't even a multi-path tower, they were merely a simple relay, and with no messages to forward, they should abandon the tower. They should leave before the Wrack arrived.

Ivrahim wasn't overly worried about that. The only visitors they ever received were the weekly supply wagons, sometimes coming with replacement seers.

When the supply wagon failed to arrive one week, that was too much for the other seers, and they fled, carrying as many supplies as they could.

Pointing out that they were fleeing south— in the direction the supply wagons came from— didn't stop them, even though it was surely the Wrack that had interfered with the supplies.

Ivrahim sighed as he poked through what supplies they'd left him. They'd taken most of the fresh goods, but he had enough dried goods, salt meat, and root vegetables to last him some time. It wouldn't be the most scintillating diet, but it would keep him alive.

His days began to take on a hint of monotony after that. At first, he spent every waking hour in the semaphore room at the top of the tower, that no messages might be missed, but before long, he resumed his long walks through the desert.

He found, in fact, that he was quite able to keep his amethyst eye on the spirit current while keeping his living eye on his paper or his subject material. At first, he got headaches from leaving his amethyst eye in longer than a shift at a time, but they slowly receded, and soon he kept his amethyst eye in even in his sleep, taking it out only to clean.

It certainly resulted in some truly strange dreams.

In the weeks that followed, he slowly began to master a rare skill among seers— the ability to turn and focus his amethyst eye even through his own head, so that he might look in two directions at once. Only one among hundreds of seers could do it, and it required the discipline to ignore a truly prodigious confusion of ripples and turbulence produced by the currents flowing through his own head. Soon, however, he hardly even noticed the difference. The only oddity was a curious tangled structure floating inside his own head, behind his eyes. It glowed faintly with its own light, not merely the light of the spirit realm, and seemed far more solid than anything else in the spirit realm.

Other seers who had his ability to look through their own heads had reported this as well, and produced a few crude drawings. There were countless debates about what, precisely, the structures were. Ivrahim merely assumed it was his soul and didn't worry too much about it. Ivrahim's drawings of the structure were far more graceful and precise than the others he'd seen, and he was sure they'd attract some interest. He was no true scholar, but he wrote a short monograph on the structure, and sent a copy south, just in case.

He received no response, nor did any supply wagons come.

Every now and then, to his surprise, messages still came through. More often than not, they were incomprehensible clusters of letters, but they were clearly man-made patterns. He wrote them all down, whether he could understand them or not.

He wasn't in any hurry to send them, of course. He merely noted them down on paper, then waited until he returned to the tower to send them onwards.

And he drew, and drew, and drew.

He'd taken to sleeping the midnight shift, during the very hours that he once had worked every night. It was, after all, the least of the shifts in message volume.

The desert grew cold even in the summer, and in the winter, it could get painfully cold at night, even though the days were balmy and pleasantly cool. To keep himself warm, he bundled himself up tightly and often kept hot coals in a brazier next to his bunk.

He wasn't sure what awoke him that night. Perhaps his dreaming mind had seen through his amethyst eye and noticed what was going on in the sky, or perhaps it was just sheer coincidence.

Either way, Ivrahim got out of bed and wandered up to the semaphore room, still half asleep.

He shivered in the night air, and he saw the messages flowing through the spirit realm. He could see many of them already far past him, rising along with the spirit current flowing south, too far away to make out now, lost to him. More marched along past him, and he could see countless more coming. The signals were all unencoded, and it only took him a second to begin reading them.

They were names. All of them names.

Sleep forgotten, Ivrahim dove for supplies, and he frantically began to write, and write, and write. Name after name after name after name. They seemed to go on forever, unending and unrelenting, and Ivrahim was still writing when dawn arose. His fingers cramped and ached, but he dared not stop, taking breaks only when he made it far enough upstream in the purple spirit current that he couldn't make out the names any longer.

The collection of paper he had up here he hadn't restocked in some time. He spent so little time up here anymore, only coming up to send messages now.

He began frantically filling margins with names, writing them in ever-smaller letters with ever smaller spaces between them, with the shrinking nubs of graphite he had left to him up here.

Some of the names were Lothaini, or maybe Geredaini, and others were Moonsworn, and others were Galicantan, and he even saw a few that he swore might be Radhan, but he didn't take the time to consider the matter.

He just kept writing.

And the names kept coming and coming, and Ivrahim knew that he would have to resupply from downstairs soon. He quickly pushed as far upstream in the list of names as he could, then he simply sprinted down the stairs, four at a time.

Ivrahim's living eye was weeping the whole way down.

He crashed into the storeroom more than he entered it, and he quickly filled his arms with paper and graphite. He ran up the stairs almost so swiftly as he ran down, tripping several times and dropping much of his paper in his haste.

He didn't bother to pick up the dropped paper, he just got up and ran.

Ivrahim nearly stumbled right over the railing of the semaphore room in his haste. He barely caught himself against the solid wooden railing. Several sheets of paper slipped from his grasp and went gliding down to the dust and rocks below.

In his desperation, Ivrahim hardly even noticed that the drop below didn't beckon him, or call him, or try to pull him. It didn't seem some great abyss.

It was just a moderate height drop from a cramped little wooden tower.

None of that crossed Ivrahim's mind, though.

He just kept writing.

He could barely see out of his living eye as tears flowed freely from it, for all the names he'd missed in his resupply trip. For all the names he'd missed in his sleep, for none of the names had repeated at all, and he knew that no tower in the world bore enough links for a message loop this long. The names were being disassembled and reformed into new names, continually.

The names he'd missed were gone, carried by the current up into the sky.

His amethyst eye still saw clearly, and his hand was strong, and Ivrahim kept writing, and writing, and writing. Noon came and went, and finally, in the late afternoon, it simply ended. No message was attached to the end, but none was needed. There was only one reason that such a monumental list of names would be sent.

Part of Ivrahim was tempted to heresy then, to hope that names sent through the semaphore made it to the ancestors since the spirit realm was how they saw the world, but he knew it was not true, for the Conclave Eidola had long since met and debated that very issue and had declared it a heresy. A minor one, but a heresy, nonetheless.

And for the first time in a long time, Ivrahim took out his amethyst eye for a reason other than cleaning, and he closed his living eye, and he wept.

The tears eventually dried, and he sat and simply breathed. He could not have told you how long he sat there and thought of nothing, but when he opened his eyes, he found himself at peace, not blaming himself for the lost names. He mourned them, and hoped they were still written down at the sending tower, but he didn't blame himself, not for sleeping, nor for running out of paper.

He thought, then, of the lives of all those thousands, and the loves they must have had, and the labors they must have toiled at, and the places they must have seen, and of even their fears they must have had, and for the first time in a long time, his world expanded past his tower, past his beautiful little patch of desert that others might see only as a dusty wasteland.

And he stood, and walked to the railing, and he looked out over the desert, and for the first time in many years, he began to think of the future. Realized he was no old man yet, that he might yet rejoin civilization— if the Wrack left anything behind it. And he thought of his drawings and his knowledge of the desert plants and desert creatures. Ivrahim began dreaming of his great work, of a great illustrated book detailing the plants and animals of the desert. He thought of attending the Collegium for training to use spinel, and his mind came alive with questions, and plans, and thoughts for the future.

And decades later, when the great scholar was in a particularly pensive mood, he would open his desk in his lavish house in Ladreis, and take out a thick, lovingly handbound volume. And in that volume lay pages filled with thousands and thousands of handwritten names, all long since transcribed to obelisks and nothing else. He had never learned who had sent them or from where. Many of the pages were spotted with tearstains, much of the writing was barely legible, and the pages were yellow with age.

And Ivrahim would sigh, and mourn still for all the names that were lost.

CHAPTER SEVENTEEN
Like Water Through A Sieve

Healer Benen cursed as he dropped his knife again. He glared at it, then at the butter, then at his hunk of bread.

He contemplated doing a bit more cursing, but sighed and reached to pick up the knife once more. His blackened fingers lacked the dexterity to pick it up off the flat table without cutting himself, so he had to slowly drag it until the handle projected off the side of the table, then try to grasp it more with his palm than his fingers, which was hardly a good position to spread butter with.

Benen actually managed to get a little butter on the knife this time before he dropped it.

Snarling, Benen picked up his hunk of bread by pressing it between his palms and jammed the whole thing into the butter, smearing it all about. He then shoved it at his face and took a vicious, tearing bite.

"I think," Nalda said, coming into his quarters unannounced, "you've quite thoroughly murdered that bread."

Benen just glared at her.

"The sentries have reported a group of people coming up the pass," Nalda said. "Around thirty or so. They'll be here within the hour."

Benen swallowed enough bread so that he could speak.

"Through this much snow? Are they insane?"

His voice was rough and rasping. He doubted it would ever heal up to sound like it once had.

Nalda shrugged. "We haven't had any communication with the outside world in weeks, Benen. Who knows how bad it's gotten on the plains? They might just really be that desperate."

"Last we'd heard, the Wrack had mostly burnt itself out, even in Seibarrow," Benen said.

"I wasn't thinking of the Wrack," Nalda replied. "How much of the harvest rotted in the fields this year, for want of laborers? The Wrack killed many of them, and scared most of the rest off. I'd wager you good money that starvation is rampant down there."

Benen shook his head. "I wouldn't take that bet. I'm guessing we'll find out soon enough, though."

Nalda nodded. "You should get changed into something cleaner so we can meet our new guests."

And, with that, Nalda left as unceremoniously as she'd arrived.

Benen looked down at his grubby chamber-robes, and, with a sigh, he began the arduous process of changing his clothes with fingers that barely worked.

Walking was a bit easier than using his hands, but Benen's blackened toes still presented a challenge. Like his fingers, they had lost most of their strength and mobility, and his control over them was exceptionally poor. Like most Wrack survivors, Benen had adjusted his stride to compensate. He kept most of his weight on one heel that remained directly below him as he stepped forwards with his other leg, then shifted his weight to that heel. It was the same way he'd learned to walk on ice here in the pass. He'd seen a few other ways of walking, some faster than his, but he liked the extra stability his waddle provided.

By the time he reached his seat in Castle Morinth's great hall, their visitors were already being led inside by the guards. He carefully took his seat next to Captain Oson, Nalda sitting on the other side of him. The irony of a Moonsworn helping to run an Eidolon fortress wasn't lost on Benen.

The three of them had divided the duties of the Mist Warden between themselves. Captain Oson had long done much of the logistical work of running the castle, paperwork not being one of Prince Arnulf's favorite activities. He'd couldn't handle it all himself, but between the three of them, they'd largely kept the fortress running, and they'd somehow managed to move the remaining villagers in for the winter. A big part of that was the fact that Oson and Benen were having to learn to write by holding graphite sticks or quill pens in their mouths, rather than their hands, which made for slow, messy going. More importantly, though, was the sense of relief all three felt in having someone to share the weight of decisions, especially in these uncertain times.

The final tally of deaths had been harsh, to say the least. One in six of the villagers had died, and that number was closer to one in five among the soldiers. That many again had survived, yet were crippled or injured by the disease, like Benen or Oson.

Worse, the Wrack hadn't vanished entirely. Every few days to a week, another screamer appeared. It was a trickle, compared to the flood at first, but it never stopped entirely.

Moving the villagers into the castle had been a struggle like no other winter Benen could remember. They'd been badly shorthanded, and while their food stores should be enough to get them through the winter, it would be more of a stretch than recent years, even with fewer people wintered in the castle. Morale was also critically low, especially whenever a new victim of the Wrack began screaming.

"We've escorted most of our visitors to guest quarters, if it pleases you," one of the guards announced.

Oson nodded at that, and the three visitors stepped forward— two women and one man.

Benen couldn't help but notice the symmetry between their two groups, as the women faced Oson and Benen, and the man faced Nalda. Almost certainly a coincidence, but he'd found himself noticing symmetry far more often since his recovery. A small number of other Wrack survivors reported the same. Unlike many of the other lingering symptoms, Benen considered this one harmless enough.

It wasn't a perfect inverse symmetry, though. The man should have had the blackened fingers of a Wrack survivor, but none of the three bore signs of the plague.

"Welcome to Castle Morinth," Oson said. His rasp was even worse than Benen's. "It's unusual to get visitors at this time of the year— it must have been hard making it up here through the snow."

The tall woman in the center facing Oson nodded. "It stretched above our heads in places, but the ancestors willed us to come, so we endured."

The woman didn't say anything after that, and Benen noted with some discomfort that her gaze never seemed to vary or twitch. There was a strange, feverish look in her eyes.

"Why, exactly, *did* you come here?" Oson asked.

"Because the ancestors willed it," the woman said, without any change in her expression.

Oson paused, clearly at a loss for words.

"What purpose do you believe the ancestors have for you here? Why Castle Morinth in particular?" Benen asked, stepping into the conversation.

The gazes of all three shifted to Benen, and he noted uncomfortably that the other two had gazes nearly as zealous and strange as the first.

"Our ancestor-given purpose isn't here in specific," the woman said, "but everywhere. Our holy purpose extends through all the Eidolon lands."

"And beyond, though the rest of Iopis," the man broke in, harshly.

"Perhaps," the woman said, glaring at him. "The signs from the ancestors remain unclear."

"What signs?" Nalda said, leaning forward.

"There is only one sign of import," the woman said. "The Wrack. Those taken by it have angered the ancestors."

Benen gave her a skeptical look and held up his blackened fingers.

The woman gave him a pitying look. "Those like you have received your punishments already. We bear no hate for you."

He forced himself not to snarl at her. He was no nobleman, and the Wrack was no punishment from the ancestors.

"You still haven't stated your purpose," Benen said.

"Our purpose is to ensure that the ancestors need not set the Wrack loose upon us again," the shorter woman, who had been silent thus far, said. "Our purpose is to weed out the sins that brought this among us."

"The Wrack in every land has struck down the nobility first," the taller woman said. "Then the wealthy after that. The ancestors have been clear about what they want. They want nobility and royalty ended."

Benen leaned back in shock at hearing that, and Oson started visibly at his side. Nalda merely continued staring intently.

"We are the Fervent," the tall woman continued. "We do the work of the ancestors."

There was silence from the six of them as they stared at one another from across the high table. The guards whispered amongst themselves in shock, but Benen ignored them.

"Does that count their children, too? What about their servants? And after you slaughter all the nobles?" Oson asked, glaring. "What then?"

"We should…" the Fervent man began, but the tall Fervent woman silenced him with a glare.

"We do not kill the servants of the nobility," she said. "As for their children, there have been some… regrettable incidents, but we believe that if raised by the faithful, they pose little threat of angering the ancestors again."

Benen could feel Oson quivering at his side, and he gently nudged him with his elbow. Captain Oson was the fifth son of a minor noble family.

"What of the Moonsworn?" Nalda asked.

The Fervent all turned to look at her. The man opened his mouth to speak, but the woman raised her hand to forestall him. "If you had your way, we'd purge the world of everyone but the Lothaini commons. You take your zeal too far."

She turned to Nalda. "You are Moonsworn, I take it? Fear not for your kin down on the plains. They have never been servants of the nobles, and the nobility's very hate of your people speak highly of you. Even if your healers didn't work selflessly to aid the common folk, we still wouldn't purge you, for our ancestors bear no hate for you, unlike your Sunsworn cousins. Your kin still live, and still do their good works among us."

Nalda nodded, her face showing only a hint of relief.

"What exactly," Benen asked, "do you propose take the place of the nobility? Some sort of government by the people?"

The tall woman shook her head. "The people lack the wisdom of the ancestors, and are no better suited to rule than they were under the nobles. The ancestors have always made it clear that the commons are to be ruled, not to rule. The ancestors will make clear what form the government will take once we have finished purging the nobility. Until then, we work alongside the remnants of the Church Eidolon to administer what remains of Lothain and Geredain. Perhaps they shall put the Church Eidolon in charge, or perhaps they shall appoint new noble families."

A cynical part of Benen immediately wondered whether, if they were telling the truth about controlling the plains, they would ever give up their control, or if the ancestors would conveniently declare the interim government to have their blessing.

"And what of the King Sigis's heirs?" Oson said. His tone was level, but his anger was obvious to anyone who had known him as long as Benen had.

"We don't know," the short woman spoke up. "We would like to have been able to take credit, but two of his sons seem to have died alongside the king during the Masquerade, and the others have been missing since then."

"So what do you want from us, exactly?" Benen said.

"That you hand over control of the castle to us— and custody of all of those in it with noble blood," the tall woman said.

Before Captain Oson could explode, Benen again gently nudged him with an elbow. "Would you give us the room for a few minutes? This is something we should discuss privately."

The Fervent man looked ready to explode, but the tall Fervent woman spoke up. "That's entirely reasonable, and we'd be quite happy to."

She didn't look happy, just determined and fanatical, but Benen didn't feel a need to mention that.

After the three had been escorted out of the hall. Captain Oson pounded his hand against the table in rage while a high-pitched noise came from behind his visibly clenched jaw.

Oson soon calmed himself and sighed, for he was a man who generally kept tight chains on his anger. "Punching something hard doesn't help like it used to. Especially without being able to feel a damn thing in my fingers or even make a proper fist."

Benen just nodded. He definitely understood the feeling.

"Captain," Nalda said, "I know what you're about to propose, and we simply don't know enough about what's happening down on the plains to risk taking action against the Fervent. If their ilk really has seized control of the plains and the capital, we can't risk…"

Oson held up his withered hand to forestall her. "You don't, in fact, know what I was about to propose, because I agree with you about the risk. As much as it infuriates me, we can't simply execute them or imprison them."

Nalda and Benen exchanged surprised glances.

"We also, however, cannot hand over control over the castle to these… Fervent. Our mission cannot be left to chance, for without us, who knows how many beasts might be left to escape the mountains and roam the plains?"

"So, what…" Benen began, then stopped, as a ripple of pain shot up his body, and a flash of memory hit him. He thankfully remembered little of the pain and delirium of the Wrack, save in his dreams, but a few times a day he was hit by these lingering surges of pain. Many of the survivors were.

Oson gave him a sympathetic look, knowing what he was going through. Nalda's look, he suspected, had more than a little pity to it.

"So what do you propose?" Benen asked when he'd recovered.

Benen quickly found himself nodding along as Captain Oson explained his plan. He wasn't happy with it, but he could work with it.

"Castle Morinth," Oson said to the Fervent triumvirate, "has always remained neutral. When Lothain and Geredain split, it remained neutral. When all three nephews of King Sigis the Second claimed the throne, we stayed neutral in the resulting conflict. We will stay neutral now as well."

The Fervent man began to redden, but before he could speak, Captain Oson continued.

"Do you know why we always remain neutral?"

"Because you're cowardly..." the Fervent man started, but the Fervent woman held up her hand to stop him and glared.

Benen would hardly say the woman's expression softened when she looked back at Captain Oson, but it was more distrustful than enraged.

"Why?" the woman asked.

Benen leaned forwards. "Because we too are on a mission from the Ancestors."

The Fervent man looked ready to explode at that, but he said nothing.

"We guard the plains below from the beasts of the Mist Maze," Benen continued. "We keep all Lothaini, common and noble alike, safe from their depredations. For generations, we've done so, and for generations we shall continue. We shall not give over our holy charge, nor shall we hand over any who aid us in it. You have your ancestor-given task, and we have ours, and it behooves neither of us to interfere with the other."

The tall woman simply stared at them, her expression inscrutable.

The Fervent man, however, had clearly had enough. "The Fervent fear no mere beasts, heretic! You spit upon the face of the ancestors to falsely claim their blessing, and you'll share the fates of all your vile..."

The tall woman, before anyone could react, pulled a dagger from her sleeve and sunk it into the back of the man's neck. He crumpled to the ground bonelessly.

The guards in the room all drew their weapons, but the woman simply folded her arms behind her back expressionlessly. Captain Oson held up his hand to forestall the guards attacking the woman.

"I had hoped Ruellen would learn to contain his zeal," the woman said. "Alas, he's been under warning for some time."

"Warning?" Nalda asked, clearly shaken.

"Some will use any political upheaval as an excuse to exercise their bloodlust," the short Fervent woman said. "The Fervent seek not to take a single life more than is necessary. We may be a movement of the commons, but do not mistake us for ignorant, superstitious peasants. We are no such thing. We've studied the history of the Sunsworn, and we know of the abuses that their fanatics have carried out. We will not dishonor our ancestors this way."

"I see," Nalda said.

An awkward silence filled the room for a moment.

"I must confess, I am not entirely convinced of your claims that you do the ancestors' work," the tall woman said.

"The nobility and the church long discouraged the idea," Oson said, "but not a soldier here has ever doubted it, nor have the villagers. Spend a week here, and you'll come to believe the truth of it as well."

The tall woman nodded. "If you speak the truth, this may serve us both. Many of the Fervent believe we need a range of punishments beyond simple execution— especially for some of the more minor nobles, who held no power or influence. Lifetime banishment to Castle Morinth to hunt these beasts of yours might serve. We had been debating conscription to guard the borders, but many of our members worried at the risk of defection to our enemies."

Benen tried not to look uncomfortably at the man's corpse as she spoke.

"That is all contingent upon you convincing us that you do the work of the ancestors, of course. I promise you, that won't be an easy task."

She turned and strode towards the door, the short woman following in her wake. Halfway out, however, she paused, and turned to them.

"If you would, I would have Ruellen's name inscribed on your obelisk. It would grieve me deeply were he to lose his chance to join the ancestors."

At Captain Oson's nod, the woman turned and strode out without another word, leaving the corpse on the ground.

Benen felt quite confident that the beasts of the pass would easily convince the Fervent of the worthiness of their cause, and they hadn't been lying that the soldiers and the villagers in the pass considered themselves to be doing the work of the ancestors. He couldn't help but feel, however, as though they'd made some dire mistake by bargaining with the Fervent.

If he were to be honest, the tall woman had terrified him as much as any rampaging beast from the mists.

CHAPTER EIGHTTEEN
Rumors at the Choke

Emiere stood guard in the morning sun, and he watched, and he listened as the rumors flew between the other soldiers.

Bandits from the collapse of Lothain had flooded over the border like locusts.

The Fractured Duchies were actually uniting, so many of their self-titled dukes and kings had died off.

The Fractured Duchies were finally being absorbed by Galicanta, as they should have been years ago.

Dannagrad and Roske, the two little eastern nations on the coast, had united.

No, they were fighting over the ruins of Geredain.

The Singers had invaded the lands south of the Krannenbergs in huge numbers with their fleets of bird-faced boats.

The Singers had entirely closed off their lands to keep the Wrack out.

The Wrack was pushing close to Ladreis.

The Wrack had stalled in the great desert at the heart of Galicanta.

The Wrack would descend among them soon, leaving the fortress filled only with corpses.

But, more prevalent than all the other rumors combined were the rumors about the Sunsworn.

Emiere just listened, and spread none of the rumors himself, for he far preferred to simply trust his eyes. The semaphore network was breaking down even inside Galicanta, and, after all, the Sunsworn could be seen with the naked eye, just shy of the horizon.

It was said there were no greater fortresses on all Iopis than On-Renza and Madracha, and they were built within sight of one another.

The narrow isthmus between the continents of Teringia and Oyansur, between Galicanta and the Sunsworn Empire, had been a place of blood and battle between the two great nations for centuries. In a distant year of unstable, watchful peace, a Sunsworn Emperor had ordered the construction of a great fortress, On-Renza, at one end of the Choke, the narrowest part of the mountainous isthmus. The Galicantan Emperor of the time had promptly ordered the construction of Madracha at the Galicantan end of the Choke.

The Choke was only a league in width, bordered by steep cliffs dropping away to the sea on either side. It was a parched desert scrubland, with nothing larger than a rodent living there— though there were usually plenty of vultures circling overhead. Emiere had never liked the ugly things, but no one on either side shot at the carrion eaters. He wasn't sure why— he'd heard rumors that it was bad luck, that the birds would remember the insult and descend upon you when you were only wounded, not dead— but regardless of why, it just wasn't done.

The seers claimed that the cliffs were slowly eroding away, and that someday the sea would break through them. Most Galicantan soldiers bragged that they'd have long since conquered the Sunsworn by then, and Emiere was sure the Sunsworn said the same about them. Emiere wouldn't admit it out loud, but a part of him sometimes prayed to the ancestors to carve away the cliffs faster, so that the two lands might be forever separated by a sea.

Not, of course, to say that there weren't battles at sea as well, but as bloody and desperate as they were, they were of little import to the great battles over the Choke, or even the quiet night raids and infiltrations. Neither side were Radhan, to sail the sea out of sight of land.

The walls of both fortresses stretched straight across the leagues of the Choke. It was hard to say which were taller or thicker, but both loomed over the rocky, dusty ground. There was little chance of even a rabbit sneaking across the Choke unseen, but Emiere kept a diligent watch regardless.

For Emiere's oldest brother had died guarding these walls. His father had died assaulting the walls of On-Renza. One uncle had died in a night raid that made it into the Sunsworn fortress itself. A second uncle, his mother's only brother, had died in a brutal, pointless skirmish in the no-man's land between the great citadels.

Emiere fully expected to die on the Choke himself someday, or at least be crippled, like several other of his uncles and brothers. Emiere was glad he had more daughters than sons, for he was sure both of his sons would die on the Choke some day.

Emiere never complained, though, for none in his family ever did. Duty had no room for complaint.

"Emiere!" one of the other guards on the wall hissed. "Did you hear they might be opening up the fortress again soon?"

They'd closed the fortress off weeks ago. No one was allowed in or out from the north, nor even supplies allowed in. Madracha was living as though besieged. And, in a way, it was— from the Wrack to the north and the Sunsworn to the south. There was no communication outside the fortress, save via semaphore. They had enough supplies to keep them going for most of a year if need be.

"They won't," Emiere said, not bothering to look at the other soldier.

"What makes you so sure?" the other soldier demanded. "The Wrack's surely nowhere near us yet. Besides, everyone knows it can't survive in this heat."

Emiere just grunted and stared out at the Choke.

"Even the generals are going crazy trapped up in here," the soldier insisted.

Emiere didn't respond, just kept watch.

"Ignore Emiere," another soldier said. "He doesn't believe anything unless it's so sour as to make your face pucker."

Emiere glanced over at the second soldier, then shrugged. The other soldiers chuckled a bit at that.

The other soldier wasn't wrong, though. Expecting the worst had always served him well.

As morning turned to noon, Emiere's fellow guards began clustering under the shade cloths, seeking what little cool they could. The sun fell like a blow against your skin at the Choke, and the air was so hot it felt like it could burn your lungs.

Emiere barely acknowledged the heat. In the privacy of his own mind, he did sometimes wish that he could be in one of the cool, breeze-filled semaphore tower rooms, where messages constantly flew back and forth between the two continents. He'd always thought it one of the great ironies of history that these two fortresses were also two of the biggest semaphore relay stations in the world, facilitating communication between the two enemy nations.

Emiere didn't say any of that, though. He just watched the Choke and listened to the rumors and complaints swirl around him.

The Radhan were spreading the Wrack, so that they could just steal Teringia's valuables to sell to the empires of Oyansur.

The Wrack was the revenge of the mysterious dwellers of the Krannenbergs, who Lothain had driven far into the deep caves of the mountains for sacrificing innocent Eidol children to their gods.

The Moonsworn were spreading the plague, for their centuries-long infiltration of Teringia was coming to an end, and the Sunsworn would be invading soon.

The Wrack didn't exist at all. It was just a lie the generals were telling them so they didn't have to give them leave.

Madracha's food supplies had been poisoned, and the Sunsworn were planning an invasion.

The Wrack was caused by the semaphores.

Ladreis was already filled with the Wrack, and the Sunsworn were planning an invasion.

The Sunsworn were planning a new invasion to take advantage of the Wrack.

The Wrack was spreading through the spirit realm.

The Quae Empire had declared war on the Sunsworn, and the Sunsworn would have to pull troops back from On-Renza soon.

The Sunsworn were planning an invasion.

The Sunsworn were planning an invasion.

The Sunsworn were planning an invasion.

Emiere just took a drink of warm water from his waterskin and stared at the Choke. He stared at the distant walls of On-Renza, where Sunsworn troops moved as little as they could, and huddled under their own shade cloths. He couldn't see the slightest sign of activity or excitement over there.

He thought of pointing that out, but sense did little to dispel rumors.

So he just watched the Choke, where he'd die someday— if the sea didn't wash it away— and he waited.

CHAPTER NINETEEN
In the Land of the Blind

Eyeless Sherra was, even among the Moonsworn, the subject of some superstitious dread. She could see it inside their bodies every time they were around her.

There were countless stories of seers who had plucked out both their eyes, but in truth, it almost never happened. Those seers who did bear gems in both eyes tended to number among those blind from birth, like Eyeless Sherra.

Even knowing that, her fellow Moonsworn feared her. They hardly showed it in their voices, but Sherra could see it easily in the Goddess Sea, in the ripples their bodies produced.

The fear directed at her wasn't because she was truly that exceptional of a seer in talent. She was good, but there were a small number that bettered her in various aspects of the discipline. She was hardly the only seer that used their gems ceaselessly, gaining effortless skill with it. Even some of the one-gem seers did that.

Having two empty sockets for gems wasn't it either. To be sure, being able to use two different types of gems at once was a profound improvement. The colors and images she saw didn't blend— instead, she saw both images simultaneously, somehow overlaid on one another in her mind. She could easily correlate what she saw in one image with the other, but this was a trait common to all two-gem seers. Likewise, her ability to see in parallax in the Goddess Sea allowed her to see things others simply didn't— in essence, she had depth perception. Something no one-gem seer would have.

Or, at least, those factors wouldn't make people as nervous around her as they were. There was something else, wasn't there?

No, it was the fact that she hadn't just been born blind. She had been born anosmic as well, without a sense of smell, and somehow, she had become one of those bizarre freaks that could perceive the Goddess Sea through another missing sense. More alarming still, she could actually comprehend what her nose perceived— something the majority of those rarities like her could not do. That would make others nervous, wouldn't it?

Sherra had no words in any of the three languages she spoke to explain what she could smell, but she was able to act on it, nonetheless.

When they came to her room and told her that she was needed, Sherra came without a word. She came expecting some poor soul no-one else could diagnose, or perhaps the first case of the Wrack in Ladreis.

Instead, she found herself being offered a new eye. Nervously, of course. She felt like she was still forgetting some reason why she made people nervous.

This wasn't an uncommon occurrence by any means— she was frequently offered new eyes. Sherra was quite certain that no other seer in all of Galicanta owned so many as her.

What she was not expecting, however, was for the new eye to be emerald.

Silently, Sherra popped out the spinel in her left socket and replaced it with the emerald. She blinked twice over the cold gem, and the Goddess Sea came into focus in a deeper, richer green than she had ever seen before.

"We're using this gem in rotation, Sherra," Raquella said. "Both the Patient and the Dedicated have agreed you deserve a slot in the rotation to use the emerald."

Sherra ignored her words and peered at her through the emerald in her left socket and the peridot in her right.

The difference was astonishing.

"Raquella, did you know that you're pushing towards a heart attack? I highly recommend you take more care with your diet. It's still some distance away, of course, but I can see the build-up in your arteries."

There was a moment of silence at Sherra's words.

"It's quite astonishing," Sherra said. "I can't see the buildup at all with the peridot yet— it would have to progress much further along for that."

"I see," Raquella said. "I'll try and follow your advice. While appreciated, though, I do need you to acknowledge what I'm saying."

Sherra whirled in place, watching the Goddess Sea spin about her.

"No," she said, "I don't think that's sufficient. One in three."

"One in three what?" Raquella said, patiently.

"Shifts in the rotation," Sherra said. "The Patient, the Dedicated, then me. Then the Patient, the Dedicated, and then me. Then the Dedicated, then the Patient, then me, because we all deserve a little variety in life, don't we?"

Sherra could see an immediate increase in stress from several of the other Moonsworn in the room. They were already quite stressed to begin with, poor dears, what with the Wrack, and their usual cares, and their fear of Sherra.

In point of fact, Sherra was absolutely sure she was forgetting some other reason why they feared her.

"We… we'll take that under discussion," Raquella said. "In the meantime, can we suggest you practice with the emerald alongside a peridot? Perhaps you might be able to learn to see the Wrack before it kicks off the delirium stage."

"Snakes, snakes, snakes," Sherra said, spinning closer to a couple of other Moonsworn.

Ah, that's right. She was mad, wasn't she? Not allowed to touch knives or be around fire or small animals unsupervised. That would explain the fear.

"Sherra, the peridot?" Raquella said, patiently.

"You don't listen very well," Sherra said. "But I do. I'm excited to hear the screaming."

When Sherra's keepers escorted the blind madwoman out of the room towards one of the infirmaries to practice with the emerald, Raquella sighed, and dismissed her rants about snakes from her mind. Dealing with Sherra always put her on edge, but it was hard to argue for doing without her— the woman's gifts as a seer were astonishing, and she could diagnose illnesses and internal injuries with ease. Her seer's nose was an especially rare gift— one that only a dozen other seers in recorded history had possessed.

When she wasn't causing injuries, at least. On no less than seven occasions she had injured other Moonsworn, usually swiping them with knives without even seeming to notice. No-one even knew how many small animals she'd vivisected.

She'd never injured a patient, curiously enough. Never even tried.

For all the dangers in dealing with Sherra, they couldn't simply lock her up somewhere safe or grant her the Goddess' Mercy. She was simply too useful.

Raquella shook her head, and returned her mind to other matters. Well, other matters than the hideous news she'd received this morning. If Raquella were a betting woman, she would imagine that they had a day, maybe less, until the first screams began. She had spent most of the last four days since meeting with the Empress working frantically, preparing the city for the Wrack's arrival.

There would not be anywhere near enough painkilling medicines, nor medicines to put victims to sleep. Tincture of the poppy was in especially short supply.

A particularly clever group of Dedicated Moonsworn had, however, thought of a useful medical treatment— namely, a way to reduce the injuries that the screamers inflicted upon themselves. It was, Raquella had to admit, a surprisingly simple solution.

Namely, a cunning canvas wrap with rope loops that could be used to keep a screamer constricted, so that they could not claw at themselves or pull muscles by thrashing their limbs unnaturally. The afflicted's struggles kept the rope loops taut and kept the canvas wrapped around them. If it worked like everyone hoped, it should also prevent the semi-frequent broken limbs.

It would do little to prevent heart failure or suffocation brought on by throat clenching, but the survivors should be in better shape than they would otherwise be.

With a simple word from Raquella, the Empress had every single weaver, seamstress, sailmaker, and anyone else who might be helpful manufacturing the wraps in Ladreis set to work on the task. It was astonishing and terrifying to Raquella— she was used to the reverence with which Galicantans spoke of the Empress, but seeing it play out so determinedly was something else entirely.

They'd set children to collecting the cloth scraps from the wrap manufacture, and bundling them with twine to manufacture earplugs. Wax, especially beeswax, was selling for an absurd premium, yet those who had it were freely sharing it with their neighbors to make even higher quality beeswax.

Ladreis had completely changed in a matter of days. From a boisterous, argumentative, bustling city, it had turned into a quiet, determined, and industrious one. Every order the Moonsworn gave was obeyed without question, and she'd even heard that duels had halted nearly entirely, which she'd never expected to happen.

Even in times of war, Ladreis usually still had…

No. Raquella turned her thoughts away from that road, for it led too close to the morning's news.

She'd also noted that the chapels, shrines, and repositories of the Vowless ancestors were packed to the brim with supplicants at all times of the day.

One of the biggest challenges had been barreling enough fresh water. At this point, the Moonsworn scholars were all but convinced that the Wrack could spread through water— hence why the poor often seemed to get it a couple weeks after the wealthy. Their access to clean, unpolluted water was poor at best, as though they still lived in the days where you drank wine or small beer if you didn't want to get sick. The Moonsworn had put an end to those days across much of Iopis, but somehow, no matter how hard the Moonsworn tried, the wealthy and powerful always managed to ensure that the poor didn't benefit from changes to society, as though they didn't deserve them.

They hadn't caught the Wrack in water yet, but Raquella was sure it would only be a matter of time. Once they could observe the diarrhea of a survivor of the Wrack's delirious screamer stage with the emerald eye, they would surely be able to identify the illness. Once the patterns were found, ideally peridot seers could be trained to do the same.

Given all that, they'd been barreling as much fresh water as they could, before the Wrack arrived. She had issued a commandment that no-one in the city was to drink from fountains or pipes, but only from stored water, once the screaming had begun. Hopefully, it would limit the spread of the Wrack to less than it had been in other cities.

They could only hope, at least.

Even as Raquella went about her inspections, she could feel the morning's revelations circling in the back of her head. While giving orders, taking care of paperwork, and responding to inquiries from the palace, she felt herself gingerly circling about the topic, like a tongue poking at a sore tooth.

She knew there was no way to avoid thinking about it, hard as she tried.

The Sunsworn Emperor had declared the Wrack a punishment from the Sun Goddess upon the heathen Vowless and had begun marshaling his armies and assembling his fleets. He declared that the Sunsworn faithful, especially the warriors most blessed by the Sun

Goddess, would be immune to the disease, as the Moonsworn had proven to be.

Raquella desperately tried not to think about the fact that plagues were not the realm of the Sun but of the nameless third sister.

Within a month at most, Galicanta and the Sunsworn Empire would be at war, and there was no greater breeding ground for plague than war. Raquella had hoped, quite realistically, that the Wrack could be contained in Teringia, that the Choke might keep it out of Oyansur.

But now, she bore no hope for that at all. Galicanta, even at full strength, could hardly hold off the Sunsworn Empire alone, and Galicanta was a shambles, half the nation overtaken with the Wrack. With the crippled condition of the Teringian semaphore network, the Empress would not be able to send for aid from the other Eidola nations. Even if they could, Raquella doubted there were soldiers or supplies to send.

The Sunsworn Empire might finally achieve its dream of conquering Teringia. A broken, plague-ridden Teringia, but she doubted that mattered to the Sunsworn Emperor. She'd spent years restraining her criticism of the man even in her own head, but in truth, she knew the man cared far more about increasing his own power and glory over any higher concerns.

She gave a brief prayer to the Moonsworn Goddess that Amazahd, the son of the Emperor, by all accounts a far more pious man, might ascend to the throne atop the Ziggurat of the Sun sooner than later.

Raquella bore no hope of that, however. Whether the Sunsworn conquered Galicanta or were miraculously rebuffed, she knew that the Wrack would cross to Oyansur in the chaos of war, and the Emperor was dooming uncounted thousands to painful death, and more again to being cripples. There was nothing Raquella could do, save for…

Her whole train of thought came to a halt, and she paused in the middle of the street she had been walking down. The Moonsworn clerks and palace scribes that had been following her stopped as well, confused. All traces of her maudlin, cynical reflections on war had vanished from her mind.

Snakes. Sherra had been ranting about snakes. Sherra might be mad, but she was anything but stupid.

Raquella turned in an abrupt about-face, and began to stride back towards the Moonsworn infirmaries as quickly as she could.

She was pretty sure she knew exactly why Sherra had been ranting about snakes.

Then, at the edge of her hearing, Raquella heard it. It was faint, and far in the distance across the great city, but it was there.

Screaming.

The Wrack had arrived in Ladreis.

Raquella didn't stop walking, even as those around her paled in fear.

She needed to speak to Sherra.

CHAPTER TWENTY
A Chorus of Screams

Half a hundred interruptions forced their way into Raquella's path as she tried to get back to interrogate Sherra.

Some were those reporting back to her on tasks she'd assigned them, and even in her impatience, she didn't begrudge them yet. The vast majority, however, had heard the screamer, who seemed to be located in the opulent manors below the palace, and merely seemed to want reassurance. So, of course, they invented business to approach her on.

Regardless of who was trying to speak to her, Raquella just kept walking, forcing everyone to keep up with her.

Several of those who interrupted her she sent out to try and find out exactly who had caught the Wrack. She could still hear the screamer in the distance, but even knowing what part of the city they were in didn't help too much, for sound echoed strangely in the city, and there were no simple, straight-line streets. The closest thing to it was the switchbacking Imperial Way, that led from the Imperial Palace atop Ladreis' highest hill down to the docks.

Other than the screams, Ladreis seemed utterly silent.

She reached the Moonsworn infirmaries to find out that Sherra was gone— she'd dragged her attendants and the Empress's Pride's guards off towards the Wrack sufferer.

Raquella was moderately confident the madwoman wouldn't try to escape into the city on her own again. A medical puzzle was one of the few things that could truly hold her attention, to the point where Sherra's keepers could hardly get her to eat or sleep until she'd solved it.

Like all inhabitants of Ladreis, Raquella had massively overdeveloped legs from roaming up and down the steep alleys and winding staircases of the city. Her lungs were equally impressive for her age. Even so, it had been years since she'd pushed either so hard. Raquella's legs were killing her, and she had trouble catching her breath, but she set out to find Sherra and the screamer anyhow, not giving the slightest allowance to her weakness.

The first screamer had been continuing off and on for nearly an hour by the time Raquella reached the wealthy neighborhood where they were from. The buildings were larger than below, but not by much, and the streets were no less convoluted, stair-filled, or steep. The plazas with their fountains were a bit more ostentatious in their carvings, but the steep hills and immense population of Ladreis governed the use of space with an iron fist, and only the Empress in her palace could defy it.

Still, though the houses were not much larger, they were each inhabited by only a single family, while the buildings below often housed as many as ten families apiece, with multiple generations inhabiting a single room. Some of the biggest families in the slums had to sleep in shifts.

If there were a single unoccupied building in all of Ladreis, it would genuinely shock Raquella.

The voice of the screamer echoed throughout those twisty alleys and winding staircases, until Raquella could hardly tell where it came from. She selected a plaza that seemed close to the sound, and sent out her attendants and clerks to find Sherra.

The instant Raquella sat down on the edge of the ornately carved fountain basin to rest, a second victim started screaming nearby.

Raquella cursed. There'd been some reports of isolated cases of the Wrack emerging as much as a couple of days before the initial, primary wave burst forth, and she'd hoped this would be one such, but with two in the same wealthy neighborhood, it seemed unlikely.

She sat, and massaged her miserable legs, and she waited. The terrified nobles of the neighborhood sometimes peeked out at her from behind their shutters, but none approached nor left their homes.

A messenger from the Empress reached her as she waited on the fountain, informing her that no less than three cases had appeared behind the thick walls of the palace, including one of the Empress's grandchildren, and that they should return with the emerald to seek a way to save her grandchild.

She sent the message back that the emerald was with the first victim in the city below, and she would send messengers to have it and its bearer sent to the palace as swiftly as she could, and she waited for her attendants to find Sherra.

And waited. And waited. It likely wasn't that long, in truth, for the shadows barely shifted, but it felt like an eternity to Raquella. A third screamer began in earshot, and then as one of her attendants returned to her at a sprint, a fourth.

"I found her," the woman gasped. "This way."

She made the attendant drink from a waterskin, then followed her through the winding alleys, up a particularly steep stone staircase where she could touch the steps above her without bending over or even leaning forward at all, and into a tiny plaza with no fountain, no great view of the city, and but three doors upon it. Several other attendants found them along the way and followed in their wake.

The attendant led her into the left-most of the doors, and Raquella found herself in a dark, musty house, crammed with sculptures, busts, and books. The kitchen was the only room well lit and well cleaned that Raquella saw as she was led upstairs.

The screaming grew louder and louder as she climbed the stairs until she could not even make out the voice of the attendant leading her upwards.

She found herself, finally, in a great bedroom that took up nearly the entirety of the top floor. An immensely fat woman writhed and thrashed in the bed, and her screams were extraordinarily loud. She was young and hale seeming, other than her great weight.

Sherra and her escorts all stood about the room. Only Sherra looked at ease, carefully maneuvering about the bed to examine the woman from every angle.

None of the emerald's guards were present.

Raquella couldn't help noticing the room's great balcony. For all the rest of the house's cramped feel and poor location, she'd seldom seen a better view than off the balcony, and it didn't surprise her that the woman could be heard from so far. Between the location and the sheer power of the woman's voice, well, it would be astonishing if there were many in the city who couldn't hear the screams.

She gestured to grab Sherra's attention. When the madwoman noticed Raquella over the screams, she smiled, both eyes glittering green. She gestured at her escorts, who moved over to the victim and began trying to get tincture of the poppy into the woman.

Raquella followed Sherra out of the room, down the stairs, and out of the house entirely. Raquella's attendants followed the two of them. The screaming was still hideously loud, but you could at least hear others speaking out here.

In the daylight, she looked at Sherra, and realized to her shock that her green gem-eye was peridot, not emerald. Which, if she didn't have the emerald, explained why the guards were not with her.

Which was better than the alternatives, to be sure.

"That woman was a singer," Sherra said.

"Where is the emerald?" Raquella asked.

"I didn't need it," Sherra said. "An interesting bauble, but the Wrack can be seen easily enough in its victims before the screaming. I gave it and its guards to… one of the Dedicated? One of the Patient? Not really sure. Do you think that woman is a good singer? She certainly was loud enough."

Raquella sighed, and sent a couple of attendants to spread the word, and have the emerald sent up to the palace to examine the Empress's grandchild.

"How have the rest of us missed it?" Raquella asked. "Is it having two gem eyes that allowed you to see it? Was it the depth perception, being able to use peridot and emerald at once? Was it your nose?"

Sherra laughed. It was a happy, genuinely amused laugh, not one of the madwoman's more terrifying laughs. Anyone who spent much time around Sherra quickly learned to identify the worst ones, but she had a great deal of others, as well. A great deal about Sherra's mental state could be carried through her laughter.

"I didn't need the emerald. The other seers all saw it. They just didn't recognize it," Sherra said, in a voice close to singing.

"Is it because they only saw the venom, and not the snake itself?" Raquella asked, following her hunch.

Her remaining attendants gave her quizzical looks, but Sherra burst into delighted laughter, even more joyful her previous laugh.

"You're not even a seer, and you understand!" Sherra said, clapping. "You know about the snakes!"

Raquella cursed.

They were all idiots. They'd been idiots all this damn time.

So many Moonsworn had thought the Lothaini healer who treated Prince Arnulf of Lothain a fool for thinking the Wrack a poison at first, rather than illness, but he'd never been a fool.

Arnulf *had* been poisoned. Not by a man, but by the Wrack itself.

"How," the Empress asked, "can something be both poison and plague?"

Raquella ran her hand through her hair, as Moonsworn healers stared at her with equal incomprehension. Only Sherra wasn't looking at her, and that's because the mad blind seer was idly dancing about the hall, as though she were attending a ball no-one else could see, with only the screaming of the palace's Wrack victims for musical accompaniment.

They weren't in the Voice of the Empire— that great hall and wonder of engineering atop the palace. That wasn't to say that the audience chamber they were in wasn't grand. Lofty columns ran down the walls, and the acoustics of the place were perfectly built to echo the voice of the Empress from her throne.

In any other palace it would be a marvel. Here, it was the next thing to intimate.

"The plague produces the poison, your Imperial Highness." Raquella said. "We've known for some time that when one is infected with the Wrack, it can take as long as three weeks or as little as one and a half before it leaves dormancy and enters the delirium phase."

"Before they become a screamer, you mean," Empress Phillipa interrupted.

"Yes, your Imperial Highness," Raquella said.

The Empress seemed to look off through the palace walls towards one of the screamers, then gestured towards Raquella to continue.

"Poisons and venoms are unliving things, Empress. They are often produced by living things, but they are not themselves living. Plagues, and most other illnesses, however, are living things that invade your body. Thus far, we've all been mistaking the poison or venom— we're not sure which it is yet— for the plague itself, hence why we've been unable to spot it before they enter… before they become a screamer. Once Sherra here made that connection and realize that what we'd identified as the Wrack was just the poison or venom it produced— and pointed out the true form of the Wrack to us— we were able to identify it swiftly."

Sherra paused her dancing just long enough to wave cheerfully at the Empress.

"How," the Empress asked, "could you simply miss seeing some foreign creature dwelling in people's bodies?"

Raquella tried to keep her nervousness off her face at the Empress's displeased tone, but she was sure the Empress could see it without much difficulty.

"I'm not a seer myself," Raquella began.

"The fact that you have two eyes rather gave that away," the Empress said.

"I… yes, Empress," Raquella said. She took a deep breath and continued. "From what I understand, there are countless tiny creatures living within everyone, and most of them are completely harmless. Seers are trained to ignore most of them, lest their vision be otherwise overwhelmed.

The true form of the Wrack seems to have been missed—it's considerably larger than most of these little creatures that live within the blood, but size isn't always a particularly useful predictor of whether something will be especially visible in the Go… in the spirit realm."

Best to use the Eidol terminology around the Empress, Raquella thought.

"So are your seers able to see the true culprit now?" the Empress asked.

"Sherra here can," Raquella said, "and she's already shown a couple other seers. Give it a day or two, they'll teach everyone else."

"Do I have the Wrack?" the Empress asked, her face utterly flat.

Raquella froze, then turned to Sherra. She was the only healer here who could identify the Wrack so far.

Sherra turned to face Raquella and smiled, her gemstone eyes glittering.

"Let's find out!" the madwoman said, and started striding towards the Empress.

"Guards," Raquella said. "Grab her. Don't let her approach the Empress with her arms free."

The guards wouldn't normally obey her order, but they were swift to respond to any threat to the Empress. They weren't gentle about it, but Sherra hardly seemed to notice them grabbing her by the arms. She didn't think Sherra would do anything to hurt the Empress, since the old woman likely counted as a patient to Sherra's strange mind.

It was too much of a risk to take, though, since an attack on the Empress would likely mean the violent end of the Moonsworn in Galicanta.

"You'll need to take her within three strides of the Empress for her to check," Raquella said. "She probably won't try anything, but it's difficult to tell when one of her impulses will seize her. And mind she doesn't get into biting range."

The guards didn't seem comforted at this, but at a gesture from the Empress, they brought the blind seer to the stairs leading to her throne.

Sherra leaned forwards towards the Empress, her crystalline eyes meeting the Empress's living eyes, and Raquella couldn't say which were harder. Finally, Sherra broke eye contact with the Empress and ran her eyes over the woman's torso and limbs.

"Move me a bit to the left and down one step," Sherra told the guards without looking away.

They looked uncomfortable, but escorted Sherra there, her arms still firmly in their grasp behind her back.

The silence stretched on uncomfortably long before Sherra shook her head and looked back at Raquella.

"No Wrack for the Empress. She's too skinny, though. Not good for her." She turned back to the Empress. "Little old ladies shouldn't be so skinny. First breeze will blow you right away. You should eat more."

Empress Phillipa's face was utterly expressionless as the guards dragged Sherra back away from her. Raquella, however, openly sighed in relief. None of the Empress's children or grandchildren seemed up to the challenge of ruling Galicanta just yet, especially not in a crisis. And with the combination of the Wrack and the looming possibility of war…

Part of Raquella had been convinced the Empress would be among the first to fall to the Wrack, because just about every other ruler whose path the contagion had crossed had died of it. She'd had nightmares that the empress would collapse into convulsions atop the Voice of the Empire, and that the whole city would be serenaded by her screams until the convulsions threw the Empress off her throne and to her death among the wires below her.

Raquella had never been so happy to be wrong.

"So does this mean we can stop the Wrack?" the Empress asked.

Raquella winced. "It's a step in the right direction, Empress, but we're not there yet. We still don't understand how the Wrack is spreading, exactly. Every sign seems to point to it spreading through water, but if that were the case, it would have spread across Teringia entirely differently— and likely much faster. It also doesn't explain why it's almost always the wealthy and powerful who catch it first. I'm sorry, Empress."

Her hands were shaking a bit, and she clutched them together. Being around the Empress was nerve-wracking, and never got any easier.

The Empress sighed. "Moonsworn, I've ruled long enough to know I can't command the tides. I don't demand miracles from you, nor will I punish you for not producing them. We fight a war against the Wrack, and no proper war is won in a single battle alone. You've won a battle today, and even if it isn't a decisive one, that's to be praised."

Much of Raquella's stress simply drained out with her next breath. As she thanked the Empress, though, she wondered, deep inside, whether they would be able to win the war at all.

CHAPTER TWENTY-ONE
He Who Would Grasp At Mist

From the Memoirs of Johannes the Wanderer, also known as Johannes of Dannagrad, also known as Johannes the Singer-Friend, also known by half a dozen other names. He was an adventurer and scholar of the highest order, with prodigious interests across numerous fields of study. This entry dates from his travels during the dreadful time of the Wrack, some ten years before his mysterious disappearance in the jungles of central Oyansur. His collection of journals, including his half-written memoir, was found a year ago in a sealed chest washed ashore on the Citrine Isles. Johannes' fate is unknown.

There is a tale that is told to children across Galicanta about a man who wished to grasp the fog in his hands. It was one of many tales told in that land, and it was far from the most popular or beloved of tales. Few children demanded it be retold to them, for it was a strange, dissatisfying sort of tale.

The learned could tell you that it was a tale found across all of Iopis, and it might very well be the oldest tale still told. Most thought it a mere curiosity.

There were a few who paid the tale closer attention, though. The Radhan, those argumentative and inquisitive nomads, were the one people of Iopis who lacked the tale, and yet they seemed fascinated by it and sought out older and older versions of it when they could. The highest ranks of the Dedicated, that impatient new sect of moon-worshippers, paid close attention to it for reasons of their own, which they held even closer to their hearts than the nomadic Radhan did— and the Radhan were famed for their secrets. The Quae Emperors and Empresses, rulers of the oldest civilization on Iopis, shared a unique version of the tale only with their heirs. Their reasons were the closest-held yet.

On the eastern coast of Galicanta, far from Ladreis or any other great cities of that arid nation, lay a single small village where that tale was told with especial interest as well. In that village, and that village alone, did children laugh and demand to rehear the tale again and again, and in that village alone was that tale truly beloved.

It has been a project of some years for me to explore this story, to chip away at it to find its heart. I've spent countless hours attempting to pluck out the splinters storytellers have shoved into it over the centuries to put their own twist onto the story, or make it more palatable for their listeners. I've systematically compared nine-score and twelve versions of the story from a half-dozen languages— and translations from a half dozen more, seeking out the most common features in all the stories, and weeding out later additions. It was only one of my many interests over the years, but it was a project I always came back to. Though my work is far from done, this is the version of the tale I have distilled so far.

There was a great man, once, whose ambition drove him ever onwards.

The boy was born to wealth, but he craved power which could not be bought, and though not born royal, he was a king by manhood.

He was not satisfied.

The king craved power which could not be inherited, and by the time he had sons of his own, he had conquered the neighboring kingdoms.

He still was not satisfied.

The emperor craved power beyond any man before him, and by the time he had grandsons, he had conquered the world.

He still was not satisfied.

Now, however, he knew not what he craved. He had more power than any man now alive— any man who had ever been alive. He had a much-beloved wife, loyal sons, and much-indulged grandchildren. He was feared as a conqueror, respected as a just ruler, and loved as a caring judge.

And yet he still was not satisfied.

The man began to worry, then, that there was some insatiable hole inside himself that could never be satisfied. That he would die unsatisfied, never knowing what it was that he lacked.

So the man sent to every corner of the world for the wise, to seek a way to plug a hole in his heart.

Some of the wise suggested taking more wives, to fill that hole in his heart. The man, knowing that his fleshly lusts were no greater than those of the simplest farmer, sent them away, for he would not dishonor his wife that way.

Some of the wise suggested that he simply indulge himself more, for the man led a strict lifestyle, seldom eating rich foods or drinking more than a single glass of wine with dinner. The man took their advice for a time, but he found only indigestion and miserable mornings. He sent those wise away, and returned to his strict ways. For their time, however, those wise were not sent away empty-handed, for the man readily forgave honest failure.

Some of the wise suggested that it was a more spiritual life the man craved, and the man immediately saw the wisdom of this idea, pursuing spiritual contemplation and funding great temples in his domains. And it contented him for a time, but he could feel that hole inside him growing again, unsated by spiritual rewards. He did not send these wise away, for they had served him well, but he sought out others of the wise as well.

Some of the wise suggested that he feared death and might seek from the alchemists and mages the means of immortality. That, perhaps, he might entreat certain beings with whom a bargain might be struck. At these so-called wise he only laughed, for he had faced death a hundred times in battle, and knew it as an old friend. At these so-called wise he only laughed, for he knew them to be not wise but cowardly, for all men faced death, and if their legacy was strong, they need fear it not. And he stripped the title of wise from them, and he sent them out naked in the world with only his mockery as a reward, bearing less than they had come with.

Years went by, and a thousand thousands of the wise of the world marched through the man's court. He was diagnosed with loneliness, and wanderlust, and a hundred other wants, and the claims began to repeat and repeat and repeat, and fewer and fewer of the wise were permitted into the man's presence. And he grew old, but his mind never faded, and his will never receded, and that hole inside him only grew. So, however, did the conviction that he would never fill that hole. That he was not lacking anything, but was just broken inside.

It was only when that conviction had grown so large that it began to turn into despair that the shepherd came to the man's palace. None knew exactly how he earned an audience with the man, but the two spoke for hours and hours. They found a curious sort of kinship, the two of them— though the shepherd's kingdom had only been a small flock of sheep and a few pastures, it was a kingdom nonetheless. They spoke of this kinship, and of other topics, but most of all what they spoke of was fog.

For the shepherd lived upon the moors, and the fog frequently hid the sharp boulders, crevasses, and pits upon the moor, and herding his sheep was a more dangerous endeavor than one might expect, and one which eventually took his whole herd from him.

The shepherd had followed his lost herd into the fog. He tracked them deep, deep into the fog. Deeper than he'd ever dared go before, for many before him had been lost deep in the fog on the moors. The shepherd kept going until he could no longer see the sun itself through the fog, and he could no longer even see his own feet.

And then he left the fog, and found himself in a new land. A hot land, with cedars taller than the tallest palace, where lumps of gold littered the stream bottoms like pebbles, where great gems protruded from the stones like moss, and where great shaggy beasts with pelts of silk roamed freely.

The shepherd had stumbled back through the fog, and wandered for what seemed like days. He never found his herd, but he somehow managed to find his way home again, and he collapsed to the ground, and slept like the dead on the moor for many hours.

When he woke, he began his journey of many months towards the palace of the great man, for all the world knew of the hole inside the great man that all the wise of the world could not fill.

And the shepherd was no wise man, but he thought, perhaps, that since conquest had once filled the great man's heart, perhaps it could do so again.

At this, the man laughed, and he knew himself again for the conqueror he was, for none of the wise had ever suggested it, for the wise all knew there was no more of the world to be conquered.

He bade the shepherd to lead him to this fog, and the conqueror and his armies followed the shepherd to the quietest, remotest, least important part of the world. And there, on the moor, the shepherd showed the conqueror the fog.

The conqueror sent thousands into the fog. Few returned, but those who did spoke of countless new lands, all hidden behind the fog.

When he asked the shepherd what reward he would ask of the conqueror, the shepherd declared himself a simple man, with simple desires. Which was to say, of course, wealth, power, women, and indolence. The conqueror laughed and granted it, and if he felt a twinge of jealousy that the shepherd's desires were so easily fulfilled, he showed it not, for the conqueror was a gracious man.

Years went by, and the conqueror grew ancient indeed, but his will and his mind never flagged, and even ruling from this remote part of the world, none dared rebel. His armies learned the ways of the fog, and began to bring back endless treasures to the conqueror. He toured a hundred lands, each more strange and wondrous than the last.

And that hole inside the conqueror filled once more. For conquest, not power, not dominion, had always been what he had craved.

At least, it filled for a time. As his limbs became frail and the end of his life approached, he came to realize there was one thing he had not conquered.

The fog itself.

Even as the conqueror's death slowly crept towards him, he set all his alchemists, all his scholars, all his mages, and all the wise upon the project of conquering the fog, of forcing it to take him where he wished, of barring passage save to those he chose.

And all those alchemists, scholars, mages, and wise ones all failed, again and again.

The conqueror still feared death not, for he was confident in his legacy and had in that way conquered death. He was, however, impatient, for he knew death was coming.

And the conqueror, in his impatience, turned to those once called wise who he had turned away in mockery, and he spoke to them of making bargains with those who might help him. Those cold, hungry beings which men spoke of only if they must, and only in whispers.

And the conqueror, in his impatience, called to those beings for their aid. He called to those beings to help him grasp the fog that so eluded him.

But the instant those beings came to the conqueror, the mists shut their ways and dissipated.

The conqueror, furious, commanded those ancient, slow beings to leave him, for there would be no bargains, and he would pay them no price.

In a quiet, unconcerned voice, the beings told him that their price was not for a bargain fulfilled, or even a bargain made. Their price was merely for being called.

And the conqueror paid that price unwillingly, and the fog slid through his grasp, as even the most common fog would slip from the grasp of the most common man, for that was the nature of fog.

Some storytellers try to impart some great lesson onto the tale, some moral of humility, of not letting ambition rule you, of knowing your place. A thousand different lessons have been attached to it— half of them contradicting the others— but somehow, every child knows that none of them fit. It is a disquieting tale that most would rather forget but end up telling their own children anyway.

Most of those that pay the story special interest— the Radhan, the Dedicated, the Quae Imperial family— know not to try and find simple morals in the story.

The little village on the southeast coast of Galicanta is the exception. They are the one group who has stuck a moral onto the tale and made it stick. Not thanks to any secret knowledge or great wisdom, though.

No, simply because they're over-proud and, to be frank, a bit thick.

Their moral isn't even particularly good. It simply consists of a single line tacked onto the end of the story.

"And that, child, is how we know Antegada is the greatest village in all Galicanta, all Teringia, and even all of Iopis— we have surpassed even the conqueror, for we alone can grasp the fog."

As I believe I mentioned, the villagers of Antegada are most certainly over-proud.

Antegada was a young village, as these things went. It was only a few generations old— not even a century, though the over-proud Antegadans always claimed a century for it.

The village was founded by, of all things, shipwrecked Galicantan sailors. Their captain— like his descendants, over-proud and a bit thick— had sailed down the east coast of Oyansur towards Quae, despite the fact that the Sunsworn and Galicanta were actively warring at the time— and despite the fact that the Quae were, by all accounts, in the middle of their own civil war.

The captain might have been over-proud and a bit thick, but he was also unquestionably lucky. Not a single Sunsworn ship came close enough to stop him, and he arrived at Quae only days after the end of their civil war. Their merchants, having lost immense sums during the war, loaded his ship with the finest of silks at shockingly low prices.

No jewel-silk, of course. That was too dear to part with cheaply even in their desperation.

The captain, because he was over-proud and a bit thick, decided to skip the long, coast-hugging voyage back to Galicanta, and instead, he decided to sail straight north back, venturing far out to sea like a Radhan. This wasn't an entirely foolish decision, in some regards— no other captains knew the civil war had ended, so if he hurried, he might beat the news back and even sail south once more. This was in the days before the semaphore network extended across the world, of course— such a feat would be impossible today.

And, to my great shock, he appears to have succeeded perfectly. One can draw a perfectly straight line due north from Quae to what is now Antegada.

Of course, the location that is now Antegada was dead center in the harsh coastal desert of that part of Galicanta, the place known as the Barren Coast. Though right along the sea, many claim it to be the driest desert on all Iopis. There were no other settlements for a hundred leagues in either direction, and no sources of drinking water along that entire coast. There wasn't even any plant life, save for moss that lived off the sea-fogs, for that coast had never seen rain in the recorded history.

And, of course, that over-proud and slightly thick captain crashed his vessel right in the middle of the Barren Coast at top speed. Broke his vessel right up on the shore.

The captain and crew rescued as much of the cargo as they could, and they spent their evening arguing over which way they should go. It didn't matter much, for they had too little water remaining to take them safely in either direction along the coast, and inland was even worse.

Their arguing went on well into the night until fatigue claimed them.

It was, according to Antegada's mayor, the captain himself who woke early and made the crucial discovery. According to the mayor's wife and several other women I spoke to, it was the ship's navigator, a woman of skill and wisdom, and the captain merely claimed the credit for himself.

I'm prone to mostly trust the women here, for a pompous ship's captain claiming undue credit is a common enough story. The one thing I distrust in their story is the claim to wisdom on the part of the navigator, because I'm ill-inclined to believe that virtue of anyone in this ancestor-forsaken village.

Regardless of who made it, the discovery was simple enough. They strode out among the wreckage, and found the morning fog settling into droplets on a swatch of silk hanging from the wreckage.

It was, I have to admit, a truly ancestor-inspired idea that occurred next. When the others awoke, the discoverer had planted timber from the wreck up and down the beach, draping bolts of silk across them. The morning fog was collecting upon all of them.

The history that followed was long-winded, self-serving, and nearly worthless— and certainly not worth repeating here. The shipwrecked men and women built a village on that brutal coast and constructed great fog-catchers for water. One would think the returns on water from fog a paltry thing, but it is not uncommon for a poorly built fog-catcher to collapse under the weight of its captured water. Antegada is truly flush with water, to the point where they have quite ostentatious town baths, and their farms and vineyards and orchards are lavishly watered. It is positively shocking to sail across the coast and then see the great shock of green surrounding the stone buildings of Antegada.

As the only habitation along that barren coast, Antegada had become quite a major stopping point for traveling ships. The beach is long, shallow, and ill-suited for any sort of pier, but ships may safely anchor offshore, where they may row their own boats in or be met by the little fishing coracles of Antegada.

In the early days of the village, the Antegadans were desperately poor for some resources, most notably wood and metal. Still, they made do during the decade it took for their new village to be discovered — in those days, few ships traversed the Barren Coast, and those that did so usually did at some remove.

My personal theory is that they were just too foolish to build any sort of signaling mechanism, but it's not one I've seen fit to share with my hosts.

As with any destination, I had many reasons to visit Antegada. First and foremost, of course, was my unending wanderlust. I'd never seen the Barren Coast, and the stories of Antegada's fog-catchers interested me. My pursuit of the tale of the conqueror drove me there as well, for I had heard mention of the village's peculiar interest in the tale, though no particulars of their interest. That part of my visit turned out to be a miserable failure, to say the least — they only retell the tale for their own self-glorification.

I had not heard any word of the Wrack yet in my travels, and for those weeks I spent in Antegada collecting their tales, exploring their farms, fishing alongside the villagers, and documenting the strange, hardscrabble creatures of the Barren Coast, I found myself content, knowing another ship would be along soon enough, and I could bargain for passage on it.

I paid special interest to the fog-catchers, of course— they were brilliant devices, and they had evolved much since their early, primitive, hung-net like form. The village was always purchasing new fabrics to experiment with, and they had long since discovered better shapes to build in. The youngest fog-catchers were curious, box-like sculptures of cloth, where the collected water would slowly seep down into the barrel below. I was told they were built like this to catch the fog from any direction.

Antegada was too small and remote for a semaphore branch to be built out to it, so we heard no news of the Wrack for some time. When finally a ship arrived to share the news, it was a fleeing Geredaini ship, which stayed only long enough to resupply before resuming its southerly flight.

And I missed it. I had ventured out with the mayor and a group of villagers to inspect a potential site for a new daughter village, for Antegada had begun to grow cramped. The mayor was filled to the brim with dreams and plans of a great chain of cities, all given life by fog catchers, turning the Barren Coast into a verdant place of beauty.

I will mock that pompous man and those over-proud villagers for many things, but I will not mock them for that dream, for it is a wondrous thing.

When we returned, some days later, it was to panic and confusion. The tales of the Wrack had the village in an uproar, and the villagers were truly convinced the world was ending, and that the Days of Hunger had come.

And, despite every bit of reason I could offer them, every bit of caution, those thick-skulled villagers closed themselves off and began chasing away every ship, in an effort to keep the Wrack from them.

Leaving me trapped in that ancestor-forsaken village for a year and a half, and unable to observe or document the most important events of our time.

What follows is a long-winded, vicious, scatological assault on the characters, ancestry, and other traits of the villagers. We can safely assume that the usually fair-minded Johannes exaggerated many of their negative traits, as he did in every instance where he felt cooped up and trapped in a place — Johannes' wanderlust was legendary, and his grudges eternal.

The self-imposed quarantine of Antegada was successful, in a manner of speaking. No cases of the Wrack occurred there, but that almost certainly would have been true regardless — given what we know now of the disease's transmission — there were no reasonable vectors for the plague to arrive in Antegada.

CHAPTER TWENTY-TWO
All Maps Lie

The irony of what Anton was about to do was not lost on him. He hadn't left the inside of the dockmaster's records depot for weeks, if not months, and he was choosing to leave in the midst of a city convulsed by the Wrack.

He hadn't needed to leave it, in truth. He had a little cot in one corner, there was a comfortable little garderobe that drained straight into the pipes that led into the harbor, dock employees brought him his meals, and he was even allowed to use the little bath-house next door. He didn't even need to go outside for that last— there was a little service door between the buildings.

Anton was rather fond of his quiet little life. He didn't have to interact with people more than absolutely necessary, and he didn't have to see the sky.

And now he was about to do both.

In truth, he would have probably needed to leave soon anyways. No one had brought him his meals in days. There were ship's biscuits and dried fruit and such in the various desks in the depot, but he'd already consumed most of them.

Part of him felt a vague disapproval that his coworkers would let the Wrack keep them away from their work. Even with the vastly reduced number of ships visiting the Ladreis harbor the last few months, there was never a shortage of work.

Anton clutched his satchel full of papers closer to him, and pulled his broad brimmed hat closer over his face.

The thin-limbed, nervous clerk must have stood by the thick oaken door of the records depot for most of an hour before he finally moved to open it. The instant he did, screams from Wrack victims echoed in through the door, and the little man flinched and began edging backward.

Then he took a deep breath, and set foot out the door.

The Wrack had only been in Ladreis a week, and it had already broken the city.

Huge tracts of the slums had burnt to the ground, and still smoldered. The rest of the city, built of stone rather than driftwood, had been left largely unscathed by the flames, but it had fared little better.

As Anton strode trembling through the streets, he found himself stepping around bodies, some fresh, and all with fingers blackened. None of the screams were close by him, but he winced each time they started anew, nonetheless.

And he kept his eyes on the ground, so they wouldn't look up at the sky.

It was easier, heading up towards the palace. Going downhill, back towards the docks, was far more difficult, to say the least. It was easy to look up just a few degrees and suddenly have your gaze overlooking the vast, empty, demanding space over the city. To see the great empty void that was the sky, have it *twist* and *pull* on the world around you, have it steal your balance out from under you, and know that if you weren't cautious it would yank you right up. And even if you fled indoors, it would be aware of you, and you would be able to feel it looking for you and waiting for hours and hours, even through thick stone walls.

Anton realized he'd come to a halt, trembling, and he forced himself to start walking uphill again. Rats skittered out of his way only briefly, then returned to their business on the streets unchallenged.

There were ways to get back down to his lovely windowless records depot without spotting the great void looming over the city or out above the ocean. Narrow, twisting alleys where the buildings ran high enough that one would have to crane their neck all the way back to see the sky. Staircases that cut underneath other buildings. There were only a couple of open spaces on Anton's safe route, and if he was careful, and moved slow, he could cross them without seeing the sky or the open boulevards or making eye contact with anyone.

He'd made a map of his route. Anton was good at maps. Maps made sense to Anton. Maps were right, and proper, and had no sky to them.

Maps were all lies, but they were useful lies. Lies by omission.

But they were lies that told the truth. You lied and lied with them to pry away unnecessary truths— truths that would only obscure and confuse the important truths that you really wanted out of a map, because the real world was a mess of too many things. It was too crowded. Lie with a map, make those things go away, the world weighed on you less and you could begin to comprehend it by only seeing what you *needed* to see.

It reminded him of the way seers talked about what they did. They didn't try to see more, they cut away all the unnecessary bits, just like a map did. He rather imagined he could have enjoyed being a seer, save for the fact that the descriptions of the spirit realm made it seem like an even more vicious void than the sky.

Anton didn't think his map that kept away the sky would work anymore, anyhow. It cut through the edge of the slums, and the fire had turned them from a wonderfully claustrophilic warren to just more open space, a chunk of the sky forcing itself down upon the city.

It didn't matter, though. He needed to get to the palace. He needed to find the Moonsworn. He needed to show them his maps, because his maps could tell them the most important lie of all.

Anton stepped gingerly around another body, accidentally meeting its eyes. He snapped his own away immediately, but then he looked back and realized that the dreadful pressure he always saw in the eyes of others wasn't in the open eyes of the corpse at his feet.

He stared at the corpse for a few moments, shuddered, and stumbled up the street, keeping his head down.

It took Anton hours to reach the palace, only to find that when he did, the guards wouldn't let him in.

He thought it was hours. Anton didn't know. He never much was one for keeping track of time. He slept when tired and ate when hungry, for time was just another lie like maps. You only really needed it when dealing with other people.

Anton's only real interest in it was putting it on maps. Time fit better on maps than in clocks or on sundials, though people always seemed to think him mad for saying it.

He wasn't mad, though. Just… broken. He couldn't ever seem to understand other people, couldn't connect with them. He'd met actual madmen, though. He wasn't one of them. That dreadful pressure behind everyone's eyes was there tenfold with the truly mad.

He was just broken.

But he was good with maps. And he was good with numbers because you could always put numbers on a map. They wanted to be on maps. They were happy there.

There wasn't a map to get past the guards, though, and the city kept screaming behind him, and he could feel himself slipping towards that lurking counterpart to the sky inside him that led deeper rather than up and pulled at him every day. That abyss inside him that would pull him in but wouldn't allow him to bring his words or his numbers or even his maps and just leave him shaking and trembling and rocking and...

Anton took a deep breath, then slowly let it out.

Then again.

Then a third time.

And he stepped back up to the guards.

After all, no matter how terrifying and painful it was to speak to the guards and make eye contact with them, if he turned around now, he'd know exactly what he'd see, looming over him, ready to pull at him and swallow him up and up and up. He could *feel* it behind him.

If he got past the guards, he could return to the blessedly close confines of the indoors.

Anton was shaking by the time the guards let him in, but they did let him in. He wasn't sure what he said, but he remembered showing the guards the maps, and one looked ready to seize them from him, and the other looked bored, but no one took his maps, and something angry and protective and hissing crept up from the hole inside him and cut through the dreadful pressure from the guards' eyes, and his words forced the guard back and then Anton was in the palace again and he could breathe again.

And he took a deep breath, then another, then a third, and then he set forth down the hallways to find the Moonsworn, because Anton's maps could save them all.

Raquella could barely keep her eyes open. She'd hardly slept in days, and she had spent most of her time managing Ladreis' healers and the crisis.

Managing wasn't the right word, Raquella felt. You could no more manage the Wrack and the chaos around it than you could manage a storm.

Though they'd managed to finally spot the Wrack— and could now identify those who had it— their fight against it was of… mixed success. Twice as many inhabitants of Ladreis were infected with it as there should have been, but that extra half simply… never got sick. The Wrack never started producing its toxins from their liver. Over time, their bodies just killed off the disease, with little to nothing in the way of symptoms.

Briefly, they'd thought that they had been wrong in their identification of the true Wrack, but every single victim who did come down with symptoms all carried it inside of them. It seemed that in a great many people, the Wrack simply did nothing. It hardly even caused any diarrhea, and provoked no fever.

And, curiously, it showed up in remarkably few Moonsworn, as always. The same proportion of Moonsworn, however, had the disease without any symptoms as those that were struck by its full force.

As if that bit of confusion weren't enough, as if she didn't have enough weighing her down already, Raquella found herself planning and preparing for dealing with battle wounded. She found herself ordering the construction of makeshift hospitals in homes emptied by the Wrack, and she often found herself near overcome with irony at the fact that she was aiding Galicanta in war preparations against her own people.

Except, for the first time in her life, she truly felt the Galicantans were her people too. When that mob had come against the Moonsworn, she had been there among the healers. And when other Galicantans stood against the mob and protected Ladreis' Moonsworn, Raquella had truly felt like she belonged.

She had always loved this city, but until the Wrack, a part of her had always known that she was only a guest. And now, she finally knew that she was home.

Somehow, though, that only made her more torn and miserable over the oncoming war.

When her assistant, Haim, led the skinny little clerk with the oversized hat into her office in the palace, she paid little attention at first. She doubted it would be a waste of her time— Haim had proved to be the best assistant she'd ever had, and she'd more than once cursed herself in the last few weeks for not noticing the boy before now, just because he numbered among the Dedicated. Haim was a decent healer, but he had a true talent for administration.

It wasn't glamorous work, but it was important. Young healers tended to hate the very idea, but non-seers who understood enough about healing to adequately serve as administrators, like Raquella, were unfortunately rare. And it was best that future administrators get some experience young.

Haim, shockingly, hadn't complained once. He'd seemed nothing but eager to please, for whatever reason. Maybe her gestures of goodwill towards the Dedicated had paid off. Maybe he was just that worried by the Wrack. Raquella had too much on her shoulders to worry about it, though.

When the shaky little clerk began unfolding maps on the table, though, she forced her attention to him.

And when he began to speak, she found she was having no trouble keeping her eyes open at all.

CHAPTER TWENTY-THREE

John Bierce
Flies Like Rain

There is a little valley, just an hour's walk outside of Ladreis. In a wetter place than the southwest coast of Galicanta, it might have been a marsh, for it lay low between hills, and had no outlet to the sea. But in that dry land, it had once been merely a dusty little field with a few scrub bushes and infrequent desert flowers, poking up where they could.

Few go there now, save for songbirds who don't understand that they're not perching on sticks and stones, but on bones. More bones than you'll see in one place than anywhere else on Iopis. More than any graveyard; more than any battlefield.

It's not a mournful place, or an ominous place, for all that few ever set foot there.

It's a place of rejoicing. A place of joy, and of triumph.

A place where once, for a time, desert flowers bloomed, watered entirely by the blood shed there, for that field was a slaughterhouse, from where no one but the flies and the rats and the wild dogs ate any meat, for not even the most desperate of men would eat meat from those slaughtered in that little valley.

That little valley where the Wrack was defeated.

"You understand how suspicious this sounds, do you not?" the Empress demanded of Raquella.

The tiny old woman looked to have aged a decade in those few days since Raquella had first met her. She'd been ancient to start with, and now she looked almost desiccated.

Raquella was convinced that she must have aged even more. She hadn't looked in a mirror in days, nor intended to anytime soon.

"I do," Raquella said, not bothering to make excuses.

Anton, the little clerk from the docks, shivered beside her and didn't look at anyone. Blind Sherra stood at Raquella's side, humming idly as she watched the little clerk. Disconcertingly, that involved her staring straight through Raquella with one eye of peridot and one of spinel.

Apparently, the strange little man had told her that her crystalline eyes were more alive than any living eyes and that they threatened to crush him under the weight of their gaze. According to Haim, who had witnessed the curious interaction, it had been the farthest thing from a flirtation he'd ever seen— Anton was absolutely terrified of the blind seer.

She, of course, seemed smitten with the clerk now. Both by his terror, and by the fact that he'd figured out what she hadn't. That little Anton, who knew nothing of medicine or scrying or healing, had been the one to solve the Wrack.

Raquella wasn't sure whether Sherra would try to seduce or murder the little clerk, but it seemed best to keep a closer eye on her than usual.

The Empress glared at all of them, tapped her fingers on her throne, and considered.

Most of Ladreis' butchers had died in the Wrack. In that little valley, where men slew the Wrack in turn, others stepped forwards to spill blood instead.

The sailors whose ships had been sunk to block off the harbor came to that little valley, and their knives spilled blood.

No soldiers could be spared to spill that blood, for they needed to prepare to spill the blood of the oncoming fleet. And no soldiers would be coming from the great fortress of Madracha, for the Wrack was not yet gone from Ladreis, and they could not risk the Choke.

The flabby merchants abandoned their pride and their fastidiousness, and they stepped into that little valley, and their knives spilled blood.

The carpenters could not be spared, for they were needed to barricade the streets of Ladreis, in preparation for the blood that would be shed there.

The prostitutes and thieves and beggars of Ladreis came to that little valley, and their knives spilled blood there.

And the city was divided, between those who spilled blood to save lives and those who prepared to spill blood to end them.

And, of course, there was that third group, who huddled in their homes and hid in fear in those last days of the plague, as they waited for war, but in the years after, everyone you asked claimed membership of the first two groups. Only the victims of the Wrack seemed to be in their houses, and that little valley, which may have held two hundred people at its busiest, must have held tens of thousands according to the stories. Years later it became, curiously enough, impossible to find anyone who'd hid in their homes while the Wrack was being slain.

It took nearly an hour for Raquella and the others to marshal their arguments and convince the Empress of what needed to be done. Impressively, even Anton found his voice to stand up to the Empress, and he had been terrified enough speaking to Raquella.

The little man was wasted on the dockmaster's offices, and if they all survived the war to come, Raquella was determined to get him and his twisty little mind working for her.

They weren't just relying on Anton's maps, of course. They'd sent out their healers to investigate his claims, with blind Sherra at their head, and they found that he'd seen right into the truth of things with his maps.

And finally, finally, they convinced the Empress of the truth of the matter, and they had convinced her of the bloody deeds that must be done. There would be riots over it, if not outright rebellions, but that was a small price to pay for the end to this plague.

And the bones and the flesh and the blood slowly began to pile up in that little valley. And those piles grew, and grew, and grew.

But not all of that bloody slaughter happened in that little valley. Hunks of flesh and bone were hauled in from the city. They were carried by hand to the edge of the city, for the streets were too narrow for wagons, and then the wagons were hauled out to the little valley. Not too close, for the horses harnessed to the wagons were skittish and unhappy with the scent of blood, but they could haul their bloody burdens up the hill to dump into the little valley.

And the mounds of flesh and bone grew and grew, until it seemed that there could not possibly be this much flesh in all of Galicanta, let along Ladreis.

And yet, for all the blood, for all the death, the men and women of Galicanta rejoiced and had light hearts, because the slaughter they did was not of their kin, nor of men or women at all.

"It's the cattle," Anton had claimed, when he stepped foot into Raquella's office. "Cattle are spreading the Wrack."

And he'd proven it.

Anton had painstakingly compared every single report of the Wrack's spread to the shipping records and reports in the Ladreis dockmaster's records. He'd spent quite literally months spending every moment of his free time comparing every movement of goods and people they had records for with the spread of the plague.

And, given how far the semaphore network had spread across Teringia, they had far, far more complete records than they might have once had from the visiting ships in the harbor alone.

The Wrack first showed up in summer by Castle Morinth, when the mountain cattle had finally gained back enough weight to start eating again. Some beast from the Mist must have spread it to the herds when it attacked them. When the cattlemen had brought their herds down to the plains to sell, they'd brought the Wrack in the cows.

Again and again, Anton showed the same pattern happening. Whenever cattle were herded to a new place, within one and a half to three weeks the Wrack would take root. The wealthy took sick with the Wrack first and most often simply because they could afford to eat beef far more often than most. Many of the poor couldn't afford it at all, and they only caught the Wrack from contaminated drinking water, hence the delay of weeks after the wealthy got infected.

In the pass below the Mist Maze, everyone could and did eat cattle, especially the soldiers defending the pass, hence the break in the usual pattern.

The Geredaini army that invaded Lothain had caught sick two weeks after seizing and eating infected cattle. The Geredaini nobility, who had their food shipped in from Geredain via supply chain, didn't catch the Wrack.

Again and again, Anton's cattle theory explained bizarre irregularities in the Wrack's patterns. The Moonsworn didn't get it because their dietary laws forbid them from eating furred animals. Their obsessive religious concern with clean drinking water kept them from getting it from contaminated water. Those Moonsworn who did catch it were often noted for their lack of piety and cheating those same dietary laws.

When Raquella brought up objections, pointed out places on the map where the cattle explanation didn't work, she found herself providing explanations instead— almost entirely having to do with the vector of contaminated water. For many routes the Wrack had taken could be explained by contaminated streams and rivers, like the Rhost through Geredain. And though Moonsworn water law had prevented the Wrack's spread in many places, it had never been intended to protect cattle from contaminated water. Fleeing infected refugees from the

Wrack shitting near streams and ponds could spread the infection to cattle.

They spoke for hours before finally, Raquella was convinced. It was a day and a half before the rest of the Moonsworn were convinced— and before the seers they'd sent out to inspect the cattle herds outside the city had found the Wrack in the animals. For, aside from perhaps a little increased skittishness, the Wrack lived peacefully inside cattle without trouble, and without producing their noxious poison.

So many questions about the Wrack remained unanswered. They still didn't know what caused the rapid mass outbreaks to occur so quickly. They didn't understand how the disease could survive cooking in meat, but be killed off with such a low fever. They didn't know how to cure it, or whether there was an antidote for the Wrack's poison, or whether its victims would ever regain use of their fingers.

But now they knew how to stop it from spreading.

And when the Empress was finally convinced, the order went out across Galicanta, to slaughter all the cattle somewhere far away from streams and lakes. The message was sent by semaphore where the network still fitfully held together, but was sent more often by rider on horseback, as it had been done in the days of the Empress's youth.

And the message was sent farther out still, across Teringia.

And it was even sent south across the Choke to the Sunsworn Empire, to Oyansur. And the courtiers in Ladreis praised Empress Phillipa's mercy and grace, even towards her enemies.

If any of them had the cynical thought that the Sunsworn, bound by similar dietary laws as the Moonsworn, would not be at much risk from the Wrack anyway, they didn't say it out loud. If they considered that explaining the plague would help tear out the foundations for the Sunsworn Emperor's religious justifications for the invasion, they didn't share those considerations with anyone.

Of course, the Moonsworn shared those thoughts everywhere and with everyone, for they considered even the calculated aspects of the matter quite praiseworthy on Phillipa's part.

And though there were more battles to be fought against the Wrack yet, for it would not die gently, the eyes and minds of everyone in Ladreis turned to the horizon and waited for the Sunsworn invasion fleet.

CHAPTER TWENTY-FOUR
Questions Like Arrows

My grandchildren ask me of those dark days sometimes. Those days when the Wrack descended upon Ladreis. They ask me if I heard the screams. If I saw the slums burn. They ask me piercing question after piercing question, and I never know how to answer, and I can't even make myself say the plague's name.

And then their mothers and fathers take them away and scold them for bothering me, and I close my eyes in my bed and pretend to sleep, and I think of all the answers I wanted to give my grandchildren but couldn't.

Then I think of all the other grandparents whose grandchildren ask them questions about those days, who find it so hard to speak of these things as well— even the ones whose fingers are blackened and withered. I think of the poets who found themselves unable to call the Wrack by its name for so many decades, and of those poets who fear it not but saw it not.

I want to tell my grandchildren that I stood with the Moonsworn, and helped them carry water in the days before the plague's arrival. I want to tell them I helped wrestle thrashing screamers into submission and wrap them in canvas so they couldn't claw and injure themselves. I want to speak of how they ran out of canvas, and how the healers began to tear down the tapestries from the halls of the wealthy and tie them about the screamers with no care for how old or rare or valuable they were.

I want to tell my grandchildren that I stood against the fires that raged in Ladreis' slums. That I stood side by side with beggars, soldiers, and noblemen against the fires. I want to tell them that I could not tell thief from merchant, heir from beggar, or priest from sailor. That we were all so tired and covered in soot that we were all brothers and sisters in that fight, hauling our buckets from ten-score fountains, and even the harbor itself, and though we lost most of the slums, we held back the fires long enough for the poor to flee.

I want to tell my grandchildren how I held my brother in my lap as he thrashed and wailed, desperately trying to free himself from the canvas. I want to tell them how I never stopped speaking to him, letting him know he was loved, that I was there, that his family would never abandon him. I want to tell them how I wept when his heart failed, though he was young and hale, and how long I simply sat alone with his corpse before I could make myself leave our home and return to fight the Wrack.

I want to tell my grandchildren how quiet Ladreis grew. Ladreis, the liveliest of cities. As the screamers dwindled in number, and the moaners slowly recovered, and the babblers regained their sense, the quiet in-between the screams started to build and build, until you had to wade through it like chest-deep water. How that heavy silence forced the words back in our lungs, and how all of us who had escaped the Wrack's clutches found ourselves secluding ourselves away, more afraid of the silence than the screams. How the streets were left to the rats and the stray dogs and all us living treated our homes like they were our coffins.

I want to tell my grandchildren of the whispered, fearful rumors that rushed through the city when we dared pass our doorsteps. For it had spread from the palace and was on every set of lips. The Sunsworn were coming. The Sunsworn had declared war. There was a Sunsworn fleet sailing for Ladreis, and Galicanta was too broken to stop it.

I want to tell my grandchildren about how the soldiers began sinking ships out in the harbor, to blockade it from invaders.

I want to tell my grandchildren how I stood alongside a hundred other men and women of Ladreis, as we faced ten times as many of our countrymen who would turn against the Moonsworn, for fear they were Sunsworn spies. How we shamed that unruly mob into turning aside, and leaving the Moonsworn unharmed.

I want to tell my grandchildren how we built blockades, passed out makeshift spears, and prepared for invasion.

There are so, so many things I want to tell my grandchildren.

I won't, though.

Because every one of those things is a lie.

I never helped the Moonsworn.

I never fought the fires in the slum, and I never joined that august brotherhood of soot.

I never held my brother as he screamed. He died alone and untended, and someone else preserved his name for the ancestors.

I never heard the quiet grow.

I never heard the awful rumors of war.

I never saw the sunken ships.

I never stood against the mob.

I never prepared for war.

Because what I never want to tell my grandchildren? The reason I don't speak to my grandchildren of the Wrack?

I fled. I fled into the hills like the coward I am before the first screams came from the Wrack, and I stayed there until the Wrack had loosed its hold on Ladreis. I stayed in those hills, and drank wine in the little shack I had stocked with food and wine and books, and I saw no one and spoke to no one until my food and my wine ran out and I'd read all the books a dozen times, and I learned of none of what transpired in Ladreis until afterward.

I tried to copy the broken walks of those who'd endured those horrible days, those stares that seem to pass right through you. I found that I needed neither, however. The more normal I acted, the more desperate I tried to seem happy, the more people just seemed to assume that I was concealing some deep suffering.

If, perhaps, I felt some deep, crippling shame, perhaps I could force myself to tell my grandchildren, or even my children, the truth.

I feel shame, but it's not crippling shame. It's not deep shame. It's a petty, slinking little shame, one I can hide, one I can conceal, and one I can lock away on command.

What do I really feel? I feel relief. Relief that I never suffered the screams of the Wrack, that I never coughed my lungs out fighting the fires, that I never had to wait upon that great Sunsworn fleet, that I will never have to see my brother in my memory as anything but the courageous man that refused to flee alongside me.

Relief that it was the better man who died, rather than the coward.

And if I could rewind time, I'd flee into the hills yet again.

-Anonymous essay, published four decades after the Wrack struck Ladreis.

CHAPTER TWENTY-FIVE
A Change in the Sky

Ladreis had always been a city that looked to its great harbor. This was certainly inevitable enough, since all the great hills of the city sloped down to it. On the day the Sunsworn fleet was expected to arrive, however, the attention of the city was pulled towards the harbor like the water was a lodestone the size of a mountain, and as though the eyes of Ladreis were iron filings. The fleet had passed by the embattled Choke already, the messages sent via semaphore had confirmed, and it was not a long voyage from the Choke to Ladreis.

The barricades at the harbor had been built, and the siege engines emplaced in the plazas that overlooked the harbor. Any ship that tried to enter the harbor too swiftly would have its hull torn apart by the scuttled ships on the harbor bottom.

The maze-like streets of Ladreis had been barricaded and fortified as well. No one who hadn't been raised in the city would ever be able to navigate to the palace atop the tallest hill without breaching them.

Screams from the Wrack still echoed in the city, but they were less in number, and the horrid grasp they had on the hearts of men was lessened. They still terrified, but their dreadful mystery was gone. The seers could tell you whether you had it or not, now, and all knew how to avoid it.

The healers and seers, exhausted by their long, sleepless struggle against the Wrack, slept on cots in the very tents they'd built for the battle-wounded. They'd be needed soon enough.

Winter was hardly a cruel thing in Ladreis, and poets often jested that southern Galicanta had no seasons, yet a wind blew across the city bearing the first hints of spring.

Those who had survived the Wrack, and whose fingers and toes could do nothing to help defend the city, merely waited. Most were too weak to get out of their beds yet, and of those that could, little more of use could be done by them but pace.

Noon came and went, and still nothing.

Early afternoon came, and a rumor raced through the crowds. The fleet had been sighted offshore a few leagues out, and one of the lookout relays had sent a message via semaphore: the Sunsworn fleet was coming.

Many argued against the rumor, of course. There was no official announcement about it. Surely, they would have sent troops ashore to seize the semaphores along the way.

The Sunsworn wouldn't want to start an evening assault. Surely they'd wait for dawn.

But the arguments all rang hollow, for there was a cynical streak running through the Galicantan spirit that hadn't been there before. The Wrack had broken something in them.

Midafternoon, and there was nearly a riot at the dock barricades. Afterwards, none could say what had provoked it, but it took Galicantan officers nearly an hour to get everything calmed down.

Late afternoon arrived, and somehow, boredom had set in. Clouds began to roll in from the sea, and seemed to wash away some small fragment of the tension. None had forgotten that an enemy fleet was on its way, yet there were dice games at half the barricades, and many of the barricades throughout the city had begun preparing feasts, as though it was a celebration. A pall still hung in the air, a sense of nervousness, and yet the city laughed, joked, and shared food with their neighbors and countrymen. Even the occasional scream of a new Wrack victim couldn't break the mood, for they knew that though some among their number would still fall to it, the dreadful plague's time was swiftly ending.

There was not a single scrap of beef at any of the feast tables set up in the streets.

Evening came, and a shout rose up from the keen of eye.

Sails had been spotted out at sea, silhouetted against the setting sun.

The silence was as thick and as cloying as it had been in the depths of the Wrack, but of a different character. This was a silence of anticipation, of dread, and of waiting.

The Sunsworn ships drew closer, and yet no-one could see their brilliant yellow and red pennants under which the Sunsworn went to war, nor even count the fleet, against the glare of the setting sun.

When the final reds of twilight were fading, whispers ran through the crowd, but they all whispered the same hope.

Surely the Sunsworn would wait for dawn to attack.

Yet the newfound Galicantan cynicism told them otherwise.

The light faded entirely as the Sunsworn fleet lay anchored out of range of Ladreis' siege engines.

Men and women slept at the barriers in shifts and lit no lights of their own, and Ladreis was dark and quiet, save for the lingering screams of the Wrack.

If you asked anyone who was there that night, they'd tell you that it was the longest night in the history of nights, that they aged a year and a day in that time.

On that cloudy, still, and moonless night, Ladreis could not see the Sunsworn fleet, nor could the Sunsworn fleet see Ladreis.

But the fleet could hear the screaming of the Wrack, and Ladreis could sometimes hear the creaking of enemy ships outside the harbor.

Even as slow as that night dragged on, it somehow ended.

But at the very end of night, just before the sky began to lighten, someone in Ladreis shouted, for there was a light visible in the harbor.

And the whole city was silent then, all watching the little light in the harbor.

It was a small light, and it bobbed up and down, as though carried in the waves. It was some time before anyone could even say for sure whether it was drawing close, but no-one shouted again. Even the Wrack seemed to have quieted at the approach of the little light.

Dawn always took its time coming to Ladreis. Long before light shone down into the city, it would crest above the palace, giving the pink marble an unearthly glow. It was one of the most magnificent sights that one of the most magnificent cities on all of Iopis had to offer, and yet none of its inhabitants saw it that day, for every single eye was fixed on the little light in the harbor.

As it often did, the light of the sun rose over Ladreis in a great rush, as though a dam had been broken, and the little light in the harbor was revealed to be a lantern, hung from the prow of a little rowboat, which contained only a single man. He rowed slowly between the sunken hulks of the scuttled ships, but he rowed steadily.

Any curiosity about what threats and demands of surrender that man might bear were quickly overwhelmed, however, with shock at something else.

The fleet did not sail under the yellow and red pennants of the Sunsworn. They were obviously Sunsworn ships, but they sailed under an unfamiliar blue and silver pennant.

And none save the Moonsworn recognized them at first, but they said nothing at first, out of fear and uncertainty at what they saw.

But the light grew, and they realized that they weren't dreaming, and the word began to spread in wonder among the Moonsworn, and others began to recognize the blue and silver pennants as well, for they were the pennants that hung over the great Temple of the Moon, in the nameless holy city of the Moonsworn, which lay distant from the Sunsworn holy city exactly halfway around the nameless holy mountain where the Goddesses had left Iopis.

And there were some that would turn on the Moonsworn in their midst, for there were always those, but their compatriots quickly hushed them, for none knew what this turn of events meant.

The little rowboat pulled up to the docks. Not to one of the great docks where war galleys or the deep-keeled ocean vessels of the Radhan might tie up. Nor to one of the more modest docks used by the coastal traders.

No, it docked at the humblest of fishermen's docks, and even still looked small.

And the man clambered out of the boat and tied it to the dock, and none approached him.

He was a tall, thin man, finely dressed but unarmed, with a great shock of black hair over skin nearly so dark.

He clasped his hands behind his back and strode down to the end of the docks. And he strode up to the barricades, and he politely asked the soldiers if he might be escorted to see the Empress.

Messengers were sent up to the palace, and the man waited patiently at the barricades. Of all things, he pulled a little book from his pocket and began to read.

Finally, the messenger returned to the docks, and the barricades were pulled aside enough that the man might be led through.

He was not bound, nor threatened with weapons, because even at a time like this, the Galicantans were fond of the polite lie, and there was no politer lie than treating an invader as an honored guest. His face was young and unlined, yet had eyes that belonged in a much older face. He walked with great dignity, but not arrogance, for he openly and frankly observed the Galicantans with the same curiosity they showed him.

No one spoke, but a few nodded to the man, and he always nodded back politely.

And the man was led up into the palace, and the waiting began once more.

When the man stepped into the palace, the city seemed to find its voice once more, and whispered rumors and speculation began, and even the Wrack seemed to stop holding its breath, and the screaming began again. Or perhaps it had never stopped, for this was one of those moments that afterward grew so confused with the stories about it, until those who weren't there remembered it nearly so clearly as those who were, and the latter would think themselves misremembering if their memories challenged the stories.

Morning dragged on and on, as the hours had seemed to since the last morning, and no one spoke more loudly than could be heard a few strides away. The Moonsworn tended to the screamers, and the soldiers and citizens of Ladreis watched the sun rise above the palace.

And then a noise shocked them all, and every citizen of Ladreis turned to face the palace.

They all knew that noise. Some had only heard it for the first time in the days before the Wrack arrived in the city. Some had heard it much more, but even a visitor to the city who had never heard it before should know that noise.

It was the Voice of the Empire.

You could not understand the wire-carried voice outside the palace— it became a discordant ringing, like the strings of a harp struck at random. Yet, inside it, all could hear the cadences of a conversation. There gaps in the ringing of the throne where the tall man with the black hair spoke to the Empress.

And as that conversation carried on, sometimes the discordant ringing of that wire throne bore anger that could not be mistaken, but those moments grew fewer and fewer.

When, finally, the conversation ended, the tension in the city grew to a fever pitch, for all knew that their destinies had been decided, but to what end, they did not know.

Midmorning arrived, and the front gates of the palace opened, and out came the palace guards, surrounding the emissary of the fleet and a little palanquin, borne by palace servants.

And as that palanquin and that emissary strode down the switchbacking road that led from the palace to the docks, the soldiers ahead of them cleared the barricades so that they might pass easily. And that palanquin bore the Empress, and more rumors flew than there were people in Ladreis.

And the palanquin and the emissary came to the docks, and servants set up a great parasol, and a pair of comfortable chairs, and a little table for tea. But the emissary and the empress did not go to that table immediately.

Instead, the Empress spoke to her people.

She told them of the Sunsworn Emperor, who craved conquest and dominion. A man who, when he heard of the misfortune of his neighbors, let his greed drive him to war. A man who was willing to take whatever measures to get what he wanted. A man who cared little for the demands of his own religion, and visibly resented even the smallest of religious duties.

A man who wouldn't even keep to the dietary laws of his people.

A man who, on the brink of launching his fleet, collapsed to the ground screaming. The first man in all of Oyansur felled by the Wrack.

And he screamed himself to death in front of ten thousand of his soldiers, for his heart, weakened by years of rich living, could not survive the strain.

The Empress told the crowd that the son of the Emperor, Amazahd, a youth little thought of in court politics, stepped forwards and was crowned immediately.

But not as the Sunsworn Emperor.

No, as the first-ever Moonsworn Emperor.

Instead of soldiers, he filled the fleet with healers, seers, food, and medicine, and sailed north on a mission of mercy.

And he stood beside her, having braved alone a city filled with his enemies, with no thought to his own safety.

And Empress Phillipa and Emperor Amazahd went to that little table, drank tea, and talked of matters that only they would ever know. And the rowboats and fishing vessels and pleasure craft of Ladreis went out to sea, and they met the Moonsworn fleet, and they began to ferry in the seers and healers of the Moonsworn fleet.

It was a beautiful morning, marred only by the screams that still rose from the city.

— —

Author's Note on Epidemiology in the Wrack

This section discusses the Wrack and other diseases of Iopis in terms of real world epidemiology.

A few notes on the Wrack:
The Wrack is a parasite— a microscopic multicellular animal— not a virus or bacteria. Like many parasites, it's a zoonotic disease, one transmitted between animals and people. In this case, between cattle and humans. The parasite is largely harmless to cattle, residing in their blood, with the only notable shift being slightly more skittish behavior than usual. The parasite is spread between cattle via fecal contamination of grasses being grazed and of drinking water. The Wrack parasite's method of entering the bovine digestive tract to spread via stool is currently unknown, but hardly unprecedented.

Zoonotic diseases, it should be noted, make up the majority of contagious diseases that infect humans on Earth.

The Wrack gets passed to humans via consuming beef— the Wrack parasite is incredibly temperature resistant, and anything less than a near-charred lump of meat will likely have the Wrack still present in it. It survives temperature extremes by producing massive quantities of a temperature-resistant protein and dehydrating itself, similar to how tardigrades survive extreme conditions. (The Wrack is a much smaller and simpler creature than tardigrades— parasite evolution often tends to reduce biological complexity over time.) Somewhat ironically, though the parasite can survive extreme temperatures, it starves quite easily— turning the meat to jerky, or merely letting it sit long enough before cooking it, will kill the parasite before long.

When the contaminated cow meat is eaten, the human body does, in fact, attempt to filter out the Wrack, recognizing it as a contaminant, but the Wrack finds the human liver to be an extremely hospitable place to live and hide itself from the human immune system. (This is similar to Plasmodium, the parasite that causes malaria, which lurks in the human liver during part of its life-cycle. Plasmodium is plant descended, however, not animal descended.) The Wrack parasite, when awakened from its dormancy, tends to be far more aggressive than usual, and begins reproducing at a wild rate inside the liver. It usually reaches a critical mass within two weeks. When that happens, the parasite then begins actively producing a neurotoxin as a stress reaction. This can be provoked by stress reactions within the human body as well. (A parasite producing a neurotoxin sounds weird, but it's not unprecedented— the botulism bacteria, *Clostridium botulinum*, produces the most poisonous substance on Earth, the botulinum neurotoxin. Botulinum toxin is also known as botox, which in small doses has both cosmetic applications and medical ones. Given that one of the main ones is treating muscle spasticity, botox would actually make for a potentially viable treatment for the Wrack!)

The Wrack neurotoxin isn't usually fatal on its own, and it's something of a distant relative to more typical terrestrial neurotoxins. The primary symptom is the characteristic triggering of skeletal muscle nerves, causing full-body convulsions. This in turn can cause other nasty symptoms, such as heart failure, fatal throat spasms (fatal laryngospasm), and rhabdomyolysis— a condition caused by the breakdown of muscle tissue, which can poison the kidneys. (Which, in turn, causes the dark urine.) The other major symptoms of the Wrack neurotoxin include severe damage to the nerves and tissues in the extremities, as well as long-lasting neurological damage leading to reduction of color vision, memory troubles, sexual dysfunction, etc.

(Loss of part of the ability to see color was a symptom of the Spanish Flu as well.)

In over half of the victims of the Wrack, the neurotoxin production phase gets skipped entirely.

After the neurotoxin phase (or skipping it), the Wrack parasite floods the body, resulting in a mild to moderate fever, light fatigue, and long-lasting diarrhea. The parasite is usually fought off by the body after this point. Rarely, it can stay and recolonize the liver, starting the cycle over again, but only in perhaps one of a thousand cases. Once the parasite has left the liver, it's quite easy for the body to fight it off over time. Though it's highly resistant to fever, it's quite easy for the body's other defenses to wipe the parasite out.

The primary way the Wrack spreads other than through eating contaminated meat is either from humans drinking contaminated water— or cows drinking it, then infecting people. Given the highly unusual attention Iopans pay to drinking water quality, thanks to the Moonsworn, the cattle vector was much more prevalent. On any other world, it would likely be reversed.

The targets of the Wrack tended to be the wealthy first, who, as they could afford to eat beef far more frequently than anyone else, were far more likely to be infected. The Moonsworn, who don't eat the meat of mammals and were scrupulous about clean drinking water, rarely caught the disease at all.

A few notes on non-Wrack Iopan contagions:
Some of the diseases mentioned in this book are fictional, but others are real-world diseases.

- **Foul Gases from a Galicantan Lake**: Some lakes in warm regions can build up massive amounts of carbon dioxide and methane in their depths produced by volcanic gases vented into the lake. This occurs when there are strong temperature differentials in layers of the lake. When an event occurs that mixes the layers, this can cause a massive outgassing, known as a limnic eruption. In 1986, Lake Nyos, in the African nation of Cameroon, had a massive CO_2 limnic eruption that killed 1,746 people and over 3,500 head of livestock via suffocation. In The Wrack, the Moonsworn are correct in attributing it to volcanic gases, despite their internal conflict over it.

- **Mudpox:** Childhood disease similar to measles, produces huge pus-filled blisters across the body, especially on the back. Can be fatal if untreated. Spreads via coughing and sneezing.
- **Sailor's Pox**: The common Iopan name for syphilis. Syphilis, though fairly easy to treat today, is a nasty piece of work. It's challenging to diagnose, often being referred to as the Great Imitator, due to its symptoms frequently resembling other diseases and health conditions. This bacterial disease can lie apparently dormant for as much as a quarter century after the initial stages of the disease, until kicking off the truly horrific third stage, which can vary in form wildly, from gross disfiguration to complete mental breakdown and insanity. (Quite a few historical figures have been speculated to have died or been driven to suicide by the latter version, known as neurosyphilis, including Friedrich Nietzsche, Leo Tolstoy, Vladimir Lenin, Al Capone, and Adolf Hitler.) Pregnant mothers can also pass it to their children, leading (tragically) to congenital syphilis. The fight against syphilis is ongoing, though far from won. As of this writing, Cuba is the only nation to have eliminated congenital syphilis.
- **Horsepox:** Fictional disease. While there is a real-world disease known as horsepox, it's a disease of horses, not humans. Iopan horsepox is a blood-borne disease characterized by huge, painful sores on the torso and limbs in humans. It's seldom fatal, though

it usually leaves distinctive, ugly scars. While most Iopans think it comes from horses, humans actually act as its main carriers, spreading it to horses, among whom it is extremely lethal. It most often spreads via contaminated water.

- **Bride's Blush**: Fictional. Sexually transmitted disease that results in a full-body rash that makes it look like the victim is blushing. While the rash goes away after a couple of weeks, the victim remains a carrier for the rest of their life. It's quite common among newly married people, and is a sure sign about their new bride or groom's past.
- **Flux:** Dysentery. Not precisely glamorous by epidemiological standards, but there've been few more reliable killers in human history, even today.

Appendix A: Galvachren's Guide to Iopis

Iopis is far more important to multiversal politics than any aether-poor world such as itself should be. This is, in great part, thanks to its seers.

There are only four known labyrinths on Iopis, though all of them are growing in junction mana wells. Counterintuitively, linear mana wells are more often found on high-aether density worlds. Three of the four labyrinths are mist-formed labyrinths. The debate on whether mist-form or tunnel-form labyrinth worlds are more common does, as usual, rage on, but, as usual, I remain convinced mist-form labyrinths are more common. The original forms of the labyrinths are now so rare as to be nearly extinct, and the other types that have evolved are quite uncommon as well, though marine labyrinths are theorized to be fairly common.

Physical Overview: Iopis is an old, small world. Earthquakes and volcanic eruptions are rare, and much of the world's geological activity has ended. Traces of past activity are everywhere, though, and the frequency of gemstones to be found on Iopis is, in part, a relic of its highly volcanic past.

Despite its small size— only about three-fourths of multiversal standard— gravity is actually a little bit higher than the multiversal average. Not so much that you'd notice easily, but enough that it can be measured.

Iopis has two major continents, connected by a thin isthmus, and a number of archipelagos of varying size, many uninhabited, though the largest of those is a stronghold of the Radhan.

Aetheric Overview:
The classification of aether is an easy enough task on most worlds, but not on Iopis. Iopan aether strenuously avoids easy classification. There's quite a bit of debate whether it's gas analogue aether or liquid analogue aether. I tend to favor the latter classification, though if grease analogue aether were an accepted part of the aetheric taxonomy, I might switch my vote.

Regardless, the aether of Iopis is near impossible to manipulate magically, and a mage filling their mana reservoir will take far, far longer than on even other comparably low aether density worlds— and, to be sure, Iopis' aether density is as low as it goes without being an aether desert.

While the aether of Iopis is notably thin and difficult to work with, this hasn't prevented a quite interesting form of local magic from arising— a form of scrying that allows one to see directly into the aether, a task usually only accomplished by the most skilled of mages on most worlds, though many of the [redacted] have developed a crude form of aether-sense that allows them to crudely perceive the aether around them. *([Redacted])'s note: I hate praising those pompous self-proclaimed godlings, but their aether sense is, though crude, damnably effective. One should never underestimate efforts that sacrifice elegance for effectiveness. Perfection is ever the enemy of success.)*

The process of becoming a seer involves blinding oneself in one or both eyes, then replacing the eye with polished spherical gems. Different types of gems allow users to interpret different types of information about the material world carried through the Iopan aether, often allowing them to look inside physical objects. It generally takes several years to be trained, depending on one's chosen discipline. The overwhelming majority of seers stick to one eye— normal sight is still far more versatile than any single seer's gem, and better at avoiding bruising one's shin. There are rare seers who choose to remove both eyes, and there are, apparently, some interesting advantages that come from using two different gems at once, or being able to see with parallax based depth perception in the aether using two of the same stone.

The difference between the stones doesn't seem to be a matter of what aether signals they perceive better, but rather what aether signals they filter out, and how. Nephrite, for instance, filters out almost everything but water.

Interestingly, the process of developing Iopan scrying seems to develop an aetheric extension of the brain's visual centers into the aether itself, which is an unusually complex aetheric structure for a mage, but as usual, the trend of low-aether density worlds having such complex structures in their magics holds true.

Political Overview:

Iopan politics are nothing particularly unusual for a human world with low aether density. The usual standard array of empires and kingdoms dominate the two primary continents, Teringia and Oyansur.

When it comes to multiversal politics, Iopis is of far greater interest. The Radhan are present in large numbers, and are definitely aware of their larger multiversal presence, unlike the Radhan on many other worlds. They actually control one of the major labyrinths granting access to Iopis, in the heart of a major archipelago a good chunk of the world away from the continents.

[Redacted's Note: There's no keeping the Radhan out of a world if they want to be there, and they can be useful allies, so we continue to seek good relations with the Radhan, despite their weak position in the multiverse.]

The [redacted] appear to be present in large numbers as well, but as usual, they bear little interest in surface dwellers, save avoiding them. There is some speculation that the northernmost human civilization of Iopis, the warrior culture known as the Singers, may have had some contact with the [redacted]. The irony of this should be obvious.

[Redacted's Note: As usual, attempts to communicate with the [redacted] are exercises in frustration. They're always preferable to their more aggressive rivals who take interest in the surface, however.]

Most important to multiversal politics is the presence of the [redacted], who have built numerous [redacted] on Iopis. Iopis appears to number among their most important stronghold worlds.

[Redacted's Note: Galvachren is even more incomprehensible at times than the [redacted]. He'll claim we're not on Anastis, a world we quite openly act on, but then outs our operations on Iopis? It's hardly the greatest secret ever, but still, it's why we make sure to be cautious with the access we allow him to our [redacted]. We certainly don't want to risk directly challenging him, and he has been useful often in the past, so we won't take any action in response to this intelligence leak.]

Appendix B: Excerpt from [Redacted] Assessment of the Wrack Crisis

If this had been an actual [redacted] incursion, with active [redacted] infections, Iopis would have fallen swiftly. The plan to feed medical knowledge to the Moonsworn, resulting in the rise of the sect known as the Dedicated, was not nearly as effective as hoped. It nearly led to a civil war among the healers, which would have been disastrous. In addition, religious tensions on Teringia weakened Moonsworn efforts to combat disease.

The overconfidence with which we held our plan could have been our downfall. We kept too few agents in the Sunsworn Empire and almost entirely ignored Teringia, instead focusing all our attention on the great empires in the south of Oyansur. Just because we consider a part of the world a cultural backwater, it doesn't mean we can get away with making excuses not to have agents there. At the very least, we should have planted observers in the Radhan fleets to keep an eye on Iopis' north.

Fortunately, the Wrack crisis seems to have played out largely in our favor. True peace reigns for the first time in centuries between the Eidola ancestor worshipers of Teringia and the new Moonsworn Empire— and the Moonsworn are more widely accepted than ever across Teringia. It's not entirely a rosy picture, of course— the new Fervent theocracy is dangerously unstable and controls the Krannenberg mistform labyrinth still. A final decision whether to help prop them up or destabilize them needs to be made. I recommend the latter, since if they fully consolidate their lands, a war intended to wipe out the Galicantan nobility is next, and that's hardly likely to go well for anyone involved.

The new Moonsworn Emperor is already facing challenge after challenge at home, but we've been covertly heading off as many of them as we can. Amazahd also takes after the rest of Moonsworn in his response to threats— he's responded to all assassination attempts with ruthless mass poisonings of the perpetrators and their families. It is an uncomfortable facet of the Moonsworn that their religious dedication to healing by no means makes them a gentle or merciful people. Regardless, the ascent of Amazahd to the throne atop their holy mountain can be seen as nothing but a net benefit for us.

As an interesting side-effect of the Wrack crisis, consumption of beef has effectively ended on Iopis, and there's a major leather supply crisis at the moment.

-[Redacted]'s commentary, written twenty-five years before the first battles of the [Redacted].

Appendix C: Galvachren's Guide to Iopan Gem Scrying

- Amethyst: The stone used by semaphore seers. While that is its most common purpose, it remains also a valued tool of researchers into the nature of the Iopan Aether, as it emphasizes turbulence within stronger currents in the aether over lesser ones.
- Citrine: The architect's left eye, this variant of quartz is perfect for seeing turbulence from metal in the aether, especially iron— though it works quite well for any metal. Works tolerably well for wood, so long as it is dry— wet or green wood can still be seen, but not as well.
- Diamond: The surveyor's eye. Diamond filters out the majority of the turbulence the physical world forms within the aether, letting the overall pattern and currents within the aether come to the fore. Highly useful to both surveyors for the semaphore network

and to researchers of aether. Due to its common nature, lesser beauty, and relatively specialized use, it ears a lower price than most gems.

- Emerald: A healer's stone like peridot, but far more effective. Emeralds of sufficient size and quality are incredibly rare on Iopis, however.
- Garnet: The architect's right eye, this gem has a singularly peculiar reaction with aetheric turbulence generated by stone— it renders it nearly opaque, save for flaws and cracks. Does not work on other garnets, spinels, or a few other minerals, curiously.
- Glass: Cannot be used to see the aether in any meaningful way. This applies to obsidian and opal as well. Glass eyes are only used to keep the seer's empty eye socket from closing up.
- Nephrite: This variety of jade is the true sailor's eye, allowing impressive perception of rocks and fish beneath the waves, as well as the shapes of sea currents. It should be noted that ship's seers using nephrite are mostly just seeing holes in the water where fish and rocks are— nephrite is strongly attuned to water, especially salt water. Despite the common belief that only transparent and translucent gemstones may work as eyes, it's the crystalline structure that channels the seer's vision into the aether, not the crystal's transparency, as proven by this opaque stone.
- Peridot: The healer's eye, finely tuned towards seeing the spirit ripples produced by flesh.
- Quartz: No particular strengths or weaknesses. Largely used as a training aid, and sometimes by especially skilled and focused generalist seers.
- Ruby: Despite being merely a beryl variant closely related to emeralds, rubies are much better suited towards viewing plant-life, especially living plants. Though nearly so rare as emeralds, they fetch a lower price, as they bear a less useful ability.

- Sapphire: Despite folklore and superstition, these are *not* the best suited towards seeing through the waves. In fact, among the learned, they're better known as the brewer's or dyer's eye— they have a strong affinity for many thicker liquids and oils, as well as fermentation. They may still be used by ship's seers, however.
- Spinel: Though commonly called the Weaver's Eye, spinel is one of the most challenging gem eyes to master. Best attuned towards seeing fibers of any sort, whether cloth, within plants, or the like. Also of use in examining muscles. Interestingly, while all spinels work for fiber, each color of spinel has a secondary use— metal, or vapor, or bone, or something of the sort. A spinel-trained seer with enough colors of spinel is one of the most versatile types of seer. Spinels cannot perceive other spinels or garnets through the aether.

There are dozens of other crystalline gemstones in use by Iopan seers, ranging from tourmaline to agate to even (oddly) polished fragments of columnar basalt, and many of the gemstones listed here have alternate uses as well. The above are simply the gemstones most widely known on the Teringian continent.

A few note on Iopan seers in the multiverse:
Most worlds' aethers are not nearly so influenced by the physical world as Iopis', rendering the traditional Iopan scrying more challenging to seers who have traveled off Iopis. Stabilizing wards and spells may still allow them to perform their traditional functions. This, however, is not the primary reason Iopan seers are of interest to multiversal powers— they have an unparalleled ability to perceive the aether among any known mages. They can see spells being constructed within the aether, tell mages from non-mages by observing their aetheric reservoirs and other internal

aetheric constructs, tell [redacted] from normal humans by their even more extreme aetheric structures, detect [redacted] incursions (at least from some of the more aggressive hordes and Khanates), and tell [redacted] from normal [redacted] (though they're surely compromised at a close enough distance to do so, and a simple visual examination from a distance can do the same. They can, however, tell the various [redacted]s apart easily, another unusual ability.) Countless mages of the [redacted], who hold this world as one of their bases, willingly remove their own eyes to become Iopan seers while stationed there.

There's a second, rarer type of seer, that may replace other missing senses with Iopan aether scrying. Deaf and anosmic mages have both picked up the magic, as have a few others. This offers some unusual possibilities, but little development of this has occurred, and the lack of a gem equivalent makes things much, much more challenging. (Non-gem Iopan visual scrying is possible, just difficult, rare, and not as effective, and still requires the removal or blinding of at least one eye.)

While rumors of Iopan seers off of Iopis using obsidian or opal eyes are common, they're also false. Those rumors spring from [redacted] gem mages, who have only recently begun making their presence known in the multiverse. Their magic is significantly more active than Iopan seers. *([Redacted]'s note: that's one massive understatement.)*

Afterword

Thank you so much for reading The Wrack, and I hope you enjoyed it! It's a weird book, I know, and I really appreciate everyone who stuck it out. (And who survived all that after-material! I might have a bit of an addiction to appendices.) Writing it has been a long, weird process- in great part due to the craziness that is COVID-19. (More on that in a second.)

As I started writing The Wrack in late summer of 2019, I began traveling the world full time as a digital nomad. And though it's been incredible to see the world like I have, it's been pretty rough on my work schedule, to say the least. Over the last few months, however, I've gotten fully back into the writing groove, and you can hopefully expect the next book on my docket, Mage Errant 4 (currently titled The Lost City of Ithos), a lot faster than The Wrack.

I was in Vietnam in December 2019 when I first started hearing reports of a novel strain of coronavirus. I'd been working on The Wrack for a few months, and had been doing heavy research on epidemiology for about a year beforehand. (On top of a lifelong interest in the topic, as well.)

You might have expected me to immediately get concerned, and peg it as the oncoming pandemic it was.

You'd be wrong. I wasn't stressed about it, save as a public policy question. I genuinely thought that China and the rest of the world had taken seriously the lessons of SARS, MERS, Ebola, and swine flu, and that it would be contained before it spread too far.

I was pretty far off on the mark on that one, to say the least.

I was in Fiji when I sent The Wrack to my editor, and four days later the WHO declared COVID-19 a pandemic.

As of this writing, I'm currently hunkered down in Vietnam again, thanks to the high quality of their response to COVID-19. I barely made it in before they closed their borders, and I actually ended up having someone with COVID-19 on my flight. Thankfully, I didn't catch it, but I did have to spend two weeks in official quarantine, which was less than fun.

I don't know how the world is going to change after this. For me, personally, it effectively means my time as a digital nomad is over for the near future. It's simply not a viable lifestyle during a pandemic. I've got plans to stay hunkered down in Vietnam for a few more months, but after that, I genuinely don't know. (Ideally, Vietnam will continue being easy-going about extending visas.) I'm at unknown/moderate risk from COVID-19, as I have congenital heart disease. There's simply not enough data to know. Sometimes it's safe to assume that people with congenital heart disease face the same risks as people with congestive heart disease, and people with congestive heart disease have significantly heightened risks with COVID-19. Sometimes, though, it's wildly off-base to assume that congenital and congestive heart disease patients will face the same health risks. I'm still young- 31 at time of this writing- and in decent physical shape, but I genuinely don't know how well I'd do if I got infected. It scares the shit out of me.

Given how badly things are going in the US, I sure can't risk coming back there anytime soon. My visa in Vietnam won't last forever, though. I don't know what I'm going to do then, but I'll figure it out.

I think working on The Wrack really helped prepare me emotionally for a lot of what's happening now, but it's still really hard. I find myself just staring at the tab in my browser that contains a tracker for global COVID-19 deaths, dreading opening it to look but still feeling compelled to. I'm reading more news articles every day than ever.

But I'm also doing my best to pitch in however I can. I'm checking up on friends and family as much as I can, which isn't always as much as I'd like. I've been buying gifts for friends and family members to try and keep them entertained and take the edge off the crazy. I've been participating in charitable sales and upping my charitable donations from my usual 10% to 15-20% of my income, mostly to Doctors Without Borders. And, well… I wrote this book. Confronting disasters and calamity head on in my reading has always helped me cope with it, and if The Wrack does even a tiny bit to help others in that regard, I'll count it a wild success.

I hope that doesn't come off as bragging or arrogance, because I don't feel overly proud of it. Mostly, I just desperately feel like there's more I should be doing, that I'm not doing enough. That I should be donating more money, spend more time checking up on my loved ones, spending more hours a day writing so I can earn more to donate. *Something.*

And then I look around, and I see so many amazing people all over the world pitching in, and I see the good in people shining out. I see people stepping up everywhere, doing their best to put a little more kindness in the world, to try and offer what helping hands they can. And maybe I don't feel especially proud of myself right now, but I'm sure as hell proud of all of you.

And that helps me remember that we get to share this burden, that we don't have to carry it alone. That we *can't* carry it alone. We might be separated physically, but we're still all in this together. And knowing that helps, it really does. It certainly deflates my hubris of thinking I need to shoulder the weight of the world. And more importantly, it gives me hope.

These are rough times, but we *will* get through them. And just a heads up, the first friend or family member I see after all this social distancing is over is going to have to put up with an hour-long hug.

Stay safe, people. We'll get through this.

For news about The Wrack, the Mage Errant series, other upcoming works, and random thoughts about fantasy, worldbuilding, and whatever else pops in my mind, check out my blog at www.johnbierce.com. The best way to keep updated on new releases is to sign up for my mailing list, which you can also find on my website. You can also contact me via my website, via email at john.g.bierce@gmail.com, or on Reddit. (u/johnbierce) Some cool folks on Reddit also started a subreddit for my books at r/MageErrant. (I regularly post updates on there as well.)

I also have a Patreon, which can be found at patreon.com/johnbierce. There, I post monthly short stories set in the worlds of my books, as well as occasional previews of upcoming books.

Cover art and design of The Wrack by Amir Zand.

Edited by Paul Martin of Dominion Editorial, who does amazing work. Any remaining issues with the book are entirely my fault.

Special thanks to my beta readers Eliot Moss, Sarah Lin, Sundeep Agarwal, Travis Riddle, F James Blair, Berkeley Franklin, Kyle Becker, and Kayla Kurin. (Also to Gregory

Gleason, who got a little overwhelmed with work and parenting during a pandemic— definitely no worries!)

Special thanks also to my epidemiological beta readers Margaret Davies and Jeremy Phillips, who made sure I didn't mangle the science too badly. Any mistakes in The Wrack are mine and mine alone. And yet more special thanks to Kelly Gillespie, who wanted to beta read the Wrack, but had to bow out because she was working at a health department and was overwhelmed with dealing with COVID-19. You rock.

(You ALL rock.)

Not to mention still *more* special thanks to my Patreon backers Josh Fink, Andrew Alves, Andrew Cogan, Cortney Railsback, Jeff Chang, Jeff Petkau, Stephen Neville, Paolo Ruiz, Jacob William Perkins, Mikal Hofstad, Jeremy Miller, Andreas F. Sørensen, Kyle Matthews, James Titterton, Andy Barnett, Ruediger Pakmor, Ryan Campbell, Daniel Williams, Joseph Lee, Leonard Bukowski, Branden Rudolph, Cory Leigh Rahman, Scott C. Adams, Diallo Bennett, Christian Nielsen, and Adam Milne.

(And yes, you all rock too.)

Further Reading

If you enjoyed this book, here are a few suggestions for other works of epidemiological fiction you might enjoy.

—*Balam, Spring*, by Travis Riddle: A slice-of-life epidemiological fantasy novel set in the town of Balam. (Amir Zand did the covers for both *Balam, Spring* and *The Wrack*, and full disclosure, Travis beta-read *The Wrack*- I asked him if he'd do so because of *Balam, Spring*.) The world Balam is set in is heavily Final Fantasy inspired.

—*The Doomsday Book*, by Connie Willis: A time-traveler is stranded in the fourteenth century when an epidemic breaks out in her own time. It's a bittersweet, depressing, wonderful book. Rightfully won both the Hugo and Nebula Awards.

—*Eifelheim*, by Michael Flynn: Aliens crash land near a medieval village during the Black Death, and establish friendly relations with the villagers— but Earth's food provides them no nutrition, and the plague creeps closer every day. Wonderful, heartwrenching book.

—*Feed*, by Mira Grant: Yep, zombie novels totally count as epidemiological novels. Most of them do pretty badly at the epidemiology aspect, but *Feed* is definitely the exception. It's an absolutely brilliant take on zombies, I can't recommend it enough. (The rest of the Newsflesh trilogy is great too.)

—*The Traitor Baru Cormorant*, by Seth Dickinson: The first book in the Masquerade series, following the brilliant and ruthless Baru Cormorant as she infiltrates the titular empire of the Masquerade in an effort to overthrow them from the inside. The Masquerade is a true imperialistic nightmare, where all the evils of imperialism and colonialism are taken as a guidebook and not a warning, and they prefer to start their conquests by wrecking their targets' economies and introducing multiple deadly diseases to weaken the population. Exploration of the role of disease in empire is a major theme of the series.

—*The Plague*, by Albert Camus: Like depressing, dry as hell existentialist French Algerian literature? Then you should read this one. If you're not already a Camus fan, though, read *The Stranger* first.

-*The Masque of the Red Death*, by Edgar Allen Poe: This short story is as brilliant of any of Poe's other works, and its influence on *The Wrack* was a major one.

-*The Strand*, by Steven King: Giant doorstopper of a novel. Deals more with the aftermath of a civilization ending disease than the disease itself, but I highly recommend it. It's one of Steven King's best novels. (Fun fact: Steven King's novel *Misery* was what first made me become a writer. Kinda ironic, since it's about an author getting kidnapped and tortured, but it was the first time I ever encountered someone describe writing fiction in-depth, and it made me realize I wanted to do that for a living.)

-*The Andromeda Strain*, by Michael Crichton: Even though later in life Crichton turned into a crazy climate change denier, a lot of his early novels are seriously top-notch. *The Andromeda Strain* follows a series of scientists studying an extraterrestrial virus that kills off a small town in Arizona. A bit dated in some regards, but an excellent read.

And, if you're interested in learning more about epidemiology in the real world, here's some nonfiction you can check out as well. (All of these influenced *The Wrack*. It's not the whole list by any means, but many of the other nonfiction works I used for research are rather more… dry.)

—*The Ghost Map: The Story of London's Most Terrifying Epidemic- and How it Changed Science, Cities, and the Modern World*, by Steven Johnson: A short, engaging nonfiction read about the 1854 London cholera outbreak. (Which, while admittedly terrifying, was far from being London's most terrifying epidemic ever.)

—*Spillover: Animal Infections and the Next Human Pandemic*, by David Quammen: A brilliant book on zoonotic diseases by one of my favorite nonfiction writers. Most of the plagues throughout history have been zoonotic diseases, including Ebola, the bubonic plage, the common cold, and more.

—*The Illustrious Dead: The Terrifying Story of How Typhus Killed Napoleon's Greatest Army*, by Stephen Talty: Honestly, the title is pretty self-explanatory on this one: Typhus was the single biggest cause of death during Napoleon's invasion of Russia.

-*The Fever: How Malaria Has Ruled Humankind for 500,000 Years*, by Sonia Shaw: Likewise, pretty self-explanatory. Malaria is a huge deal when it comes to the its effect on human history.

-*The Great Mortality: An Intimate History of the Black Death, The Most Devastating Plague of All Time*, by John Kelley: …Look, a lot of epidemiological fiction is just has really self-explanatory titles, alright? They're definitely worthwhile, though.

—*Pale Rider: The Spanish Flu of 1918 and How It Changed The World*, by Laura Spinney: …You get the idea. Despite being the most recent major global pandemic, the poorly named Spanish Flu is one of the least studied and understood major pandemics in history— despite it being the single biggest cause of death of any event in the 20th century. (It definitely killed more people than either World War, and some experts believe it might have killed more than both combined, by quite a large margin.)